M

Hello Alexina.

His lips did not move, but his voice was there in her mind, not like the impersonal flow of mindspeech, but exactly as if he had spoken. It struck terror into the very core of Alexina's soul.

Don't be afraid.

Alexina closed her eyes, but this was a dream, and she could still see him. *Go away*, she thought miserably. *Please leave me alone. Oh, why can't I shut you out?*

I couldn't shut you out, he replied to her thought. *Why should you be able to shut me out? What befalls one befalls the other in equal measure. The link is not merely spiritual. It is physical as well.*

No, she thought. *No*.

You will soon be where I am. Come to me. . . .

WORLDSTONE

VICTORIA STRAUSS

A SIGNET BOOK
NEW AMERICAN LIBRARY

PUBLISHER'S NOTE

This novel is a work of fiction. Names, characters, places, and incidents either are the product of the author's imagination or are used fictitiously, and any resemblance to actual persons, living or dead, events, or locales is entirely coincidental.

NAL BOOKS ARE AVAILABLE AT QUANTITY DISCOUNTS
WHEN USED TO PROMOTE PRODUCTS OR SERVICES.
FOR INFORMATION PLEASE WRITE TO PREMIUM MARKETING DIVISION,
NEW AMERICAN LIBRARY, 1633 BROADWAY,
NEW YORK, NEW YORK 10019.

This is an authorized reprint of a hardcover edition published by Four Winds Press, Macmillan Publishing Company, and simultaneously in Canada by Collier Macmillan Canada, Inc.

SIGNET TRADEMARK REG. U.S. PAT. OFF. AND FOREIGN COUNTRIES
REGISTERED TRADEMARK—MARCA REGISTRADA
HECHO EN CHICAGO, U.S.A.

SIGNET, SIGNET CLASSIC, MENTOR, ONYX, PLUME, MERIDIAN and NAL BOOKS are published by New American Library, 1633 Broadway, New York, New York 10019

First Signet Printing, March, 1987

1 2 3 4 5 6 7 8 9

PRINTED IN THE UNITED STATES OF AMERICA

prologue

It was midafternoon by the time the dark man reached the place of the Gate. It was a cave partway up a mountain, opening off a rocky ledge. For a moment he stood still. All around lay pine-forested mountains, rising and falling toward the horizon, interspersed with grassland and the occasional gleam of water. The wind rushed down from the heights and swept through the passages between the hills, flattening the grass of the valleys and ruffling the dark waters of the lakes. Directly below lay a meadow and a cluster of farm dwellings; the dark man and his servant had had to waste quite a bit of time avoiding them, trudging around the foot of the mountain where the pines offered concealment.

The man pushed back the hood of his enveloping cloak. He was tall and slender, with strong features and dark eyes, a jawline beard, and hair braided in a club at the nape of his neck. He wiped his damp forehead with his sleeve. Despite the wind it was breathlessly hot.

There was a scrabbling sound and involuntarily he snapped around toward it. So long had he been in flight that every sound seemed to herald the approach of his pursuers. But it was only his servant, panting along the ledge, bent beneath the weight of a shoulder yoke. He lowered it to the ground, groaning.

The dark man set down his own burden, a leather pouch containing a roughly spherical object about the size of a man's head. From beneath his cloak he produced a closely written sheet: instructions for the opening of the Gates. He had chosen the Gate of this wild northern land because it was the country of his youth, and he could travel it much faster than could his trackers. They were far behind him now; as yet they could not know that he had dared the mindlink and discovered the secret. But they would know soon. And they would also know that they were too late.

He began the formula. First he arranged a pattern of stones before the entrance to the cave. Then he uttered a series of phrases, touching different and precise points of the pattern with each set of words. There was a cracking noise, a sharp odor that pierced the nostrils, and the Gate sprang into existence. Where before there had been the mouth of the cave, its interior dimly visible, now the entrance framed pitch blackness, dark as the inside of a well and shot at intervals with darts of bluish light.

The dark man turned to indicate to his servant that it was time. But he was caught by the view, by the beauty of the lands and the mountains of his childhood, and for a moment he stood still, gazing outward. It was a great step he was about to take, and it was dictated not so much by desire as by necessity. It would be dangerous and difficult, and very strange. But, on balance, he was not sorry to leave his world. The new world would teach him much. And with him went the object that would help to bring his visions to fulfillment—in a way those of his world could never accept, in a way those of the world he entered would never believe. Involuntarily his hand moved upward, to the empty space below his collarbones where the medallion had hung. It was the lightness of freedom, he told himself. The badge had always been a burden.

"It's time to go," he said to his servant. "Wait for a moment after I'm gone and then follow me."

The servant nodded, obviously terrified. The dark man turned to the Gate, the leather pouch cradled in his arms. In one step he was through. There was a sensation of rushing winds, of being wrenched apart, of traveling with immense speed though his feet remained in the same place. He felt himself fall, landing as one does in dreams, with a mental rather than a physical impact. He opened his eyes to find himself inside a cave exactly like the one he had just left. Had the Gate failed? But then he felt the air around him, alive with alien currents, and knew he had succeeded.

There was a coalescence nearby and his servant appeared, stumbling as he did so, tipping some of the gold pieces out of the bags that swung from the shoulder yokes. His eyes were wide and he was panting, and if he had had a tongue he would have cried out. The dark man went to him and placed soothing fingertips on his forehead. Closing his eyes, he sank swiftly into the deep meditation that restored powers sapped by the difficult journey through the Gate, the touch of his fingers passing some of that peace to his servant. Next he set about the task of building a barrier against this unfamiliar world, surrounding himself and his servant and the thing he carried. Already he could feel the difference, and forces of this world dragged at him even as he wove his protective net.

Opening his eyes, he felt the barrier strong around him. The forces were still there, but outside. He hoped to adapt quickly so that protection would no longer be necessary. In his arms the object rested, dormant, deep in the sleep into which he had cast it. Later, when he had learned more, he would know when to wake it and how to use it, and just what, beyond his barriers, it would ultimately become.

He motioned to his servant, who gathered up the spilled gold and shouldered the yoke. They stepped out of the cave, into intense heat and a landscape identical to the one they had just left. The dark man looked about, intrigued. There was even a cluster of buildings in the meadow, their shapes and functions unfamiliar, but their placement identical to the farm buildings in the world he had just left. Could parallelism be complete?

Barricaded within his net, he allowed himself to drift a little. And so he was not prepared for what he encountered halfway along the ledge. It was power, a blast of power that punched right through the net and into his mind before he was aware it had happened. Instinctively he threw up his inner barriers; whatever it was bounced off and away and was gone. He stopped and looked around him. Below was the meadow and the buildings, above was a sheer stone cliff and the sky. Dropping his protection a little, he sent out his mind—but now there was nothing. Nothing and no one, no trace of power. Uneasy, he thought: It must be the world-forces. They are stronger than I expected, and I will have to be more careful. It had felt . . . human. He might almost have believed that the Guardians had anticipated him and awaited him already, but he knew that could not be so.

The dark man motioned to his servant and once more they moved on. At intervals he cast out his mind, and each time he encountered nothing unusual. Yet he had an uneasy feeling that did not fade, as if the blast of power had found him out and a thread had been hooked into his mind, unreeling now behind him as he went.

In the world the dark man had left, the Gate blinked out of existence. The cave stood empty and unremarkable, winds playing around its mouth. The sky had turned gray and lifeless; clouds hung heavily upon the peaks. And far to the south a group of travelers came abruptly to a halt. They did not need to look at one another or speak to know what had happened. It was as if a sound, so low as to be inaudible yet so pervasive as to make up a permanent substratum of all other sounds, had ceased, leaving in its wake only a vast and spreading silence.

1

Alexina Taylor trudged up the hill that led to the farm. It was a sweltering day, unusually hot for June in upstate New York. The sun beat down out of a sky the color of steel, and dust rose from the rutted dirt road, drying her mouth and irritating her eyes, already burning from the glare. Across the meadow at the foot of the mountains rose inviting stands of trees, cool shadows dark at their base. Alexina's schoolbooks were heavy in her arms, and sweat trickled down her sides beneath her blouse.

The farm came in sight as she mounted the top of the hill. It had been built at the turn of the century and improved in the 1920s, but since then it had been left untouched, and time and weather had worked inevitable transformations. The barn and other buildings were a faded pink, with warping boards and trim that showed only a ghost of their former white. The house, though large and attractive in its proportions, was similarly dilapidated. Its paint had long since peeled away, its shutters sagged, and the porch was lopsided. Long ago a stand of magnificent trees had been planted—maples, oaks, a copper beech—thriving as steadily as the house decayed. Julia kept it all spotlessly clean, of course, and there were flowers along the front walk and tubs of geraniums beside the steps. But nothing could really cheer it up or alter the look of age and poverty and defeat.

Even now, six months after she had first arrived, Alexina's heart sank slightly each time she crested the hill, a reminder of the dreadful plummeting sensation that had gripped her then. She had been shocked by the meagerness, the shabbiness, the sheer *oldness* of it. Of course she had known it was isolated, that the Krantzes were not rich—but even her most dismal imaginings had not conjured up anything as dismal as this. Why hadn't Jessica prepared her? Alexina had looked at Jessica, not knowing what she expected—sympathy, perhaps? But her guardian, sitting straight in her seat and maneuvering carefully past the ruts in the road, did not return the glance. As usual, Jessica had simply forgotten to think about how Alexina might feel. Busy with the details of her appointment to a scientific exchange team that would spend the next two years in Russia, she had spared no time to worry about her ward.

Alexina reached the house and went in through the kitchen door, letting the screen slam behind her. The inside was as shabby as the outside, but at least it was wonderfully cool in hot weather. She put her books down on the scrubbed wooden table, stained and pitted with decades of use, and poured herself a glass of the iced tea Julia Krantz kept in the refrigerator. In a moment she must begin her chores. Oh, the tediousness of the constant chores! That was perhaps the worst thing about the farm. The work never ended: The more you worked, the more work there seemed to be. Life was a constant struggle simply to keep on top of it all; getting ahead was too much to hope for. Not that her own chores were so strenuous, she reminded herself. The family, she knew, made allowances for her, and everyone else worked much harder than she. But they took up so much *time.* Alexina rarely had a moment to do the things she enjoyed most—reading, thinking, spending hours daydreaming. She had thought herself lonely in New York, but she had not realized how much those long solitary hours meant until she no longer possessed them.

Alexina finished her tea, washed her glass at the cracked kitchen sink, and went upstairs to change out of her school clothes. Her room was flooded with afternoon sunlight. There was a single bed of white-painted iron, covered with a faded red patchwork quilt. A massive wardrobe with a dark, cracked finish leaned against one wall. A bureau, lopsided to match, stood beside it. The floor was painted a utilitarian shade of brown, and a small red rag rug lay on the floor next to the bed. The walls were bare. Alexina had tried to hang up a few of her prints and posters when she had first arrived, but they only made her more homesick and she took them down again. Always when she entered this room, she saw for a moment the superimposed image of her room in New York, with its comfortable furnishings and wall-to-wall carpet. She would go back to that room in two years—no, in one year and six months. This room, like the farm, was a sort of way station, to be endured until her time was up.

Alexina deposited her books on the bed, put on her chore clothes, and braided her long brown hair so it would not get in her way. Downstairs, she set to work. First she laid the dining room table for dinner, using the chipped white ironstone that dated from the twenties. Next she began to peel potatoes, saving the skins for broth as Julia had taught her, leaving the peeled potatoes to soak in a bowl of water. When she was done with that she had the chickens to feed, the laundry to fold, and the large vegetable garden in the back to water. Then she must help Julia with dinner. After dinner there was washing up, and after that there was homework. If it had been vacuuming day or ironing day or any of the other regimented work days that made up Julia's life, she would have been expected to help with that too. Fortunately, it was not. Today, with luck, she might manage to fit in a free hour somewhere.

There were footsteps on the porch, and the screen door slammed. Alexina glanced up: It was Toby. Please let him be on his way somewhere else, she thought. But Toby poured himself a glass of tea and sat down at the kitchen table, propping his feet on a chair and showing no signs of haste. Only four more potatoes to go. Alexina could feel him looking at her.

"Whew," he said at last. "It's hot as an oven out there."

Alexina dropped a potato into the bowl of water and did not reply.

"How was school today?"

"Lousy," she said shortly.

There was a silence. She could hear him drinking. "Did you hear the joke Pete told this morning?" he said. "The whole back of the bus was on the floor."

She looked around with what she hoped was a withering expression. "I thought it was stupid and puerile. Only an idiot would have laughed."

His face took on a very credible look of wronged innocence. "Boy, are you nasty. I was just trying to make conversation."

"Well, don't bother on my account." One more potato to go.

"Alexina, Alexiiiiina," Toby singsonged. "Awful Alexina. Atrocious Alexina. Abysmal Alexina."

"We've been reading the dictionary again," she said as sarcastically as she could.

"Oh, my! Miss Superiority! Who was it who said 'puerile'? *Puerile*!" he mimicked in falsetto. "I bet you don't even know what it means."

"I do so!" cried Alexina, stung out of her lofty pose.

"The chickens are calling you, Alexina. They're hungry. Better do your chores! Alexina! Alexiiiina!"

"Oh, can't you leave me alone for once?" She had meant it to sound superior and quelling, but it came out petulant. There was a hateful grin on his face and he did not reply. He was satisfied now that he had produced a reaction. Blinking furiously, Alexina scraped the last bit of peel off the final potato, dropped it with a splash into the bowl with the others, and stomped out of the kitchen to do the rest of her chores.

Why could she never learn not to react? she thought as she fed the chickens. Never, never in all her life had she met anyone as unpleasant and sarcastic as Toby Krantz. She felt tears behind her eyelids, but she refused to shed them. No one had ever treated her the way he did—it never seemed to stop, the merciless teasing that reduced her to speechless rage. And he only did it when the adults weren't around, so she could not appeal to Julia or her husband, Charles, for help. What made him so hateful? I hate you, Toby Krantz, she thought fiercely, throwing a handful of corn with unnecessary force and sending the chickens flapping and squawking. If only there were someone I could talk to! But there wasn't: There were only Julia and Charles and awful Toby. A familiar wave of self-pity swept over her. I can't stand it, she thought. I can't.

She was not much calmer by the time she finished

watering the back garden, but after the hose was coiled and put away, she found there was over an hour before she would be expected to help get dinner. She could do the laundry later. She felt, suddenly, that she must get away, away from the farm and its people, away to her own secret place.

Alexina had discovered her secret place one afternoon in late March. She had used a free hour to explore the mountain that rose behind the farm at the edge of the back meadow, wandering through the pines that covered its slopes, moving up the relatively gentle incline until she came to a sheer rock face. About fifteen feet up there seemed to be a ledge. It wasn't too difficult a climb, and she breasted the top to find herself on a wide rocky shelf that curved for quite a long way around the side of the mountain. Following it, she rounded an outcrop and found herself at the entrance to a cave.

Spring had come early to this sheltered place. A small stretch of soft grass grew from its mouth to the lip of the cliff, ferns unfurled around the opening, and tiny yellow flowers clustered in the mossy crevices of the rock. The cave extended into the mountain for about forty feet, slanting down at the back so it became impossible to stand upright. The floor was of dry rock, bare except for the pine needles that had sifted in around the entrance.

Alexina fell in love with it. Here was a refuge, a haven from Toby and chores and dreariness. She began escaping to it as often as she could. She stuck candles on outcrops around the mouth; she rescued a few old cushions from the attic, and a little kerosene burner so she could make tea in a chipped mug. In the solitude of the cave she could read as she liked, devouring whole books in an afternoon. She could dream to her heart's content without being asked if she was done with her work or if she felt all right. But it was more than solitude or the chance for escape. The cave had given her a gift.

There was a feeling she had had, on and off, for as long as she could remember. She thought of it as the *waiting* feeling. She could not define it, exactly. It was made up of many feelings, a jumbled combination of anticipation, breathless excitement, suspense, as if somehow she were standing on the brink of something wonderful about to happen. She could not say what it was she waited for. She only knew the feeling had always been there, a bright thread of continuity stitching through the gaps and changes and bereavements in her life. But at the farm, for the first time ever, it ceased to visit her. She told herself it was temporary, that the daily dreariness and her own depression blocked it. But as the days passed and it did not return, another possibility began to suggest itself. Could it be that this strange new life was changing her somehow, turning her into someone who no longer *waited?*

But then she found the cave. The very first time she entered it the feeling was there again, as strong and sure as ever. She could remember her happiness, the deep relief of knowing that she had not changed after all. She was still herself. The farm could not touch her. She was not like the people here and she never would be.

Today, hurrying through the meadow, her pride still smarting from Toby's teasing, Alexina hugged this knowledge to herself with a sort of fierce determination. No, she was not like them. She was not like anyone. She was *different*—not just because she had no parents or spent most of her time alone, but in a deeper, more mysterious, more essential fashion. She had always known this, but before, in New York, it had simply been part of her, like breathing, taken for granted. Here, it had become something more. It was a last line of defense, an assurance that she would make it through the next two years. When things closed in around her, she could repeat it to herself over and over, a litany or a promise.

Alexina stepped around a bramble, swearing as it hooked through the heavy denim of her jeans and bit into her leg. She stopped to disengage it and moved on, but her train of thought was broken and instead the image of Jessica rose up before her, face serious, mouth forming the word "escapist." It was a word Jessica often used. She felt Alexina was too dreamy, too solitary, read too much—and worst of all, read the wrong kinds of books. Periodically, Jessica tried to make changes. She enrolled Alexina in a science-oriented school, bought her a computer, sent her to camp. She gave her books on science and mathematics, which accumulated unread beside Alexina's own collection of science fiction, legends and mythology, discussions of parapsychology and the possibility of life on other planets. Alexina found it fairly easy to ignore these sporadic efforts, and derived a certain satisfaction from Jessica's frustration. But Jessica's statements had a way of intruding at odd moments, and sometimes Alexina would hear that dry, detached voice inside her head, saying things like, Computers are the language of the future, or You should read less and socialize more, or You can't bury your head in the sand if you want to be a success.

Today was one of those days. The voice would not be shut out, and, as always, it produced the familiar, nagging doubts. *Was* she escapist? But who wouldn't be, here? She certainly didn't read too much any more, she thought bitterly. The farm had seen to that. Well, maybe the reading *had* begun as a kind of escape—from the lonely apartment, from the long grieving for her parents. But, she thought stubbornly, it was much more than that. She had always been fascinated by the other worlds, other realities her books described; she was sure there could not be so much literature if these things were purely imaginary. Too many people had experienced magic and ESP and other dimensions—even famous scientists speculated on the possibility of life on Jupiter. No, these wonderful things were somehow real. Alexina read her books as a sort of quest, a search for some clue as to how the wonderful things might become real *for her.* They were hidden, she knew, hidden behind the dense confining fabric of the daily world. But they could break through, the books attested to that. Alexina knew that most people were like Jessica: Lack of imagination and skepticism drew a curtain around them and made them blind. But Alexina's eyes were open. If ever something should break through, she would be ready to see it.

She reached the shade of the pines at last, passing gratefully into their relative coolness. She began to climb the gentle slope, the needles slippery beneath her feet. Already she could feel the calming atmosphere of the cave, the restful silence of its cool interior, the special sense of herself she could regain there no matter how dismal her hours at the farm. Determinedly she thrust Jessica's voice away, pressed her lecturing image down to nothing. I'm *not* escapist, she thought. It didn't matter what people thought, not Jessica, not Toby, not anyone. She would read what she liked and think what she liked. She would never change, never become dull and skeptical and reasonable. She would not allow the farm to drag her down. And someday . . . someday she would know everything, understand why she was different and what she waited for. Jessica's voice would be quieted forever then.

Alexina scaled her way up the rock face to the ledge, pausing for a moment to rest before going on. It had been perfectly still all day, with not the breath of a breeze, but now the wind brushed down from the heights, stirring the ferns in the cracks of the rock. She felt almost chilly. There was a rustling sound that seemed to come from all around. Then the wind died and abruptly everything was still.

It took a moment for Alexina to become aware of something strange. Partly it was the silence. It was *too* silent, as if all of nature, like an animal dozing in the sun, had come suddenly to full alertness, head up, frozen. Slowly Alexina looked around. She could see nothing out of the ordinary. But as her eyes swung toward the cave, she *felt* it. There was something there, something not visible: an outpouring of some unseen atmosphere. It was as if a river boiled from the mouth of the cave, made not of water but of stillness, and with it came a slowing, a suspension—as if the world had stopped breathing. Alexina's own breath deepened. She felt the blood slow on its path through her veins, and everything else seemed to deepen and slow as well.

With a sudden shock, almost an explosion, everything started up again. The wind rustled, the ferns swayed, and Alexina found she was breathing hard. She put her hand to her forehead. Am I ill? she wondered. She felt dizzy and sat down to let the faintness pass. And then she heard a muffled noise. It came from the direction of the cave. It was the sound of footsteps—footsteps approaching along the ledge.

Alexina was stricken with absolute and unreasoning terror. She leaped to her feet and flung herself up the cliff until she came to a smaller outcrop. She crouched there, her back against the rock, panting. After a moment she leaned forward slightly, just enough for a view of the ledge below.

Moving along it were two men. The taller one wore an enveloping cloak that reached to his ankles. His long black hair was braided in an unfamiliar way at the back of his neck. The other man was shorter, more muscular, dressed in tunic and leggings and carrying a sort of yoke from which hung two heavy bags. Curiosity got the better of caution, and Alexina craned forward for a better view. The tall man was carrying a wrapped object in his arms, and as he passed below her she caught a flash of something she could not identify, a sort of subliminal pulsing, like the thrumming of a generator behind heavy doors. She concentrated on it, reaching forward with her mind in the way she had always done with things that interested her. There was a peculiar sense of meeting a barrier, a resistance that held for a moment and then yielded, and then all at once she felt a blow, like meeting solid rock at the end of a long fall. It was not physical, but reaction to it pushed Alexina back against the cliff as if she had been physically thrown.

The man stopped dead. He looked around, carefully, his narrow eyes lingering on the ledge where Alexina crouched, willing herself to be invisible. After an endless moment he gestured to his companion, and once again they proceeded along the ledge. They reached the rock face that led to the meadow and disappeared down it. Only after they had gone did Alexina realize that she had not actually seen all this with her eyes—rather, she had somehow sensed it without looking, in images as clear as sight.

Alexina was shivering, despite the heat of the day. Her head ached as if someone really had hit her, and she stayed on her little ledge for some time. Eventually, when she was quite sure they were not returning, she climbed down and cautiously made her way to the cave. She shone her flashlight inside. It was empty. There was an odd sharp smell, like ozone, which she did not recall ever having been there before. At the back of the cave her flashlight caught the glint of a small object half-concealed in a crevice of the rock floor. She went forward and picked it up. It was a golden disk about the size of a half dollar, stamped with a curious design. She hurried back to the ledge, looking out over the meadow to see if she could catch a glimpse of the two men. Nothing. And yet, she *felt* something. It was a sort of tugging inside her head. An image of the men rose behind her eyes; she saw them quite clearly walking off around the foot of the mountain, keeping to the pines so they would not be seen. That was what they had done, she was sure. Yet how could she know that? She had not actually seen them.

Some of the fear was returning. The landscape around her was suddenly hostile, the cave at her back a gaping mouth ready to swallow her up. She beat a hasty retreat, climbing down the cliff as fast as she could, running through the pines and across the meadow, slowing only when she passed through the gate that marked the boundary of the Krantzes' backyard. Breathless, she pushed open the screen door and entered the kitchen. Julia was already at the stove.

"What's the matter?" she asked, turning around. "You look like you met a mountain lion."

"I . . . I thought I was late for dinner," Alexina gasped, trying to calm her breathing.

"Well, you're back just in time. What's that in your hand?"

Alexina looked down and realized with an unpleasant shock that she was still clutching the golden disk she had found. Instinctively, she pushed it into her pocket. "Nothing," she mumbled. "I . . . I found a rock. In the meadow."

"Well, wash your hands and put on an apron. There's some beans over there that need washing."

For once glad to be enclosed in the deadening normality of daily routine, Alexina got to work. The meal seemed to go on forever. All through it she was aware of the lump of the disk in her back pocket. But at last the food was eaten, the dishes washed and put away, the laundry folded, and she was free to escape to her room with her homework.

She put her books down on her bed and took out the disk, tilting it toward the light of her bedside lamp. The design was stamped on both sides, a symmetrical geometric ornamentation that reminded her a bit of ancient Celtic designs. It was heavy for its size, a deep and lustrous yellow—for all the world like real gold. Gold, she knew, was soft and easily dented. She scored at the disk with her nail file. A definite mark appeared on the shining surface.

Alexina stared at it. Could this really be gold? Could the bags the shorter man carried be full of disks like this one? An amount of gold that big staggered the imagination. Could the two men be thieves, robbers? But why had they been at the cave? A storage place for their loot, perhaps? Alexina searched her memory for anything she had seen on television recently about big heists, but could recall nothing. However, they could have done it a long time ago, hiding the gold until the statute of limitations had passed. Maybe it had been in the cave all along, all the time she had been going there. Alexina felt cold. If she had left just a few moments earlier today she would have met them face-to-face. Should she tell Charles and Julia what she had seen? Should she call the police?

No, she thought slowly. There had been more to it, more than gold or thieves or heists. The men had been dressed very strangely, and the one with the yoke had looked positively medieval. Not like a bank robber at all. And . . . what about her odd feelings? The slowing before they appeared, the weird non-physical blow that threw her against the rock, seeing them without actually looking at them . . . Did I imagine that? she thought. In the turmoil that came to her as she remembered, in the traces of panic, she knew she had not imagined it. It had happened. It had happened just as she recalled.

But *what* had happened? She had felt it so clearly—yet there had been no understandable physical cause for any of it. Could it have been . . . could it have been ESP of some kind? Telepathy? Alexina felt breathless, as if the air in the room were too thin. Could it possibly be that, at last, something had broken through to her? Yet it had not been the way she thought it would be. There had been no sense of exhilaration or wonder—only something alien and immensely powerful. Behind that blow she had sensed a force quite beyond her experience, something that could have eaten her up if it had caught her. Alexina shivered, in spite of the heat of her room. The gold disk was a hard weight against her palm.

Suddenly she did not wish to think about it any more. She got up and went to her bureau, and pushed the disk into the back of a drawer.

Opening her books, she tried to study. But she could not concentrate. Finally, still chilly, she turned out the light and got under the covers. The darkness—country darkness, much thicker than city darkness, with its own special scent of dry mountains and damp meadows—came inside and enclosed her, and she felt the familiar loneliness clamp down. This was the worst moment of the day, when the lost, desperate feeling—the farm-feeling, she had come to call it—rolled over her with an intensity that never seemed to decrease. She no longer cried, as she had at first—what was the point, after all—but lay dry-eyed, staring out at the starry rectangles of sky framed by the windows and listening to the silence, the country silence with no background of city noise to disturb its depth.

On the border between sleep and waking, the image of the two men composed itself again inside her mind. She saw them walking, moving through the night, this time not on the ledge or in the meadow but skirting one of the lakes. And she felt it again, that slight tugging, as if she were a fish at the end of a line. She grew cold briefly and passed swiftly into sleep.

2

School let out the last week in June. Alexina had looked forward to summer, for she found the small local school intolerably boring after private school in New York. But she soon found that the free time she had anticipated rarely materialized.

The farm was one of the small subsistence operations common to that part of the country: a few head of cattle, some pigs and chickens, some corn and soybeans, an apple orchard, and the major source of revenue—a large field of produce grown for local markets and several acres of pick-your-own strawberries, peas, and blueberries. The family also had a stand beside the main road where they sold fruit, vegetables, and honey from their hives. In the summer, besides the usual tasks of animal-tending and maintaining the farm, there were additional chores—cultivating, harvesting, and storing the bounty generated by the fields.

Everyone pitched in, with the help of local teenagers hired at minimum wage. The worst task was weeding the long fields of vegetables grown for market—yard after yard of green and yellow squash, tomatoes, beans, and peas. A Rototiller was run between the orderly rows, but it was still necessary to weed around each plant by hand. Spending hours bent over in the dirt under a blazing sun was no fun, and Alexina hated it, even though her mirror told her that her muscles were firmer, her hair was acquiring attractive red highlights, and her skin was spectacularly tanned. She preferred to tend the booths in the pick-your-own fields, because at least she could be in the shade, sitting down, for some of the time. The fields bore peas first, then strawberries, then blueberries, with apples and pears to come in the autumn. They attracted large crowds and made quite a bit of money, but costs and overhead ate up the profits, and the Krantzes would be lucky to make more than a ten-percent gain on the entire operation.

Toby graduated from high school in June with high honors—it surprised Alexina to realize he was such a good student—and now that his schooling was over, he had taken on a substantial portion of the burden of running the farm. Much as she disliked Toby, Alexina could not help but be impressed with his dedication to a brutal schedule. He labored from dawn until dinner in the fields; at six o'clock he ate a hasty meal and then, at six-thirty, he left the house for his paying job in a restaurant in the small town nearby. He worked there until midnight.

Embarrassingly, Alexina had unintentionally overheard part of the quarrel which followed Toby's announcement that he planned to work off the farm. She had come into the kitchen to get herself a drink, vaguely aware of the sound of voices in the basement where Charles had his workshop. Abruptly, they seemed to move closer to the stairs, and she could hear them clearly. There was a surprising note of desperation in Toby's voice.

"But why not? If I can still keep up my farm work, what harm can it do?"

"You won't be able to work your best this way." It was Charles. "You'll be exhausted. You won't get more than six hours of sleep a night."

"It'll just be for the summer! And if my farm work's affected, I'll quit the job whenever you say. Just let me give it a try!"

"What do you need money for? If you become my partner, you'll get a share of the profits."

"That's my business! And the goddamn farm doesn't make any profits!"

There was a silence. When Charles spoke his voice was level, but there was a lot of anger in it. "Don't think I don't know what all this is about, Toby. We've been over it a hundred times, and my answer's still no."

"You just can't accept that I am different from you!" Alexina was transfixed by the emotion in Toby's voice. "You want to force me into your mold. If you'd just look you could see it's not right for me! I'm eighteen—I have a right to make my own decisions!"

"Toby, you will inherit the farm." Charles too had raised his voice. "You can't afford to take time away from it for some . . . some pipe dream! You've got to face reality!"

"It's not a pipe dream! It's as real as the farm is!"

"My answer is no, and that's flat." There was a sound, as if Charles had struck a table to emphasize his words. "You get more like your grandfather every day."

"Oh, what's the use." There was the sound of rapid footsteps on the basement stairs. Before Alexina could move, Toby was in the kitchen. He stopped short and Alexina tensed, expecting him to lash out at her for having overheard. But he just looked at her for a moment, his face utterly bleak, and then walked out of the kitchen, the screen door slamming behind him. Thoughtfully, Alexina returned to work. All at once Toby seemed human. She understood the frustration of being forced into the wrong mold—Jessica had tried to force her often enough.

Apparently Julia intervened, for Toby was allowed to take the job after all. But the tension between Toby and Charles was very apparent. They quarreled frequently, usually over trivial matters, and always beneath the arguments remained a deep anger that was expressed but not addressed through their outbursts.

Julia was busy with preserving and canning and freezing as produce from the family's own garden ripened. By the end of June she had put up pounds of strawberries and quarts of peas, and was beginning on the beans and every conceivable kind of relish and pickle made from squash and cucumbers. One of Alexina's summer tasks was to help with the preserving process. It was the one job she did not mind, for it was cool in the house and she could sit down while she worked. And beyond that, she genuinely enjoyed Julia's company. From the beginning, Julia had, taken real pains to make Alexina feel at home, including her in the warmth she extended to her husband and son, making allowances for Alexina's unfamiliarity with hard physical work, never scolding her for mistakes. Yet Alexina still felt a slight constraint in Julia's presence. She was not quite sure why.

In July the first tomatoes were harvested and prepared for canning. Julia stood at the stove, dropping them into boiling water to blanch, and it was Alexina's job to peel off the skins, cut the tomatoes in half, and place them in sterilized jars. The growing rows of clean glass jars full of scarlet fruit were beautiful, and produced a pleasant sense of accomplishment.

"I'll bet you never did anything like this when you were in New York," said Julia after a while.

"I certainly didn't. I've never worked so hard in my life."

Julia smiled. "It *is* hard work. I'm used to it—I've been doing it most of my life." She glanced at Alexina. "But I know it's been tough for you to adjust."

"A bit," agreed Alexina tentatively.

"Frankly, when Jessica asked me to take you while she was gone, I had my doubts. I wondered if a city kid could be happy here." She paused. "But you seem to be doing okay."

Alexina did not respond. She was not sure if Julia were asking a question or making an observation. The farm-feeling threatened briefly and receded.

Julia was looking at her again. "Alexina," she said, "I know you're *not* happy here. I've been wanting to talk to you about it for a while now, but it never seemed to be the right time."

Alexina kept her eyes on her hands. Julia stopped blanching and came to sit down at the table.

"Stop peeling for a moment. I just want you to know that I understand, that I know how hard it is for you. I know you feel out of place and lonely. And I know you resent being here. I just hope you don't resent Jessica for bringing you."

Alexina felt ashamed. She truly hadn't meant, no matter how bad she felt, to go around broadcasting her emotions. "I'm sorry," she said, not meeting Julia's eyes. "I just . . . well, it takes some time to get used to it all. The work and, and—," she stopped awkwardly, not knowing how to go on. "And I don't resent Jessica, I guess. I know she couldn't take me with her to Russia, and she couldn't leave me alone in New York. I know she didn't have any choice." But she *did*. Alexina could not stop the thought. She could have not gone at all.

Julia reached out and patted Alexina's hand, then

got to her feet and went back to the stove. "It will get better, you know. It did for me. I felt all those things too, when I first came here. I haven't lived on the farm all my life."

"Really?"

Julia nodded. "I came to like it, of course. But Jessica always hated it. She was dreadfully lonely."

Alexina tried to think of Jessica being lonely, and failed. Jessica was as close to being completely self-sufficient as anyone Alexina had ever met. "I can't imagine that," she said. "I mean, she's so wrapped up in her work she might as well be in Antarctica with the penguins most of the time."

"It was a different kind of loneliness for her, Alexina. A loneliness of the mind. She needed people around her as intelligent as she was, people who shared her interests. That's why she left." There was a pause. "She works pretty hard, then, does she?"

"Pretty hard!" Alexina laughed a little. "She works *all* the time. Even when she's home. She goes to work at seven and sometimes she doesn't come home until ten. Everything is computers, computers, nothing but computers! All her friends are just the same. She gives parties sometimes, and even then they talk about computers—computers and the company." She stopped, suddenly aware of the resentment in her voice. Julia was so easy to talk to: Her sympathetic silence held no judgment or censure. It was the longest conversation they had ever had.

"You don't sound as if you're too keen on computers," Julia said.

"I'm not." Alexina finished filling one jar and began on another. "I'm really not. Jessica wants me to be, of course. She gives me books and things, and she tries to talk to me about her designs and what the company's doing in the field. She got me a computer for Christmas a couple of years ago. I think she thought that if it was sitting right there I'd get interested. Well, I did, sort of. I mean it was interesting figuring out how to use it. But there's just so far you can go with a computer before you have to add on whole new gadgets to expand its capacity. And then you run into things you can't teach yourself, and you have to go to school or something. And there are only so many games you can play! So I didn't use it at all after a while, and I think she got mad. She sent me to computer camp that summer—you know, where you spend eight hours a day with a bunch of kids with glasses a foot thick and nothing but numbers in their heads. It was perfectly *awful.*" She glanced at Julia. "I don't mean to sound nasty."

But Julia shook her head. "Don't worry, Alexina, I know how frustrating Jessica can be. We aren't very close any more, you know. Sometimes she seems to be speaking in a foreign language." For a moment her hands were poised above the kettle and her eyes were far away. Then she shook her head slightly. "I take it you don't want to follow in Jessica's footsteps."

Alexina shook her head emphatically. "We're on completely different tracks. She thinks the only important interests are scientific ones, but there's so much more to the world. I mean . . ." Alexina struggled to put her feelings into words. "It just seems to me that people who are into computers think like computers. All they see is numbers. They don't see all the other things out there, all the wonderful things in the world. They can't accept anything that can't be proved—preferably on a computer. The really important things don't exist for them. I don't ever want to be like that."

"What sorts of things are you interested in?"

"Oh . . . lots of things," said Alexina vaguely. "I

read a lot—science fiction and stuff. And I go to museums, and movies—I love all kinds of movies. There's always something to do in New York." She stopped, not wanting to imply so clearly that there was nothing to do here.

"Tell me, Alexina, has Jessica always left you alone so much?"

"Yes."

"Even when you first came to her?"

Alexina nodded, looking away. Even after eight years, the awfulness of that time could still reach out and grasp her. She remembered the numbing shock of her parents' deaths, the pain of the funeral, the strangeness of Jessica's impersonal apartment. Jessica was her mother's best friend, and as her parents had no living relatives, Jessica was named as guardian in her parents' will. Alexina had known Jessica from babyhood, in an aloof and unemotional way, and that was the nature of their subsequent relationship. Since Jessica was rarely home, a succession of babysitters had been arranged. The baby-sitters stopped when Alexina turned fourteen and was, in Jessica's opinion, able to "do on her own." As she grew older Alexina realized that Jessica wasn't unfeeling, as she had assumed in her first unhappiness, just utterly wrapped up in her own world. She wasn't unkind either; she simply had not known how to deal with children or with grief. Still, Alexina had needed someone, and Jessica had not been there. She had never been there. The old resentment bit down, as sharp as ever.

She became aware that Julia's eyes were on her. She began to work again, her face still turned away.

"It's her way, Alexina," Julia said gently. "She's just . . . not very emotional. She never was, you know. I love my sister, but I'm aware of her limitations."

Alexina looked up. She saw Julia's handsome, aging face, like and unlike Jessica's, lined with care and hard work. It was as if she had spoken aloud and Julia had answered her: Julia had sensed her feelings as keenly as if she had expressed them. How could one sister be so unlike the other? Alexina's loneliness rose up inside her and reached out.

"You know, I don't think she . . . I don't think she cares about me really. Oh, I know she cares *for* me—but it's sort of like I was a house she inherited by accident and had to keep up so the value wouldn't drop."

"But she does care," said Julia gently. "Don't think that because she doesn't show it she doesn't care. She does."

Alexina turned her face away. Perhaps Julia was right. But deep within her, she could not believe it. "Oh, well," she said after a moment to dispel emotion. "Things turned out okay for me. I know plenty of kids who have parents and normal families and are completely screwed up anyway. I'm better off than they are."

"Your friends?"

"Some of them."

"Well, I'm glad you have friends in the city. It's not good for a young girl to spend a lot of time alone. It makes you morbid. Believe me, I know." She finished her blanching and came over to the table to help with the peeling. "You're alone here a lot. I worry about you sometimes. I'd hoped you'd make some friends at school."

Alexina shrugged. "I know some people."

"Acquaintances aren't like friends, Alexina. Maybe if you spent some time with people your own age you'd feel more at home."

"I don't mind, Julia, truly I don't. I'm used to being on my own. Don't worry about me."

Julia was silent for a few moments. Then she smiled. "It'll work out, Alexina. Everything does, in the end."

"You know . . ." said Alexina, her voice trailing off. Julia looked at her enquiringly. "You and Jessica are so different. It's hard to believe you're sisters."

Julia smiled. "I guess so. But it's always been that way, even when we were growing up." She shook her head. "Things were awfully tough then."

"You mean tougher than they are now?" said Alexina, before she thought. But Julia only laughed.

"You must think we're poor," she said frankly. "But no one who hasn't experienced it can know what real poverty is. Why, I can remember my mother selling her wedding ring to buy us meat during the winter, and there was a time when we had no machinery and we had to use a horse-drawn plow."

"Why were you so poor?"

"Partly the Depression. And partly my father." Julia shook her head. "My father wanted to be a lawyer, not a farmer. My grandfather sent him to law school. He found a good job. But then the Depression came, and there was no more work. My father and mother had to come back here because they couldn't afford to live in town. I was about six then, and Jessica was five. My father hated it—here he was, stuck on the farm, not able to do the thing he really wanted. It ate him up inside, and he began to drink. He never got another job, and we stayed on the farm even after the Depression was over. The farm was in my family for three generations before me, you know. When my grandfather was alive it was a pretty profitable operation. He managed to keep it up even through the thirties and into the forties. But when he died my father just let it all go to waste, let the buildings rot and the machinery fall apart. My mother wound up carrying most of the burden. She sold parcels of land when she could to keep us going. The farm was quite a bit larger than it is now."

"Wow!" said Alexina. "It sounds like a novel."

"You and your books. But I suppose it was like a novel, a sad one. Jessica couldn't wait to get away from here, of course. She left as soon as she could. But I got to love it, and I stayed to take care of my parents and the farm, too, as much as I could. But things went on getting worse and worse—there was so little I could do. And then I met Charles. I'd almost given up hope of marrying by that time! He'd been to agricultural college and he was pretty sure we could bring the farm back. And we did. But you have no idea how hard we had to work in the beginning."

"Everyone seems to work so hard now."

"You should have seen us then. Why, the first five years were spent just getting started. We had to buy a lot of machinery and equipment. That was the 1950s and interest rates were low, but we're still paying off some of those loans. Things were in awful shape. But we had the land, and we had faith in ourselves. It was Charles's idea to have the pick-your-own fields—he was the first around here to do that, and now everyone's imitating him. And we had Toby. He's been such a help. Though his heart's not in it."

"Really?" said Alexina, curious.

"Yes." Julia's face clouded slightly. "He just has his heart set on going to college. But Charles doesn't want him to. He wants him to stay here on the farm and inherit. Charles is very set on not having the farm go out of the family." She glanced at Alexina. "You and Toby don't get on."

"That's an understatement."

"It's too bad, you know. You're more alike than you realize."

"It's just that he's so sarcastic. He never seems to stop teasing me. It doesn't matter what I do, he finds something to make fun of."

Julia sighed. "Yes, I know. Toby's tongue is too quick. But he doesn't mean a lot of what he says. And you get too angry, Alexina. If you could go along with him a bit, it wouldn't be so bad."

Alexina was silent. That she would never believe.

"Partly it's his frustration coming out. There's a lot of my father in him. And it's a defense mechanism—if he laughs at the world, it can't hurt him. He makes fun of himself too, you know."

"Well, I just wish he wouldn't make fun of me!"

Julia looked at her. "Would you like me to talk to him?"

"No. Probably that would make it worse."

"That's a wise thought." Julia surveyed the tomatoes. "We're almost done here, Alexina. Why don't you run down to the produce stand and open up for the afternoon."

"Okay." Alexina got up and wiped off her hands. She started to leave the kitchen, but at the door she paused and turned. "Julia?" Julia looked up. "I enjoyed our talk today. I really did."

Julia smiled. "Get along with you," she said, and returned to screwing the lids on the tomato jars. But Alexina thought she looked pleased.

Tending the produce stand was the job Alexina liked best. It was a shallow shed with shelves up the back on which sat baskets of fruit and vegetables from the family's fields. Often it did a decent business, and Alexina might be quite busy with customers. But more frequently there would be long pauses between cars, and she could sit in her chair in the shade, free to read or daydream to her heart's content.

She was aware that she felt more cheerful today

than she had in a long time. Talking to Julia had really helped. She hadn't realized how much it would mean to have her feelings understood and, moreover, be told they were perfectly natural. She had liked Julia from the first, but today Julia had also become someone she could talk to. In the course of the afternoon that slight awkwardness had vanished for good. It was interesting, she thought, the degree to which things were a matter of perception. She would never have imagined that this life, which seemed to her one of incredible hardship, might seem one of ease and comparative comfort to Julia. She could not begin to visualize living as the sisters must have during their childhood. Perhaps, she thought, mathematics and computers were as much of an escape for Jessica as books and fantasies were for her. It was a strange idea.

The day was beautiful—hot, but with a pleasant breeze and a brilliantly blue sky. No cars appeared. Alexina let her thoughts drift away on the heavy summer air, too lazy even to read. Dreamily, she watched the pocked pavement of the road. It shimmered, and mirage oil slicks appeared far down its length. The meadow grass shimmered too, as if smoking from an invisible ground fire. And the mountains, shaded and dark and a relief to the dazzled eye, breathed out a promise of coolness that was almost tangible.

3

Alexina had not forgotten the two men she had seen almost a month ago. She had not returned to the cave since that day. The immediacy of the experience decreased with time, and her fear lost some of its power; but she retained the uneasiness of something unexplained, something encountered that for a moment had taken her right out of her normal frame of reference. As days passed, she could recapture less and less what it was she had felt. A slowing feeling? A blow? The more she tried to pin it down, the more nebulous it became, and she was left at last with only the certainty that something *had* happened, something she did not understand.

She had two dreams about the men. In the first, she saw them camped by an enormous body of water. Its farther shore was lost in distance, but it was not the ocean. The men were dressed in normal clothes now. The second dream came a week later. They were walking along a country road that seemed vaguely midwestern, heading north. These dreams were different from ordinary dreams, both in the clarity with which she recalled them afterward and in the feeling that accompanied them, a tugging at her mind like that of a thread unreeling. She woke from them cold, frightened, tired as if she had not slept. But there had been only the two dreams, and none since then; she hoped there would be no more. The gold coin lay at the back of her bureau drawer. She was aware of its presence sometimes, but she did not take it out.

One Thursday toward the end of July, Alexina woke up to a gray sky. By nine o'clock it was pouring, the heavy rain sweeping across the fields and the wind whipping at the grass until it lay almost flat. She was supposed to open the produce booth, but Julia looked out at the storm and told her to wait until the rain slackened.

It was still raining after lunch, and the family busied itself with indoor activities. Charles disappeared to his workshop, Julia took a pile of mending and sat down at her sewing machine, and Toby sequestered himself in his room. Alexina settled in the window seat of the front room to read. The storm showed no signs of abating as the afternoon wore on. The wildness of the weather stirred in her a restlessness, an undefined feeling that there was something she should do. The antique clock on the mantel ticked steadily, chiming the half hours. Her feeling of restlessness grew, and gradually she began to realize that it involved the cave. It was almost a compulsion to act, as if she had left the gas on or the water running. She was aware of the strangeness of it, but the impulse was not to be denied. It brought her to her feet and took her up to her room. Quickly she got into raingear and crept quietly down the back stairs and out the kitchen door.

She ran through the backyard and across the meadow. The force of the wind was intense, and despite her slicker and hat she was soon wet through. Cautious now, she reached the pines and climbed the cliff. She put her nose over the top of the ledge, looked about until she was sure no one else was there, and hauled herself upright.

The compulsion disappeared all at once. Alexina stood on the ledge with the rain beating on her head and shoulders, unable to remember exactly why she had wanted to come out in a downpour to a place that made her nervous. Well, now she was here, she thought, she might as well wait out the storm. She walked along the ledge, shivering in the wind. Inside the cave, she shrugged off her slicker and wrung out her hair.

It was a moment before she noticed that there was something in the air, something familiar. It was the smell, the smell that had been here the day she saw the two men. She froze, her skin crawling. Instinctively she turned her head toward the back of the cave. It was too dark to tell for sure, but it did not look as if anyone else was there. Fumblingly she felt for the flashlight that lay on the floor just inside the entrance, and shone it around her.

Empty. It was just a smell, she told herself. What could a smell mean? But she was still uneasy. And when she began to light the candles, their uncertain glow showed her what the flashlight had missed. There were several footprints in the pine needles at the mouth of the cave. She stared at them, feeling like Robinson Crusoe. You idiot, she told herself, they're *your* footprints. But when she put her sneaker down beside them it was obvious that the feet that had made them were larger than her own. They pointed out of the cave.

It's happening again, thought Alexina, cold with sudden conviction. She wanted all at once to be far away. She put on her raingear, not pausing to blow out the candles, and hurried back along the ledge. Her breath sounded oddly in her ears. Reaching the cliff she paused, feeling weak. The rain still fell, a gray curtain obscuring the view. It was slowing as she watched, each drop distinct, and the sound it made was barely audible.

It was there again, the sensation she had felt a month ago, a river rolling silently over the world. Almost, she could see it coming toward her; powerless, she stood as it reached and engulfed her. There was a moment of dreadful terror and then, abruptly, nothing, nothing but a dreamlike, floating suspension. Alexina turned, each motion graceful and precise, and moved back toward the cave. She pressed against the current; it became necessary to lean against its force, and by the time she reached the cave entrance she could move no farther. She was aware that something was coming, approaching on the crest of a strange wave that carried it closer and closer to this place, this instant of space and time. She held on to the rock beside her. The candles were still burning on their outcrops, unaffected, their flames rising straight up. Her blood sounded in her ears, slowing, slowing. . . .

And then came the explosion, the outpouring as whatever it was arrived. It wrenched Alexina's fingers from their hold and she was flung backward, losing consciousness as she fell.

* * * *

When she came to she was prone on the grass outside the cave. The rain had stopped. She had no idea how long she had been unconscious.

She sat up, then got slowly to her feet, bracing herself against dizziness. The world felt normal again. What had happened? It had felt like an explosion, but there were no signs of damage or debris. Cautiously, Alexina approached the cave. The smell was there again, very strong this time, assaulting her nostrils with a sharpness that made her gasp. She peered inside. Was it her imagination, or was there a dark shape at the back? Oddly, she was not afraid. Perhaps it was the lingering numbness of unconsciousness, which made everything seem slightly distanced. She was sure now she could see something, but the candles did not cast enough light. She felt for the flashlight, pointed in the direction of the shape, and switched it on.

It did not stir in the sudden illumination. Carefully, she moved closer. It was only a boy—certainly older than herself but probably not yet out of his teens. He was unconscious, lying on his back with his arms and legs flung about, as if he had fallen from a height. He wore a tunic of thick, dull-colored material, leggings crosstied with leather thongs, and a short cloak. About his waist was a leather belt with a number of ominous-looking utensils attached to it, including a dagger; around his neck hung a pair of heavy silver medallions. His features, with high Scandinavian cheekbones, were regular and handsome, and his skin was extremely fair. His blond hair, spread out around his head, seemed to be at least shoulder length. It was twisted in front into several small braids.

Alexina knelt down a short distance away, staring at this apparition, feeling a bit as if she were dreaming. She had never seen anyone so odd looking—fully as odd as those two men. The men, and now this boy—what was going on? She had been quite sure the cave was empty before—where had he come from? It was almost as if he had arrived on the crest of the explosion, but of course that was impossible. He must have been here all the time, hiding, either in the cave or around it, and like her had been overcome by the explosion. The footprints in the pine needles must have been his.

The boy's eyes opened. There was an instant's pause, in which she had time to notice that they were a brilliant green, and then he sprang up and away with a suddenness that made Alexina jump backward also. The flashlight swung wildly for a moment, creating enormous leaping shadows, then steadied and picked him out crouched against the opposite wall.

Alexina's heart pounded. The boy was staring at her, motionless, his eyes wide open and his face very pale. Why, he's terrified of me, Alexina thought with some puzzlement. Slowly she lowered the flashlight and placed it on the ground so it would not shine in his eyes. She saw now that there were rips in his garments and that his cheek and forehead were grazed as if he had scraped them against the rock. Apparently he decided she was not going to attack him, for he slowly relaxed his tense posture and sank down against the cave wall. He let out a gasp of pain as his left hand touched the ground.

"Are you all right?" Alexina asked softly.

He stared at her, unblinking. She tried again.

"I won't tell anyone you're here if you don't want me to."

He still stared, as if he had not understood. Slowly she rose to a crouch. Back here the cave was too low to stand upright. He tensed.

"I'd like to help you," she said. "You're hurt. Let me take a look at your cuts. I can get some disinfectant."

She began to move slowly toward him. He let her get about halfway and then, in a movement so swift it was almost invisible, whipped out the dagger and pointed it at her. She froze. His lips pulled back from his teeth in a snarl that, with his wild hair and bizarre clothing, made him look truly ferocious. It occurred to Alexina that he might be mad, or sick. She began to back away, very slowly, as one did from an angry dog. As the cave roof lifted she stood straight, still backing, her eyes fixed on his. All at once he leaped up and charged at her with the dagger outstretched, letting out a bloodcurdling yell. She screamed and ran for her life along the ledge.

She was nearly to the ground before she realized he had not followed her. In fact, he had not even left the cave. Alexina clung to the cliff, indecisive. He had not actually attacked her, only chased her away. She remembered his look of terror; perhaps he charged at her because, for some strange reason, he was afraid, not mad or dangerous. He had limped badly. He was injured—perhaps he was sick. He needed help. She thought again of the puzzle of his presence. They were all connected in some way—the boy, the men, the coin, the strange feelings. She was sure of it.

Alexina climbed back up to the ledge and tiptoed along it. Rounding the curve, she peered into the cave. The flashlight, still on the ground, showed her that the boy was sprawled out, again unconscious. The cut on his forehead had reopened and was oozing blood.

As Alexina turned to head back to the farm, she knew that her curiosity was stronger than her sense of caution. The boy was a link in a chain, and she meant to find out what was going on. There was still over an hour before she must help get dinner; she would get bandages and disinfectant, and some food if she could manage it, and return to treat his wounds. She was aware of a strange excitement, as if a momentous event were about to occur.

She managed to get into the house without being seen, but when she reached the upstairs hallway,

Toby emerged abruptly from his room. He stared at her.

"You look like a drowned rat, Alexina."

She scowled. "Shut up, Toby."

He cocked his head. "It's not exactly a perfect day for a walk. What were you doing outside?"

"None of your business!" she snapped.

A wicked smile settled on his face.

"Aha, it's a secret. Alexina has a secret. Well, you're making puddles on the carpet." He raised his voice. "Ma! Alexina's dripping all over the upstairs rug!"

"Shut up!" Alexina hissed, but it was too late. Julia had come into the downstairs hall and was looking up.

"Be quiet, Toby," she said. "Mercy, Alexina! You certainly are wet. You'll catch a cold for sure. Get into some dry clothes and I'll make you some cocoa to warm you up."

Alexina felt she could cheerfully wring Toby's neck. Now she would not be able to get back to the cave this afternoon. She shot him a silent look of hatred, putting into it every ounce of her frustration. She was satisfied to see it had made an impression; his smug expression turned puzzled as she squelched toward her room.

She would just have to wait, she thought. She could sneak out tonight, when everyone was in bed. . . . No, that was not wise. She must wait until it was light. First thing tomorrow, then, before anyone was awake. Not Toby, not anyone, was going to stop her from going back to the cave.

* * * *

Alexina set her alarm for 4:00 A.M., and when it rang she was awake at once. Dressing quickly she crept downstairs, avoiding the creaky boards. In the kitchen she put together as substantial a package of food as she could without Julia noticing: half a loaf of bread, several hunks of cheese, some assorted fruit. As an afterthought she also took two cans of soda. All of this she placed in a backpack beside the bandages, disinfectant, cotton swabs, and ointment she had collected the previous night.

She let herself carefully out the back door and tiptoed across the yard. Dawn was just breaking and a semitwilight lay on the meadow. The sky behind the mountains was beginning to turn pale yellow. Past the fence she broke into a run, not slackening her pace until she gained the pines. She hurried through the wisps of mist that rose from the damp needles. Let him still be there, she thought as she climbed. Reaching the ledge, she moved cautiously along until she could see inside the cave.

He must have come to during the night, for he lay against the cave wall with his wadded-up cloak for a pillow. The candles had burned out, leaving congealed pools of wax on the outcrops. Alexina began to unload the backpack outside the cave, for she did not wish to alarm him again. She arranged the food invitingly just inside the entrance, then sat back and cleared her throat. The boy's eyes flew open and in almost the same motion he was on his feet, crouched in a defensive stance against the rock.

"It's only me," said Alexina.

He watched her. He looked even worse this morning: His skin was pasty beneath blood and dirt, his long blond hair matted with pine needles, his green eyes bloodshot.

"I brought you some food," Alexina said encouragingly. "Aren't you hungry? I meant it last night—I didn't tell anyone you're here."

He stared at the food, then back at her, then back

at the food. Finally he pulled out his dagger. Holding it warningly before him, he sidled up to the food, grabbed it, and scuttled back inside the cave. Had the dagger not been quite so obviously real, it would have been almost comical. His apparent fear of her allayed any lingering nervousness Alexina might have felt.

He ate ravenously, examining everything as if it were slightly unfamiliar. The cans of soda seemed to perplex him completely: He tapped them, scratched at them as if trying to peel them, and finally shook them against his ear. Alexina observed all this with puzzlement. Was it possible he had never seen a canned soft drink before? Or—might he be slightly retarded? His eyes were too intelligent for that. She gestured toward the can to indicate he should bring it to her. After a suspicious pause he did, leaving it just outside the entrance. Alexina picked it up and pushed back the tab. She poured a bit out on the ground to show him there was liquid inside, and then drank. He watched her and for an instant there was something in his expression—amusement?—but then it was gone and Alexina could not be sure she had really seen it. He seemed to like the drink. After a start of surprise at its carbonation, he drank it all and, after examining the first can, popped the tab on the second and drank it too.

Finished, he looked at her again. Alexina took the medical things out of her pack and held them up, pantomiming swabbing and bandaging his cuts. He seemed to understand, but still did not wish to approach her; he gestured that she should leave the things where she left the food. She obeyed. He did not bother to retreat this time, but clearly he could not figure out the screw top of the disinfectant bottle, or the wrapping of the bandages. He hesitated a moment, looking at her carefully. Then, giving in, he indicated that she should help him.

She was aware of his fear, his body tensing each time she touched him, his wary eyes never leaving her face. Again she wondered why he found her so alarming; she should be the one to feel nervous. There was a good deal of caked blood on his forehead and cheek, but when she removed it the cuts did not look serious. He was fascinated by the adhesive tape and kept touching it, as if he expected it to fall off. His hand, which he continued to favor, was scraped and swollen. Alexina was pretty sure it was not broken, but it was certainly badly sprained. There was nothing she could do for it. She thought of people in books who improvised splints out of unlikely materials, but did not have the first idea how to go about it herself.

She began to put the medical things back in her pack, together with the soda cans. What to do now? She looked at him; he looked back at her as if he were thinking the same thing. *I wonder who you are,* she thought, unconsciously reaching forward with her mind as she searched for a way to communicate. *I wonder how I can talk to you.*

He jumped suddenly, as if someone had stuck a pin into him, and reached out with one hand to grasp at the rock of the cave wall. Eyes open wide, he stared at her. Alexina stared back, perplexed.

Who are you?

It was a voice, very clear and so close it seemed almost inside her head. It was her turn to jump. She looked around, searching for the speaker, but could see no one.

Who are you? it repeated.

Alexina felt the first touch of fear. The voice had a strange quality, neither male nor female, without tone or timbre. But there was no one here, only the boy, and his lips had not moved.

"Did—you hear that?" she whispered to him. An expression very much like impatience appeared on his face.

I can't understand your words, the voice said, slowly and with exaggerated clarity, as if speaking to a child. *We must use mindspeech. Who are you? Why do you have the power?*

For the rest of her life Alexina would remember that moment of realization, the intuition beyond rationality dawning far back in her mind. A shaft of sun fell along the mouth of the cave, and she could feel the cold seeping up into her knees from the hard stone on which she knelt. The boy sighed and began to turn away. Without conscious volition, Alexina reached forward again, wordlessly.

His head snapped around. *You can understand!* They stared at each other, Alexina still numb, he with an expression that moved from eagerness to an impatient frown. *What's wrong with you?*

She took a deep breath. Not quite believing she was doing it, she began to think, fumblingly shaping words inside her head and projecting them forward. *Are—you—telepathic?*

His frown deepened. *Telepathic?* It came back slowly, as if he were turning an unfamiliar phrase over on his tongue.

I mean able to talk by thinking.

Of course. He looked puzzled now. *I don't understand. You bespoke me first.*

I did? Alexina felt as if she were in a dream. All the reading, all the technical phrases—parapsychology, ESP, telepathy—they were all just words. This was the real thing. And here was this boy, behaving as if it were a completely everyday occurrence.

Why do you have the gift? Your people are not supposed to have it.

She hesitated. *I don't know. I didn't know I could do it until this minute.*

It was his turn to stare. *Do you mean you didn't know you had the gift? You didn't* know *you could mindspeak?*

Alexina shook her head.

He sat still for a moment. *This is very strange. They told us your people didn't have the gift, so naturally I didn't try to speak to you, but the power's not supposed to exist here! I don't understand!*

The thoughts came at her quickly, bombarding her, slipping past almost before she could grasp them. They were not separate words, exactly, more like images or concepts. She shook her head and reached forward, still thinking in words because she knew no other way: *You must go slowly. I'm not used to this.*

Sorry. All at once he grinned. *This'd give my teachers something to think about. One of the handpower-born with the gift!*

Why can you understand my thoughts but not my words?

We speak different languages. But thoughts are not in words, they only seem that way. So no matter what language we speak, we can understand each other's thoughts.

Wait a minute. She looked at him, alarmed. *Do you mean to say you can read my mind?*

He shook his head. *No. Everyone has natural barriers. I can receive only what you Project toward me. Besides, it's forbidden to do that sort of thing. Now tell me, who are you?*

My name is Alexina Taylor. It was difficult not to speak the words she thought, and she had to go slowly, but it was becoming easier. It was just an amplification of the *reaching forward* she had done since she was a child, without being aware she was doing anything special. Could she have been projecting thoughts all her life without knowing it? She shivered, struck suddenly with a vertiginous sense of unreality. *Are you sure you can't read my mind?* she repeated, watching him.

He didn't smile, but she knew he was amused. It was amazing the way thoughts carried shadings like spoken words. *I promise I can't.*

How do you *know how to mindspeak?*

I have the gift, he thought, as if that were explanation enough. He looked puzzled again.

She tried another approach. *Where are you from?*

I'm from . . . from far away.

Well, where? And what are you doing here?

A hesitation. *I'm on a journey.*

Are you . . . with anyone? Do you have companions?

Why, have you seen anyone?

Well, yes. Some men—

He did not let her finish. He sat forward and his thoughts slashed across hers, fast and sharp. *When? Where did they go? Are they still here? What did they look like?*

Stop! Alexina projected over the torrent of images, unconsciously putting her hands to her head. There was an echoing inside her mind—the mental equivalent of ringing ears.

Sorry—I keep forgetting. He sat back. *Please tell me, when did you see them?*

About a month ago. They were here, at the cave. Are they your friends?

No. It was emphatic. *They're . . . part of why I'm on the journey. Did you see where they went?*

Alexina prepared to answer and then thought, Why is he interrogating me? *No,* she projected. *I won't tell you anything else until you tell me what's going on. I want to know who you are.*

I can't tell you that.

Why not?

I just can't.

Then I can't tell you anything either.

He looked at her for a moment. She met his eyes defiantly, refusing to drop her gaze. *Tell me why you helped me,* he thought at last. *I want to know why you're not like we're told your people are.*

I'm . . . I'm not sure what you mean. I'm not sure who you mean by "my people."

Your people. He gestured. *The people of this. . . land. We're taught you're unfriendly, hostile, even evil. We're taught your people have no power and hate people like me who do have it.*

There was a challenging expression on his face, as if he were testing her. *Well,* Alexina began, *I don't know who told you that, about people here being hostile. But I guess maybe some people, people who don't believe in what your people can do—mindspeech, I mean—might be hostile, or even hate you, because it would make them afraid. Most people don't believe in things like mindspeech. But I do, I always have. I always knew it could happen. I guess that's why* I'm *not afraid.* She took a deep breath. *As for helping you, that's pretty obvious. You were hurt and sick. You needed help, so I helped you.* She hesitated. *I also thought you might be able to tell me about those two men.*

There was a silence. He watched her steadily, and Alexina wondered what he was thinking.

I don't know what my teachers would say, he thought at last, *but I think I trust you. I don't know why, I just have a feeling. . . . Anyway, you have the gift. All who have the gift are brothers, even if you do come from this place. . . . But you must swear you won't tell anyone about me or what I tell you. You must swear.*

I swear. Alexina tried to project as much conviction as she could.

My name is Taryn. I'm from . . . from another place, a place far away. I'm sorry, but I really can't tell you where. I'm following those two men. They're thieves, and they have stolen something very valuable from my people. Something priceless, something so important I can't express it. They escaped. There were several places they could have gone, but we don't know exactly which one they chose. So we sent search parties to each place to find the men and get back what they stole. It's absolutely vital. What they took means everything to us. Everything.

The images were coming fast again, conveyed on a powerful tide of urgency. What he told her carried a truthfulness that could not be doubted, despite its lack of concrete detail. *What was it they stole?* she asked.

He looked uncomfortable. *I can't tell you. But it really is as important as I say. The whole future of my people is involved. Those men are criminals and they must be brought to justice.*

What could it be? Surely not the gold; he had made it sound too important. Secret papers, perhaps? Knowledge of some kind? She looked at him doubtfully. *So you're with a police force? Or a detective?*

He seemed puzzled for a moment and then his face lighted up. *Oh, I understand what you mean. Yes, that's what I am. And that's why I want you to describe everything you saw—maybe it'll give me a clue I need. At least it'll confirm that this is the right place to start looking.*

All right. And Alexina told him, first describing just the two men and what they looked like. But it felt good to discuss it at last, and after a hesitation she also told him about the slowing sensation, the blast of power, the two dreams and their strange tugging feeling. She concentrated on communicating as fully as she could despite the awkwardness she still felt with the mindspeech, and it was not until she had finished that she saw Taryn's expression.

Is something wrong? Don't you believe me?

No. Taryn shook his head. *It's not that. I just don't understand. Your people aren't supposed to have power. Yet you have it . . . and not just that, you* punched right through *into that man's mind. You did something that's incredibly hard to do.*

Is it something bad?

Not bad . . . only I wonder how much more there is that I don't know. He shook his head again. *So far nothing is the way it's supposed to be.*

Well, I don't understand either. What happened to me?

I'm sorry, I can't say any more.

But you know.

A hesitation. *Yes. At least I think so.* Another pause. *You see, I'd get into dreadful trouble if I told you. I've told you to much already.*

But no one would know!

Believe me, they'd know. I shouldn't have said anything to you at all, Alexina.

I don't understand. Why can't you tell me what all this is about? What's the big secret?

But Taryn did not reply. Alexina felt impossibly frustrated. He had told her just enough to whet her curiosity but not enough to clarify anything. She stood on the brink of a revelation, only to have it pulled away even as she reached for it. She was suddenly very tired. Her head was splitting.

Have you seen anyone else? came Taryn's thought. Alexina looked up. *Besides me and the two men, I mean.*

There were others?

My search party. They got here just before I did. Three people.

No, I haven't seen anyone else.

I have to find them. He sounded anxious. *I should*

have gone last night, but I felt so sick. . . . I'll need food for my trip. Can you get me some more?

Alexina nodded. Taryn pushed himself to his feet. His face, which had regained a more natural color after eating, paled, and he staggered slightly. Alexina jumped up to help him, but he put out a hand to hold her away.

I'm all right. Just a little dizzy. I feel quite all right now.

Are you sure? You don't look very well. Maybe you should stay here another day.

No. I have to find my friends. The longer I wait the more risky it is. There are forces here. . . . I'm all right, really.

She had no choice but to take his word for it, and they started back toward the farm. It was broad daylight now and the sun filtered through the pines, stippling the ground beneath. Alexina glanced back at Taryn: He was following her, limping, a set expression on his still rather pale face. He was tall, she noticed for the first time. She looked at her watch. It was only five-thirty. With any luck no one would be downstairs yet.

She left Taryn among the trees and ran across the meadow. She peered into the kitchen: It was empty. Quickly she filled a bag with food, not caring now if Julia noticed: cheese, fruit, leftover pot roast. She went down to the basement where extra groceries were kept for another loaf of bread and some cookies. Coming back up the stairs, her eyes fell on the pile of laundry by the washing machine. Clothes, she thought. He must have some normal clothes. Quickly she sorted through the laundry until she found a pair of Toby's jeans and a T-shirt. They were muddy with field dirt, and Taryn was slightly taller than Toby, but they would do.

Taryn was sitting against a tree when Alexina returned, his eyes closed. At the sight of his drawn face she felt a twinge of concern.

I've packed you a lot of food, she thought to him. *It should last a couple of days at least. I'm giving you my pack; it's easier to carry. And I brought you some clothes. People around here don't dress like you, and if you run into someone there might be questions.*

Thank you. He shouldered the pack, grimacing as he used his injured hand. *You went out of your way to help me, Alexina. My own people couldn't have treated me any better.*

Awkwardly, she held out a slip of paper on which she had written her name and telephone number. *If you need help, this is a way you can get in touch with me. And, Taryn . . . be careful.*

He nodded. Then he turned and walked swiftly off through the trees, still limping slightly. Alexina watched him move out of sight, standing until she could no longer hear his muffled footsteps. He was gone, as finally as if he had never been there. Her head ached fiercely. She heard the chirping of the birds, the faint whir as the early morning breeze brushed through the branches. The sounds seemed tiny and far away, echoing in the great silence that settled now on her mind.

4

After breakfast, Julia sent Alexina out to open up the blueberry field for picking. The misty dawn had given way to one of those brilliant summer days unique to the Northeast. The sun shone down out of a sky as blue and hard as an Egyptian faience bowl, edging everything it touched with gold. Shadows lay in liquid pools beneath the trees and the wind swept between the mountains, smelling of the lakes and of warm grass. Alexina sat in the shade of the booth with the cash register. There were a lot of pickers today—mothers and small children, teenagers—and she was kept occupied, handing out baskets and weighing fruit. She did it all without really noticing, her mind far away.

Something had happened to her this morning, something almost beyond grasping, something right out of all her books and fantasies. It was like a dream. Yet it had been *real,* and she hugged the reality to herself with a kind of incredulous wonder. Today, she had met a telepath, someone who possessed the powers even the people who wrote about them didn't really accept. With triumph she thought of Jessica, scoffing at all that lay beyond conventional scientific proof. She was wrong, she had always been wrong. Alexina had always been right. And as if that were not enough, she had discovered that she too was a telepath. Within her existed some of that reality she had always sought outside herself. She closed her eyes for a moment. At last, here of all the places in the world, the curtain had been breached. Was it this which had made her feel different, this dormant power inside her, present and sensed but never realized because there was no one to use it with? Until now. Until Taryn.

She had known Taryn barely an hour, yet she felt as if she had known him always. She had not wanted him to go this morning. He had been unwell, of course, and she was sure he had no idea where he was heading—but it was more than that. She did not want to let go of the experience, or of the living confirmation of a new power. Her thoughts turned to the story he had told, to the two men, to his people, whoever they were. She had an image of a secret community of telepaths, living on some uncharted island perhaps, guarding their gift. She thought of the search parties, risking discovery of their power to follow the precious thing they had lost into the hostile outer world. What *was* it the two men had stolen? Really, Taryn had told her remarkably little. She had so many questions.

But he was gone, she thought, gone in search of his people. When he found them they would disappear, their secret safe once more. She stared out at the blueberry field, seeing it more clearly than she had all morning, her elation seeping away. She would never see him again. She would never be able to ask the questions that teemed in her mind; she would never hear what he could tell her about his people—or about herself. How could it have been so brief? she thought disbelievingly. How could it be over, this experince for which she had been waiting all her life? It wasn't fair. Could it really be that she must go on now as if nothing had happened? She rubbed at the headache which had never entirely disappeared.

At one o'clock she closed the field and went slowly back to the house for lunch. Tiredness was catching up with her, and the headache was becoming worse. The mail had just arrived; there was a letter from Jessica. Upstairs, Toby stood in the doorway of his room, reading something, a smug expression on his face. Alexina walked past, ignoring him.

"Alexina, Alexiiiiina!" came his hateful, teasing voice behind her. "How's Astonishing Alexina today?"

Alexina was swept with a rage so intense it made the blood rush to her head. Deliberately she turned and, not knowing what she intended to do, walked back toward him. His reaction was surprising. With a startled "Hey!" he clutched the letter to his chest and backed up against the wall. Before she thought, she had reached out and ripped the letter from his hands.

"State University of New York at Binghamton," said the imprint at the top of the page, and then, "Dear Mr. Krantz: We are pleased to inform you that you have been accepted into the class of. . . ."

Alexina looked up, realizing what it was, her anger suddenly gone. Julia had told her how much Toby wanted this. She opened her mouth to congratulate him, but when she saw his face, the words died on her lips. He looked, not furious as she would have expected, but nakedly vulnerable. She had never before seen him wear such a human expression, and she remembered that Charles did not want him to go. Belatedly, she wished she could take her action back. She paused, irresolute. Should she apologize? But the vulnerable look was gone; in its place was a cold mask. Toby reached out, twitched the letter from her grasp, and disappeared into his room.

The incident faded from Alexina's mind in the

heavy listlessness that had replaced her earlier elation. After lunch she took some aspirin and returned to the blueberry field. The long day dragged at last to a close, the sun setting slowly between the mountains in a glory of peach-colored cloud. After dinner, Alexina went up to her room and tried to read. But she could not concentrate, and after a while she turned off her light and went to kneel by the window, gazing up at the thickly starred sky.

Oh, she thought, with a wave of indescribable longing, why isn't anything ever the way you want it to be? She had always expected that if she were lucky enough to encounter the wonder of another reality, it would work some kind of irrevocable transformation. The miraculous things that hid behind the curtain of disbelief would be laid bare, and she would suddenly understand how it all fit together, the humdrum world she lived in and the world she believed in, but had only read about in books. Today the books had become real, the imaginings gained a shape. In a way things *were* different: She had been proved right, and she had discovered in herself a thing she never dreamed she might possess. But in a larger sense, nothing had changed. The curtain had closed again. That other reality had been moving away from her even as Taryn receded beneath the pines. He had taken everything with him, even her newly found gift. For what good was the gift if there were no one to share it with? Alexina thought of the *reaching forward* she had always done without understanding it. All her life she had been stretching into a vacuum, sending thoughts where there was no one to hear. All her life she would go on doing so, the only difference being that now she knew it. Perhaps there were other telepaths, she thought hopefully. Of course there were. There were Taryn's people. But she might never find them again.

Alexina felt so alone she could hardly bear it. This was a new kind of aloneness—not the dreamy solitude of her New York days, or the exciting isolation brought by the feeling of being different. It was a desolate sense of alienation and of waste. I wish it had never happened, she thought, and then took it back. No, she did not wish that. But the prospect of the waste of her gift was almost worse than the thought of never having known at all.

It grew late. After midnight a wind sprang up and clouds drifted in over the mountains, obscuring the face of the moon. The long meadow grass rippled, darkening with the shadows of the clouds, hissing faintly. The world seemed all black and silver, and Alexina forgot her woes for a time in watching it.

A motion caught her eyes, a tremor of shadow over by a tree close to the pines. She peered at it. Everything was still; the swatch of shadow around the tree was unbroken. Yet all at once she had an uneasy feeling. She swept the area with her eyes. There it was again, a slight stirring. She was sure it came from that tree, though when she looked right at it she could see nothing.

She withdrew from the window and was halfway to her bed when a different noise came from outside: not the random sighing of the grass but a purposeful regular sound, as if someone were walking softly around the house. Petrified with supernatural fear, she stopped in her tracks. The sound was coming closer. She crept back to the window. A figure was crossing the backyard. Alexina leaned out a little to get a better look, and the creepy breathless feeling vanished. It was just Toby, home from work. She must have made a noise; Toby looked up and saw her. It was Toby under the tree, she thought. Or was it? He had come around the house from the other direction, from the road.

She heard his footsteps mounting the stairs and moving along the hall, and then, surprisingly, continuing on to her room. There was a pause, and then a light tap. She put on her robe and went to open the door.

"Can I come in?" Toby whispered. "I want to talk to you."

His face was serious; there were no traces of sarcasm or malice. For a moment Alexina hesitated. Then, wary, she let him in. She reached to turn on the light, but Toby put out his hand.

"No, leave it off," he whispered.

He sat down on the end of her bed. The moonlight streaming through the unshaded windows was bright enough to illumine the room fairly clearly; it lay in a long bar across the floor, a subdued image of afternoon sunlight. Her bed, however, was in darkness, and it bothered her that she could not see Toby's face. The silence grew. Outside, the wind made rustling noises.

"About what happened this afternoon," Toby whispered at last. "Did you tell anyone about the letter?"

Alexina shook her head.

"Well, I've got to ask you not to say anything. I have to trust you not to."

"I won't say anything if you don't want me to." There was another pause, and after a moment she hazarded a question. "Why? Is it because of your father?"

For a moment he looked down, tracing the patchwork squares of her quilt with his finger. Then he raised his head. "How did you know that?"

"Julia said something about it," Alexina replied guardedly.

"He's dead set against my going to college. There'd be the fight to end all fights if he knew."

"That must be why you've been in such a hurry to get the mail every day. So your father wouldn't see the letter."

He nodded.

"And why you need the job. To save money for college."

He was still tracing the patchwork. "For my living expenses."

"Can you earn enough in just one summer?"

"No." He sighed. "You might as well know everything. I've had a job for the past year in the afternoons. I arranged it so all my classes were in the morning."

"At the diner?"

"Yes. Pete works there too, and he brought me home so Dad wouldn't find out. So now you know it all." He raised his head. "You won't tell anyone, will you?"

Alexina looked at him. Nasty as he might be, this was his dream, and she would never puncture someone's dream. Fleetingly, it occurred to her that she had unexpectedly acquired a card to hold in the endless teasing game. Maybe things would get better now that he had to trust her.

"I won't say a word. I promise."

He nodded and looked down again. This subdued mood was something new. They had never before had such a straightforward conversation. Suddenly Alexina felt bad about her previous thought, and about how she had discovered his secret.

"Toby," she began hesitantly. "Toby, I'm sorry I

grabbed the letter." He looked up and defensively, she added, "I was just so mad at you."

He shrugged, "I guess I sort of asked for it."

She could hardly believe her ears. Was this the Toby she knew? Impulsively, genuinely curious, she asked a question. "Toby, why is your father so much against your going to college?"

"A lot of reasons." He paused. "It isn't the money—the college is giving me a full scholarship. He's just set on me inheriting the farm. I think he's afraid if I go away I won't want it anymore. But *he* went to college! Maybe it was agricultural college, but it was college just the same."

"Well, would he like it better if you went to agricultural college like him?"

"But I don't *want* to go to agricultural college!" He was still whispering, but his voice strained with barely contained frustration. "I want to be a scientist. I need something besides the farm in my life! He just doesn't understand that it's not education that turns people against the land, it's what's there inside you! I just don't fit in. It's *in* me, like the land is in him. But he won't see it!" He stopped, as if biting off more words. Then he sighed. "I don't even know if it's worth it to go."

"Are you thinking of that? Of not going?"

"I don't know. I just don't know if it's worth all the fighting. Dad would never speak to me again."

There was a silence. He was watching her now. It made her uncomfortable not to be able to see his expression. "You know, you don't fit in either."

"I guess not."

"I picked up on that right away. There's a kind of shell around you, Alexina. It comes off as snootiness. Maybe you're not trying to be snooty, but that's how it comes off."

"You're pretty snooty yourself," Alexina hissed, stung. For a moment they glared at each other, reawakened hostility hanging in the air like the dust motes in the bar of moonlight. Then Toby turned away.

"I'm tired," he said. "I'm going to bed now. I get little enough sleep as it is." He got up and tiptoed across the bare wood floor, briefly silvered as he passed through the moonlight, fading into darkness again. As he reached the door, Alexina whispered, "Good night."

He turned toward her, his face still in shadow. There was a pause, and then he whispered back, "Good night."

Alexina sat for a moment, contemplating this latest turn of events. What a day it had been. She felt as if a lifetime had passed since this morning. She was exhausted by it all. She no longer had the energy to think. There would be plenty of time tomorrow.

5

A night's sleep has a way of distancing experience, of putting it on a more objective plane. When Alexina woke the next morning the events of the day before had receded. It was difficult to believe she had not dreamed them. She descended the stairs to breakfast, the ordinary world reasserting itself with leaden insistence. She no longer felt the goading frustration of the previous night, but rather a dull resignation.

After breakfast Alexina and Toby went out to weed the vegetable fields. Hoe in hand, Alexina chopped between the plants, hating the work and the sweat that ran down her sides beneath her T-shirt. After about an hour, Toby's shadow fell across the zucchini vines. She looked up. He seemed uncertain, as if he wanted to say something, but did not know how to start.

"Well?" she said after a moment, giving vent to the irritation produced by fatigue and boredom. His gray eyes narrowed and his face became hard.

"About the things I said last night. You won't tell anyone, will you?"

"No. I already promised I wouldn't."

"Anyway, I just want you to know that in case you're thinking of it, I saw you come out of the woods very early yesterday morning. I also know you stole a whole bunch of food."

Alexina stared at him, open-mouthed.

"I won't ask you what it was all about. This just makes it more of a bargain, see."

He turned to go. Alexina stared at his departing back and was overwhelmed with rage.

"You jerk!" she yelled after him, as loudly as she could. "Don't you know anything?"

He turned, startled, and she marched up to him, heedless of the rows of vegetables.

"I can't believe you said that to me. I can't believe you could be so petty. Don't you know I'd never, never give away someone's secret? I can't believe you think I'm that kind of person!" By now she was shouting into his face. He looked gratifyingly taken aback.

"I . . . I didn't mean that," he said rather feebly.

"Oh, yeah? You didn't mean it, but you're trying to blackmail me just in case!"

"Well . . . you did take the letter and we don't get along that well—"

"I said I was sorry! And in case you don't know why we don't get along it's because you're the nastiest, most sarcastic person I have ever met! Nothing is good enough for you! You make fun of everyone and everything! You make everyone's life miserable, especially mine! I don't care if you like me or not, just leave me alone. And if you don't trust me, don't talk to me! I wouldn't miss it if you never spoke to me again!"

He was getting mad now; his fists were on his hips. "You're not exactly Miss Personality, you know," he said, glaring at her.

"Oh, what's the use." Alexina began to turn away, but he reached out and grabbed her arm.

"Hey, wait a minute. If you can have your say, I can have mine. Did it occur to you that you're not the innocent martyr you think you are? Maybe it's your fault too!"

"*My* fault! I'm not the one with a nasty comment for every occasion!"

"Well, I admit I tease you a lot. But can't you see it's a joke? You're so uptight you can't even take a joke. You can't see I don't really mean it."

"You could have fooled me! What am I supposed to think when someone makes fun of every word that comes out of my mouth?"

"Okay, Miss Holier-Than-Thou. You say nothing's good enough for me. Well, have you looked at yourself lately? You walk around here looking like you expect someone to throw you into the pigpen any minute."

"I do not!"

"You act like you're a princess locked up in a dungeon somewhere. *You're* from the big city, and we're all country bumpkins. Everyone at school thought you were incredibly stuck-up. You don't say two words to anyone."

"No one says two words to me!"

"Have you ever wondered why? And anytime *I* try to talk to you—just talk, like a normal human being—you say something rude or snotty. Can you blame me for not trusting you? How did I know you weren't going to go to Mom or Dad after all? I was real tired last night, and I said too much. When I thought about it again this morning, I figured maybe I'd better show you I had something to bargain with, because I'll just bet you were thinking about bargaining yourself!"

This struck too close to home. Alexina felt herself threatened with humiliating tears. "You didn't have to tell me any of that other stuff. I promised I wouldn't tell. Isn't my word good enough for you?"

Her voice cracked on the last word and she stopped abruptly.

"I don't know. I really don't know." Toby looked at her for a moment, his face a mask, his gray eyes like bits of mirror glass. Then he turned and walked off. Alexina watched him go. The held-back tears made her head feel swollen. I won't cry, she thought. I won't. She picked up her hoe and began to work again, hacking savagely at the weeds as if it were Toby, and not they, she was cutting into tiny pieces. Her eyes burned from the tears she would not shed, burned and burned like the sun on her back.

She spent the rest of the morning in the field, and the afternoon at the produce stand. She did not see Toby again until dinner. He was unusually silent, going out of his way to avoid her eyes, but she was almost too exhausted to care. She went upstairs after she had finished the washing-up and lay on her bed, submerged in a cloud of gloom and self-disgust. Some of Toby's bolts had hit home, and over the afternoon she had not been able to help wondering if he were right. Not completely right, of course—but could that really be the way others saw her?

It's so unfair, she thought. I'm *not* stuck-up and I'm *not* snooty—I just don't know how to fit in. I'm not the kind of person he thinks I am, I'm not. It was the accusation that rankled most. Never, never would she destroy someone's dream, because she understood dreams. She could not forgive Toby for thinking she was the kind of person who would. Maybe she hadn't given him a chance to think she was any other kind of person; maybe he actually had been trying to be nice some of the time. But how was she supposed to know when? He had made her so miserable with his teasing, the teasing that started even before she really knew she was here. It had forced her to put up a guard she was unable to drop.

Everything washed over her at once, all the accumulated hurts and frustrations and disappointments and yearnings, and she gave in at last to the tears that had haunted her all day. It felt as if she had held them back for far longer than that, and she wept into her pillow, muffling her sobs so no one would hear.

At last there were no more tears, and Alexina lay for a long time face down on the bed. Later she went and sat by the window with the light off, staring toward where she judged the cave to be. It was another night of bright moonlight.

There was a stirring at the base of her vision, in the shadow around—could it be the same tree? Yes, it was, she was sure. As it had before, the motion disappeared as soon as she glanced toward it. But the moon was brighter tonight, and after prolonged peering she was almost positive she could see something, a darker mass against the shadow. As she looked it moved again, a small shifting as if from one foot to the other. It's probably only an animal, a deer or something, she told herself. Logically, what else could it be? She returned to bed. But the irrational side of herself was sure it was someone, not something. Pulling the covers over her head did not help much, and as she fell into sleep she was still conscious of the feeling of being observed.

* * * *

It was there the next night too. Almost against her will, Alexina rose from the bed after she had turned off the light, and crouched at the window to watch. Whatever it was stood in the same pool of shadow beneath the same tree, dark against dark, shifting a little now and then. Alexina watched until fatigue overcame her, and she fell asleep against the window sill, awakening some time later, cramped and chilly. As she raised her head, her eyes caught something moving slowly away from the tree, disappearing among the pines at the foot of the mountain. The moon had set by this time and there were only the stars to see by, but she could tell it was a human figure, very tall, clad in some sort of dark, flowing garment. Cold fear galvanized Alexina's stiff limbs, and she flung herself across the floor to huddle under the covers of her bed. She had suspected it was not an animal, but it was still frightening to have that so clearly confirmed.

She woke the next morning to another round of wearying tasks. The forest that stretched in a circle around the farm seemed to ring her with invisible observers. The figure had worn a dark cloak like that of the man she had seen coming from the cave. Could it be he? But why would he watch the house? Taryn had said he was a thief, a criminal. . . . She had seen him with his loot. Perhaps he knew it was she who had been there. Perhaps he had even overheard her conversation with Taryn. If he were connected with Taryn and his people, he might very well have the same telepathic powers. He might think she knew more than she should. Or perhaps he was looking for Taryn. Alexina felt a chill, despite the hot sun.

That afternoon she remembered the gold coin buried in her bureau drawer. Could whoever it was have come for that? Maybe they had seen her take it, and wanted it back. She waited until she was alone in the house to retrieve the coin. It was heavy in her hand as she carried it out to the backyard and placed it on top of the gatepost that faced toward the mountain. It would have been better to do it when the figure was there to see her, of course, but her courage wasn't quite up to that. She resolved to stay up all night watching, to see if she had been right. But lack of rest took its toll and she fell asleep as soon as she got into bed, waking up the next morning with the bedside light still burning. She could see from her window that the coin was gone. There was a moment of excitement before she realized that a bird or animal could just as easily have taken it; or it could have fallen off the post and disappeared in the long grass. She went out and looked, but could not find it.

After lunch, Alexina began the clearing up. Julia was in the garden, gathering the daily bounty of vegetables, and Charles and Toby were off in the fields. Halfway through the dishes, the phone rang.

"Is this the Taylor residence?" a man's voice enquired.

"You must have the wrong number," said Alexina without thinking. Then, "Wait a minute, I'm Alexina Taylor."

"Is this the Taylor residence or isn't it?"

"Yes. Yes, it is."

The voice sounded cautious now. "Are you related to or familiar with a male Caucasian, about eighteen years old, long blond hair, tall, muscular build?"

"Taryn?" she said incredulously.

"Can I assume you know him?"

"Yes, yes, I know him. Is something wrong?"

"It certainly is, miss. This is the Bradenton police station. We picked your boy up this morning for vagrancy. We thought he was drunk, but he seems to be sick. We had a doctor in to look at him. Seems to be some kind of virus. He looks like he was robbed, too—he hasn't any money or I.D. Is he some kind of foreigner?"

"Ah . . . yes. Ah . . ." She searched for a plausible

explanation. "He's an exchange student. He's staying with my family for the year. He went out last night and we were getting worried. He doesn't know any English, you see."

"Can someone pick him up, miss?"

"Yes. Yes, I can. What's the address?"

For a long moment Alexina stood still after the man had hung up, staring into space. What a stroke of luck, she thought, that she had been alone in the house when they called. To think she had almost hung up when they asked if it was the Taylor residence! Now, how was she going to get there? There were buses. She could get one into the village and from there catch one into Bradenton. She would need money for tickets, and she would need to check bus schedules.

She was still holding the receiver. Carefully she replaced it on the hook. Her heart was racing. She had told herself that it was all over, Taryn and her power and his people gone forever from her life, but she knew now that she had never really believed it. Somehow she must have known he would come back, that she would be given another chance. Asking herself what she should do and how she should do it, she had not once, after the initial shock, felt any sense of surprise.

She took a deep breath to steady herself, and dialed the bus station to check schedules. Then she counted her money. Jessica provided a generous allowance and there was little to spend it on: Alexina found she had just over forty dollars. She was all set now. There remained only the question of Julia, to whom she must explain her absence. In the end, she decided to say that a school friend had invited her over for the afternoon and evening. She would tell her that the friend was picking her up on the main road. Julia gave permission, pleased to see Alexina undertaking some social activity; Alexina felt a twinge of guilt but told herself she had no choice.

Afterward, she found it hard to remember the journey. It seemed to take much longer than the two hours her watch told her had passed between the time she caught the bus from the farm and the time the second bus deposited her in the Bradenton terminal. She made her way to the police station, a large brick building in a more depressed part of town. She could feel her nerve evaporating as she entered its dirty waiting room.

"I'm Alexina Taylor," she said to the desk sergeant. "I've come to pick up the person you called me about?"

He looked at her for a moment, unfriendly, and then flipped through some papers on his desk. "Wait over there," he said, indicating the benches. "I'll call the officer in charge."

Alexina chose an empty bench and sat down to wait. There were only a few other people: a couple of men, a nervous-looking woman with a small child, and a very old man who appeared to be sleeping. Harsh white lights cast a flat, unpleasant glare over them all. Alexina looked anxiously at her watch. At last a tired-looking man in shirt-sleeves approached her.

"Alexina Taylor?"

"Yes." She got to her feet.

"I'm Sergeant Mackenzie. Come with me, please. I have to ask you a few questions before we let him go—got to have a complete report. He's listed as John Doe at the moment."

Alexina followed him into a large, noisy room full of desks and people. He led her to a desk, indicated that she should sit down, and rolled a form into his typewriter. "What's his name?"

Alexina had worked out a story in advance. Taryn would be an exchange student from Holland—she chose Holland because Dutch was a language no one would be likely to know—and she would tell them his real name, which was dissimilar enough from common names to pass as foreign. She answered the sergeant's questions as calmly as she could, gave him her own name and address, and wound up by explaining her situation at the Krantzes. At last he rolled the form out of the typewriter, putting it on top of a stack on his desk. He leaned back in his chair and looked at her.

"Why did your guardians send you up to get him alone?"

"Ah . . . they work. No one was home but me, and I didn't think I ought to wait until they got back—sometimes it's not until late. I took the bus."

He stared at her for a moment, then nodded. "I told you on the phone we had a doctor in to look at him. He's confused, and he has a fever. Not a very high one, but you'd better get your own doctor to look at him when you get home."

"I will."

"And tell your guardians not to let him go around on his own. It could be dangerous for him until he learns English. He's lucky he had your name and number in his pocket. Without any I.D. he could have been here for quite a while." He paused. Alexina was beginning to get a little nervous. She looked at her hands in her lap. After a moment he pushed back his chair and stood up.

"I'll get someone to bring him out for you. You can go back to the waiting room."

Alexina nodded. "Thank you."

It was fifteen minutes before they brought Taryn out. The first sight of him after four days was a shock; Alexina had forgotten how tall he was, and he looked bizarre even though he had put on the jeans and shirt she had given him. His long hair was dirty and tangled. He seemed sicker than the policeman had said: His face was flushed and he was unsteady on his feet. Standing in the ugly waiting room, unfamiliar sounds and smells all around her, Alexina felt a moment of dreadful desperation. Now she must get him home, get him the medical attention he needed, keep his presence a secret. How on earth was she going to do it all? She had not really planned beyond this point.

Taking a deep breath, she thought, One thing at a time. She went up to Taryn and said his name. His eyes opened and he looked at her. An expression of enormous relief came over his face. She nodded and projected a warning: *We mustn't use mindspeech here.* She had the impression he had not received the thought.

The man who had brought him out indicated that Alexina must sign a paper for the desk sergeant. The sergeant pointed out a pay phone, from which Alexina called a taxi. Then, taking Taryn's hand, she led him at last out of the police station.

She never forgot the last leg of the journey. Most of all, she remembered the fear: fear that the taxi fare would come to more than the few dollars she had left in her purse, fear that Taryn would become sicker, fear that the driver of the local bus would be the one she knew. They waited for the first bus, Taryn half-slumped in his seat in the waiting room. It was as if the relief of knowing himself rescued had been a signal to let go. He appeared barely conscious, his eyes half-closed, muttering now and then in a strange, guttural language. Alexina endured the looks people gave them, on pins and needles lest someone try to interfere. From time to time she attempted mindspeech, but Taryn seemed quite out of reach now and she met only blankness. By the time they reached the village and caught the second bus, his breathing was hoarse, and Alexina had to support almost the entire weight of his heavy body with her own.

It was after eight o'clock when they reached their stop, and almost dark. Lucky it was so late, she thought. The twilight would hide their arrival. Taryn leaned slackly against her, muttering. The heat of his fever was intense. They staggered along the road, but halfway along it Taryn's legs gave out altogether and he collapsed, carrying her down with him. *Taryn!* Alexina cried in her mind. But he could not be roused. Alexina began to sob with strain and fatigue. She gripped him under the arms and pulled, dragging him along bodily. Thinking about it afterward, she realized that only her desperation could have given her the strength.

At last she got him into the barn, depositing him in a pile of hay in one of the unused stalls. Panting, she sank down beside him. She could not have gone another step to save her life.

What now? The sense of urgency had decreased with the achievement of her first goal—getting him home. It was too early for her to go inside without provoking awkward questions about why she was back so soon from the fictitious visit. But Taryn must have a doctor—his breathing was very labored and even at this distance she could feel his fever. She would have to wait until later. When they were asleep, she could use the pickup to take him to the hospital. Charles always left the keys in the ignition. The truck was parked on a hill so she could just release the brake and roll most of the way down the road. With luck, she could get back before morning.

Some time later she jerked awake. The fluorescent dial of her watch read 12:30. They must be worried about her. Maybe they had even called the police—and what if they had called the parents of the girl she had said she had gone to see? She sat up quickly, ready to dash out of the barn. Only then did she realize that Taryn's harsh breathing, a half-heard accompaniment to her sleep, had ceased. In panic she felt about for him, found his chest. It rose and fell regularly, easily. The terrible heat had disappeared. His forehead and neck were quite cool, and he was drenched in sweat. The fever must have broken.

Alexina fully expected to see the farmhouse in a blaze of light as she left the barn, but all was dark. She leaned against the door for a moment in relief. Amazingly, it seemed they had not waited up for her. She did not have the strength to deal with questions and explanations anyway. They were probably waiting to hear her come in, though; she should go up to her room. Then she could place pillows strategically under the covers and make her escape.

She walked around the house, taking no particular pains to hide her passage. It was a still and beautiful night. The moon was spotlight-bright. Country silence lay thick on the world. Alexina could barely hear the hiss of her footsteps, and the breeze she felt made no sound. Her stiff muscles relaxed and her steps were buoyant, but strangely slow. A heavy dew had fallen, and her jeans were soaked to the ankles by the time she reached the back of the house. Rounding the corner she caught a flash of motion, a darting of darker shadow against the dark walls. She froze. The watching figure flew back to her mind. It was several seconds, very slow ones, before she recognized Toby, in the act of opening the kitchen door. He had frozen at the sight of her just as she had at the sight of him. Over the pounding of her heart, Alexina felt a wild impulse to laugh.

She walked up to him, watching him relax as he recognized her.

"Hi," she whispered.

He looked at her for a moment, undecided, and then smiled slightly. "Here we are again," he whispered back.

"My sentiments exactly."

"What are you doing out here, anyway?"

"It's a long story." What was she going to tell him? It was a second before she noticed that his expression had begun to change. His eyes widened and his mouth opened with an odd, underwater slowness. His gaze was fixed on a point just beyond her shoulder. Alexina felt a creeping start at the base of her scalp and spread down her back like cold water. Slowly, slowly she turned around. . . .

It was there, like a bad dream: the dark-robed figure of recent nights. It seemed immensely tall. The shadow it cast reached out toward her, jet black, engulfing her feet and knees. In her fear she stumbled back against Toby, clutching at his arm. The fabric of the figure's cloak swirled around it, muffling it completely. Even the hood hung so far down over its face that nothing at all was visible. On its breast glinted a disk of gold on a heavy chain. The moment in which they stood was endless; the heavy silence of the night seemed to weigh the seconds down.

Don't be afraid.

The voice broke the stillness yet did not break it. There was something familiar about it. The figure raised sleeved arms to its hood and pushed it back. The cloth revealed not a monster but a man, a middle-aged man with dark hair and sharp features. She heard a rush of breath and realized that she and Toby had exhaled at the same time.

Don't be afraid, the voice said again. The man's lips did not move. Of course—mindspeech! That was what was familiar. This was not the dark man she had seen first. Could he be one of Taryn's friends?

Who are you? Alexina thought to him.

A friend, he answered. *Taryn's friend.*

One of his people?

His friends, the man repeated. *Will you take me to him?*

Yes. Alexina nodded.

Beside her, Toby whispered, "What's going on?"

Of course: He could not catch the mindspeech. For some reason this pleased her.

"Toby, I'll explain later. I have to go with this man for a little while. You stay here."

"No way." He shook his head emphatically. "What's happening here, Alexina?"

"I just can't explain now!" Alexina hissed at him. "I've got to go. Stay here."

"I'm not going to let you go off with this guy alone! You don't even know who he is!" He paused. "Or do you?"

The man's thought cut across Alexina's protest. *Is there some trouble?*

She turned to him. *No. No trouble.* She looked at Toby, realizing that he was not going to cooperate no matter what she said. It might be simpler to let him come along. He had already seen the man, anyway, and knew something was up. It wouldn't make much difference if he saw Taryn. She could think of something to tell him later.

She began to lead the way to the barn. Toby and the stranger followed. She could hear the sounds made by her feet and Toby's, but the man made no sound at all. The grasses seemed to part silently before him.

It was very dark in the barn after the brilliance of the moonlight, and Alexina realized that the lantern was outside. She projected toward the man her intention to go get it, but he shook his head. He held out his hands, cupped upward as if to receive a gift. For a second nothing happened, but then light began to glow within the hollowed palms, slowly at first and then more brightly. She heard Toby gasp, and she realized that the source of illumination was not a lamp; rather, it was a ball of light resting directly in the man's hands. He seemed to have called it out of the air. After a moment he lowered his arms. The light hung suspended. His hands left a faint luminous trail, like a photographic afterimage. Toby pulled at Alexina's elbow.

"Do you see that?" he whispered.

She nodded.

"What's going *on* here, Alexina?"

Alexina shook her head. The light throbbed slightly, sending a soft golden glow over the area where they stood, fading away toward the corners of the barn. It irradiated the pile of hay and Taryn lying in it asleep. The man knelt to examine him, and Toby saw him for the first time.

"Who the hell is that?" Then, in a lower tone: "You've been doing some strange things in your spare time, Alexina."

"Oh, shut up, Toby."

The man looked up. *Do you know how long he's been this way?*

Alexina shook her head, aware of Toby's scrutiny, not caring. *The police said he was sick when they picked him up this morning. Can you help him?*

We will try. Although this is not sickness as you would understand it. He got to his feet, towering above them in the pulsing, tawny light. Involuntarily they both stepped back.

Thank you for caring for Taryn. You have the deepest gratitude of myself and my companions. Thank you also for your discretion.

Alexina nodded. *I didn't tell anyone about him.*

The man seemed to hesitate. Then, *I wish there were some token of gratitude I could give you. But I'm afraid we can leave you with nothing, not even the memory.*

Alexina felt a stirring of alarm. *What—what do you mean?*

Taryn has been . . . indiscreet. He has told you something about himself, yes? Reluctantly, Alexina nodded. *And even if he had not, your knowledge of him and us is dangerous. You could betray us without meaning to.*

No, no, I never would! Alexina was shaking her head, stepping backward. Toby took her arm protectively.

"What's wrong? What's happening?"

I'm sorry. Though you have the gift, I cannot allow you to remember. Don't be afraid. I won't harm you. I shall just remove the images of Taryn and myself.

"No!" cried Alexina aloud. "I don't want to forget!"

"Forget what?" cried Toby frantically. "Alexina, forget what?"

The man was advancing on them, his hands outstretched. Alexina backed away, pulling Toby with her, but his shadow reached out for them, enfolded their feet and legs, held them fast. Unable to cry out, Alexina could only watch those fingers, closing on them until they touched, one hand on her and one on Toby. She felt Toby try to twist away, saying, "Hey, take your—," before he was abruptly silent.

Stillness flowed from the man's fingers, reaching inside her head. He stepped back.

Watch the light, he thought gently. *Watch the light.*

Alexina could not disobey. The beat of her heart sounded loud in her ears; a fuzziness began to grow around the edges of her mind. Her vision indistinct, she saw the man lift Taryn in his arms as effortlessly as if he had been a child. The light was shrinking now, a little dimmer with each pulse, and consciousness shrank with it, the fuzziness spreading inward, pressing down like the night. With the last of her strength, Alexina watched as the man moved across the meadow toward the pines. Taryn lay limp in his arms. She saw the blond hair, white in the moonlight, trailing over the dark shoulder that supported it. Consciousness was a pinpoint now, contracting like the view behind a closing door. The globe of light pulsed a final time and winked out, and there was only darkness.

6

Alexina woke the next morning with a headache, dull and heavy behind her eyes. When she sat up, the pain increased and her stomach lurched. She rested for a moment, groggy, on the edge of her bed. Her thoughts were slow and there was an odd blankness behind them.

She took a shower and some aspirin, and went downstairs. Charles was finishing breakfast and Toby was toying with his food, looking listless and a little pale. Julia was doing something at the stove. Alexina paused in the doorway, looking at the scene before her. It seemed wrong, a little off, as if there were something missing. . . . She started across the kitchen, feeling worse with each step. She had just enough time to see Julia turn, when the world twisted suddenly and the kitchen imploded into darkness.

Alexina came back to consciousness, caught in a whirlpool that swung her sickeningly up toward the light. She was being carried, then set gently on a firm surface. Opening her eyes, she saw that Charles had laid her on the living room couch. Julia was bending over her.

"What happened?" Alexina managed weakly.

"You fainted," said Julia. "I thought you looked pale when you came down, and then you just keeled over. Charles is calling the doctor. Now just lie quietly until he comes."

Julia disappeared and Alexina closed her eyes, feeling very ill indeed. Distantly she heard footsteps and saw that Toby was standing beside her. He was drawn, as if he had not slept, and there was an expression of real concern on his face. How strange, thought Alexina vaguely. She remembered the time she had strained her back when she first arrived—it had been good for a lot of jokes. But he only looked at her for a moment, uncertainly, like someone who has gone into a room to fetch something and, once there, realizes he has forgotten what it is.

"Go on, Toby, leave Alexina alone now. She doesn't feel well."

"I wasn't going to do anything," Toby said. "Ma, I don't feel well either."

She put her hand to his forehead, frowning. "You don't feel as if you have a fever. I'll have the doctor take a look at you too."

The doctor arrived, took their temperatures, prodded their glands, and listened to their chests. There seemed to be nothing wrong, he said, perhaps a touch of twenty-four-hour flu. Julia was to keep them in bed and call him if things got any worse.

After he was gone, Julia helped Alexina to her feet and upstairs to her room. She tucked in the covers and pulled down the blinds. Then she came back to the bed.

"Will you be all right? Can I get you anything, a glass of water maybe?"

"No, thanks. I think I'll just go to sleep for a while."

"All right then." Julia hesitated for a moment and then, stooping quickly and awkwardly, dropped a kiss on Alexina's forehead. She walked swiftly to the door and closed it gently behind her.

Alexina lay on her back in the comforting dimness, looking at the ceiling. How long had it been since someone kissed her on the forehead before she went to sleep? Years . . . not since her mother. She felt tears gather in the corners of her eyes, a sudden welling up of the old grief—the feeling of something precious gone from her life forever. She did not want to think about it. She closed her eyes and let the familiar emptiness take her down, down into sleep.

Much later, she awoke to darkness and discovered the headache and attendant nausea were gone. The clock on her bedside table read 3:00 A.M.. She couldn't believe she had slept so long. She turned over, luxuriating in a feeling of well-being. But the closed blinds bothered her. She did not usually draw them, for she liked to watch the rectangles of evening sky they framed. So she got out of bed and padded across the floor to pull them up. At the second window she paused, gazing out over meadow and mountain. . . . Wasn't there something, something she should look for? It hovered just out of reach, an image that had slipped away. The effort to call it back made her feel sad again. She returned to bed, curled up, and closed her eyes against the blankness of the night.

She felt well the next day and to Julia's pleasure ate a large breakfast. Toby too seemed quite recovered. He looked up from his plate to ask her very civilly how she felt. "Fine," she replied, thinking: Here it comes, some smart remark about passing out on the kitchen floor. But he just went back to his breakfast, and left her alone for the rest of the meal.

Alexina was puzzled. You'd never know they'd had such a terrible fight so recently. She frowned to herself. There was something else, something that had happened the day before. . . . What had she done late in the day? She couldn't really remember. She looked up from her eggs to see Toby's eyes on her. He dropped them at once, but she had time to see that his expression was the one he had worn yesterday by the couch: questioning, slightly searching, as if he too were looking for a misplaced memory. She wrinkled her brow. Now that was strange.

* * * *

Alexina woke to a sense of light, dawning somewhere far away. She opened her eyes. But there was no light at all, only the darkness of her nightbound room and the silver patch the moon cast over the floorboards. She turned her head and saw more darkness, darkness solidified into an inky form beside her bed. She clapped her hands to her mouth to stifle a scream. It was the tall figure, it had somehow gotten into her room . . . and then she remembered that its hood had fallen back and there had been a man, a man who had taken Taryn away—Taryn! And he had put his hand on her forehead and caused her to forget everything. That was what the odd blank feeling of the past two days had been about. But why was she remembering now? All this ran through her head in a few seconds, seconds in which the man moved to the foot of her bed where she could see him better.

"Why?" she whispered and thought toward him.

He shook his head. *No questions yet. I've come to take you to my companions. And to Taryn.*

Taryn? He's all right?

Yes. He is well.

I'll come. She scrambled out of bed. He waited outside her room as she got into her clothes, and then led the way down the stairs and out of the house. Again his footsteps made no sound, and this time, neither did hers. They moved within a pocket of their own silence; Alexina had the strange feeling that they were invisible.

When they reached the pines he turned to her. *We have some way to go. I am able to move much faster than you, and it will save time if I carry you.*

Before she could speak he had swept her up into his arms. She stiffened instinctively, her hands against his chest, but his grip was very firm and she knew he could overcome her easily if she struggled. And after an instant she realized that she was not in fact afraid. Somehow she sensed he would not harm her.

They seemed to be going a good deal faster than should be possible for a person on foot, especially when burdened by another, and Alexina rapidly became disoriented. When at last they came to a stop, she did not know where she was at all. They were in a wood—that was not unusual—but it was not one of the woods near the farm because there were too many deciduous trees. Just ahead was a clearing. A small campfire burned in it. She could hear the wind in the trees, and something else, a sighing or lapping. It took a minute to recognize the sound as water moving against a shore.

The man put her down. *I will let them know we're here.*

There was a pause, then a kind of blast of thought, the mental equivalent of a trumpet call or a whistle. There was meaning in it, but it flashed too quickly through Alexina's mind for her to understand. It was answered, after a moment, with a similar call. The man turned to her.

Come. His eyes were on hers. *Don't be afraid, Alexina. We will not harm you. To us, the power is sacred, wherever it may occur.*

I'm not afraid, she thought back. But she was not quite sure what she was feeling now. Curiosity, caution, eagerness to see Taryn—did it add up to fear?

She followed him into the clearing. The small fire, ringed with stones, cast enough light to illumine the three people around it. She saw Taryn at once. His hair was combed and freshly braided, and he was dressed again in the clothes he had worn when she had first seen him. He seemed completely restored to health. But instead of the recognition she expected, his expression was impersonal, almost as if he did not know her. His face was shadowed by the shifting firelight, older than she remembered. His eyes held no trace of warmth.

Alexina's eager smile died. She had not thought beyond this moment. She was aware for the first time of her own vulnerability. She did not know where she was, and she knew nothing about these people except that they were strangers, people of power against whom she was probably helpless.

She felt a hand on her shoulder, and could not control her nervous start. It was her guide. *Come,* he thought. *Sit down with us.*

She obeyed, glancing warily around the circle at the others. There was a man in his early middle years, with dark eyes and shoulder-length brown hair. Beside him sat a woman of similar age and features. They wore tunics and leggings like Taryn's, uniform in color except for the bright slash of red scarves circling their waists. Gold medallions gleamed on their breasts. Their calm expressions were unreadable.

She shifted her eyes to her guide. This was the man who had made light from nothing, who had taken away her memory. He was older than the others, in his forties perhaps, with a well-defined aquiline profile and a face that was thin almost to the point of emaciation. His light brown hair was cut short. His mouth was firm and did not look as if it smiled very often. He had thrown back his cloak, revealing clothing identical to the others' except for the shimmering green band that was tied around his waist. In the firelight his eyes glowed tawny amber, only a few shades darker than the gold medallion he wore. They met Alexina's; she could not hold them for long. She heard the crackle of burning wood, loud in the quiet night.

Let me introduce my companions, he thought. *The man is Loran. The woman is his sister Gwynys. Taryn you know. And I am Marhalt.*

They inclined their heads gravely as he thought their names, even Taryn.

And now, thought Marhalt, *you must be wondering why we have brought you here—why we've given your memory back.*

Alexina nodded.

We need your help.

My *help?*

Taryn has told us that you saw two men come from the cave where you found him. We are looking for them—you know that, yes?

Yes.

You understand that one of them has stolen something from us, and that this thing is very valuable. We need to know everything you saw and felt.

Alexina looked at him, then at the others, then at Taryn, the only one who did not meet her gaze.

What will you do after I've told you? she asked. *Will you take my memory away again?*

Our presence here must remain a secret. We cannot risk betrayal.

Alexina shook her head vigorously. *I wouldn't betray you. I want to keep my memory. It's very important to me.*

He did not reply. Alexina took a deep breath.

I . . . I don't know if I can tell you anything if you're going to take my memory afterward. It's . . . it's not fair to me.

She stopped, steeling herself for his response. She saw that his face was not angry, but could not read what lay behind it. *I must speak to my companions,* he thought at last, and turned to the others.

A discussion followed in a language Alexina recognized from Taryn's delirious mutterings a few days earlier; Taryn, she noticed, did not take part. At last Marhalt turned back to Alexina. His expression was still unreadable. When they came, his thoughts were neutral, devoid of identifiable feeling.

We seem to have reached an impasse. We cannot force you to tell us what you know. It is forbidden for us to enter the mind of one with power, unless permission is granted. And you do have power, even in this place, for you felt the call.

What call?

Mine. It was I who watched your window these past few nights. Only your power allowed you to see me.

Why were you watching?

We wished to be sure who possessed power, here in a place where none can possess it. We felt the disturbance when you and Taryn used mindspeech. We knew Taryn had passed through the gate, and we thought that perhaps he had found the man we seek. But when we traced the disturbance to its source, we found it was not that man, but someone else. We located you and I tested you. Your memory was removed because we could not risk discovery. When Taryn recovered, he told us what you had seen. We knew then that you could help us. And so we have brought you here tonight.

You knew Taryn was here the whole time? But why didn't you come get him, instead of letting him go off on his own and get so sick?

Taryn is not supposed to be here at all, Marhalt thought. For an instant his eyes rested on Taryn. Alexina sensed some current in that gaze. Taryn's shoulders stiffened. *He is only an apprentice. He does not have the full training that would qualify him for the quest we follow. He came after us disobediently, in secret, and we did not know it until we felt the Gate open again after we had passed through. We would have rescued him ourselves, of course, had you not arrived there before us. However, we also wished him to learn the consequences of diobedience and excessive self-confidence. So we let him be on his own for a time. We feel he has learned a valuable lesson.*

How did he get well so fast?

He was not sick, Alexina. Not as you understand sickness. You see, this place is very dangerous to any of us who are unprotected. Each of us here has barriers which shield us. But Taryn's training is not complete, and his barriers are not strong enough to sustain him. That is why he became ill. Under our protection, behind our barriers, he could become well again.

Alexina shook her head. *I don't understand. Why is it dangerous for you here? What is this Gate you're talking about? And . . . and why isn't anyone here supposed to have power? I have it, after all. And so do you.*

For a moment Marhalt did not answer. The firelight flickering over his face emphasized its hollows and straight lines, and lit his eyes so it seemed as if they possessed their own illumination. Abruptly

Alexina felt a touch of fear. It coursed quickly through her and then was gone.

I can answer all your questions, he thought at last. *Or I can tell you nothing at all. You may choose. But if you choose knowledge, remember that all knowledge demands a price.*

A price?

A payment in kind. Your knowledge for ours.

Would you really tell me things? About yourselves? About why you're here?

I would tell you everything you wished to know, or could think to ask. But the choice must be yours.

Could he mean it? Could he really be offering her the chance to find out about these mysterious people and their power and what had been taken from them . . . and perhaps about herself too? Her sense of caution told her there must be a catch. It seemed too easy a bargain. They must already know, through Taryn, most of what she had to say. And mightn't they just take her memory after she had told them, erasing anything they had revealed, leaving her once again with nothing? With renewed acuteness Alexina felt her own defenselessness, her ignorance of these shadowy people around the fire. And yet . . . and yet, she thought, everything is a risk. Wouldn't it be better to know, even for a little while, than never to have known at all? Resolutely she met Marhalt's eyes.

I want to know.

For a moment he did not reply. Alexina could feel the blood beating in her throat. At last, shadows dark upon his angular features, Marhalt inclined his head.

You are brave, Alexina. Only the brave choose knowledge. But you must prepare yourself for what I will tell you. For I warn you, it will strain the bounds of your belief. Your people do not come naturally to such things.

I'm ready.

Good, Marhalt thought. *Listen well, now. For we are not of your world.*

7

There was a silence. Marhalt's thoughts had stopped, but Alexina could still feel them, echoing inside her mind. The night seemed to have become immense; the world centered upon the smallness of their firelit circle, as if time had suddenly halted.

Do you mean . . . do you mean you're from another planet? she managed after a moment.

No. Another world, but a world next to yours. Side by side.

A parallel world. Her eyes opened wide.

Marhalt nodded. *These worlds, these parallel worlds, are profoundly different from one another. They are physically the same, and governed by the same natural forces. What makes them different is the powers that rule them. Here, I will show you.*

He leaned forward swiftly, and thrust his arm deep into the heart of the fire. Alexina gasped. But his face registered no flicker of pain. When he withdrew his hand, a live coal rested in his fingers. As Alexina watched it licked into flame; the flame grew, enveloping the hand that held it, reaching upward until it became a tall column, a fountain of sparks. Slowly it sank back down to a glowing ember and, abruptly, winked out. Marhalt held up his palm. It was empty and unmarked.

That is the power which rules my world. It is called

mindpower. *And this is mindpower also.* He looked at the man Loran, and Alexina saw the knife at Loran's belt unsheathe itself and drift to Marhalt's outstretched hand. *And when we speak with our minds, that is also mindpower. Mindpower is the ability to control the forces and the objects of nature through the power of the mind alone. Do you see?*

Alexina's throat was dry. She swallowed and nodded. *Magic,* she thought. If she had spoken it would have been a whisper. But Marhalt shook his head.

Not as you mean. Your concept of "magic" implies something that goes against nature. But mindpower does not go against nature. The forces that govern the worlds are the same, and mindpower is a way of controlling them. The proper way. He held out the knife, which still rested in his hand. *This is the power that rules your world, Alexina. It is the lesser, improper power, the power of tools, of things worked with the hands, and it is called* handpower. *It means your people use tools and their products to shape their world. Your people have lost the powers of the mind that would enable them to live by any but external means. I can make light with thought alone, but your people must use a lantern. I can make fire through the force of my will, but your people must use flint and tinder. I can cut through a branch without a tool, but your people must use this knife.* He lifted his arm suddenly and threw the knife straight at Loran. It whistled wickedly through the air, almost too fast to be seen, but Loran put up his hand as swiftly, and without effort the knife rested in his grip, point upward. He sheathed it slowly. Marhalt looked at Alexina. *Do you understand?*

I . . . I think so. She recognized the dichotomy between science and what she had always thought of as "everything else." She thought of that other reality for which she had searched despite the evidence of her senses and the assertions of people like Jessica, imagining it to be obscured only by people's disbelief—hidden, but still present beneath the things she knew, if only she could discover where or how to look for it. Marhalt was telling her that it was not hidden at all but actually separate, that this reality dominated its own world, a world physically apart from her own. It was almost beyond grasping. But the glow of spectral flame was still in her eyes, and her mind held the thoughts of another. Reality had become like the infinitely expanding horizons of a dream, a landscape that stretched far beyond any boundaries she had ever imagined.

There is . . . there is one thing. You said the people here have lost the powers of the mind. And yet I can mindspeak. Why is that?

I must admit that we do not know. You're a throwback, perhaps, like the man we follow. It's very rare, but he has shown us it can happen.

But that doesn't make sense! If I have power, there must be others who have it too. There must be some *mindpower in this world! Otherwise, how would people here even know about it? And there are people who do, people who write about it and think about it and even try to prove it exsts. I mean, I can't be the only one!*

Her thought trailed away. Their faces were all turned toward her, even Taryn's. Suddenly she had the impression of a blank featureless wall.

I am sorry, Alexina, Marhalt thought at last. *You must accept what I tell you. Your possession of the gift is very strange, but it means nothing. Long ago your people threw away the powers of the mind and built a wall around themselves, a wall of handpower so high that they could no longer feel the true rhythms of reality. They remember mindpower because once, long ago, their ancestors possessed it; but they no longer believe in it or possess it themselves. Mindpower and handpower—your kind of handpower—are simply incompatible. They cannot exist together. Power is impossible in this world.*

It was an assertion beyond contradiction, the more brutal for its very lack of emotion. Could it really be that she was the only one, the sole possessor of power in the whole world? It did not seem right. She thought of the things she had searched for, the different order whose shadow she had sensed behind the fact of the way things were. Perhaps her own latent, useless power had been at work, making her dimly aware that something vital was no longer present in her world. She felt a terrible loneliness. If it were true, that other reality was as inaccessible to her as if it were in fact as unreal as Jessica and the others believed.

Marhalt must have sensed something of what she felt, for his next thought was gentle. *Let me tell you the Tale of the Worlds, Alexina. It will help you to understand how these things came to be.* He leaned forward in the firelight. A change came over his face; it turned inward, and, though his golden eyes still rested on her, she had the impression that they were seeing something else. When his thoughts came again, they rose and fell within her mind with the cadenced rhythms of spoken phrases, of a story often told.

Once, in a time lost in the mists of beginning, the worlds were one. There are few records of this golden age, and we know only that it was an age of harmony, an age of balance. Mindpower and handpower existed side by side, and the people had the capacity for both. Yet they existed in the proper proportion, for handpower is the lesser power and must always be secondary. Mindpower ruled then, ruled all the world.

The people were innocent then. No limits were set on handpower, and they thought the balance would last for-

ever. But tools are a fatal temptation, to which the weak succumb and the ignorant fall prey. They seemed to promise great things, a life of ease, comfort and wealth unlimited to the imagination. And, drawn by greed and slothfulness, the people began to seek the way of tools. Gradually handpower began to develop, to gain a foothold in every region of the world. Those who adhered to the way of tools became corrupt, blinded and obsessed with the power of the hands; they did not perceive that they paid for their comfort with the rhythms of the world, that they exchanged for their ease a power so precious it cannot be measured. For those who chose handpower left mindpower behind. Handpower was the new way; they no longer valued any other. At last they bred out of themselves the ability for mindpower, and often even the memory of it. If they recalled it at all, it was as a dream: vivid, perhaps even frightening, but no longer real.

Yet there were some who were not beguiled. These people saw the falseness of the way of tools and clung to the paths of mindpower. They withdrew from the others and their insanity, attempting to preserve the proper balance and the proper ways of life. Often they were persecuted and hounded, burned and tortured and imprisoned. Yet they held firm.

No one can say for certain when it happened, when the balance tipped forever. But at last the very fabric of reality began to fray. A person might leave his village and find himself in a wild and uninhabited forest where once there had been a handpower town. Familiar roads began to disappear from one day to the next. A village which had been three days' travel might suddenly be only one. Somehow, the difference in the powers the people followed was changing the very nature of things; two entirely separate worlds were forming and, slowly, sealing off from one another. Those who followed handpower were probably not aware of what was occurring. But those who followed mindpower understood and used understanding to survive. Now they could find shelter behind the barriers of their own world, where others could not go. Over the centuries, the division has become almost complete. There are only nine gates left. One day they will all be gone, and all contact between the worlds will be lost.

Those who followed handpower, those who broke the balance, those who ripped the original world apart—they were your people, Alexina, and that became your world. In your world mindpower has been thrown away, shut out forever. Do you understand now? Do you?

For the first time his thoughts carried real emotion, a great current of sadness, the consciousness of waste and of something precious lost. It was his own personal sorrow, but it was also the sorrow of an entire people, an entire world, which he carried as his own. Alexina was shaken by it. She thought of the powers, the possibilities, the wonders of the mind, set aside for tools and technology and science, for vacuum cleaners and can openers and automobiles and toxic waste. Yes, she understood now. She *had* known it all along. Her people had been greedy, fatally greedy, and they still were. The old was still destroyed by the new, its value forgotten in the pursuit of novelty and of the myth of progress. She felt a surge of anger. She had been cheated, cheated of her true heritage. She despised those who had thrown it away.

The other world is ours, Alexina, the world of those who chose mindpower. Marhalt's thoughts resumed their flow. *We guard the true ways. We keep handpower in check, for we do not wish that ancient error to occur again in our world. There are strict Limits on handpower now, governing tools and their use and manufacture. Thus temptation is removed from those who might succumb, and handpower cannot grow. We are the Brotherhood of Guardians. It is our task to keep the Limits, to preserve them throughout the lands so that the people may understand them and live by them and the balance may never tip. The worlds cannot be one again, but in our world we keep a balance as close as can be to that original one.*

Marhalt's eyes rested on Alexina, and they seemed to reach out to her. *Would you know our world, Alexina? Would you see that which your people threw aside?*

Yes, she whispered.

Then come with me. Give me your mind and I will take you there.

Was there a tiny breath of hesitation? Held by the golden cord of Marhalt's gaze, Alexina was not aware of it. She surrendered her mind to his. His eyes became larger, larger, until they were all that existed; she felt herself falling, plunging toward a landscape that materialized suddenly below her. It was his world, and she knew she would not fall all the way, for he would hold her up above it. Gripped by his unfaltering power, she soared over hills and valleys and plains and rivers identical to those in her own world. But the terrain supported a very different way of life, an older and more primitive one, where people ground their grain between stones, farmed with hoe and horsedrawn plow, fought with bow and arrow and sword and spear. It supported many races, too, many animals; some she knew from her own world, some only from myth. She saw gnomes living in caves deep below a great mountain range. She saw ethereal beings who inhabited streams and forests. She saw creatures which were half man, half animal. She saw skies darkened with great flying reptiles, seas that boiled with huge snakelike monsters.

They soared at last above a vast range of mountains, and below them a great Fortress became visible. It was the Fortress from which Marhalt and the others had come, the Fortress of the Brotherhood of

Guardians. Here resided the most powerful of all those in that world of power, guarding their heritage, keeping safe forever the powers of the mind. And something else too, something that pulsed deep within the Fortress like a heart, a muted thrumming that was somehow familiar. And then a surge, a surge of power so great it seemed larger than the world itself, limitless, greater than the mind that held it could conceive.

The strange landscapes disappeared all at once, and Alexina was aware again of the fire and the night. She felt dizzy, as if a support had been unexpectedly jerked away. She put her hand to her forehead. There was nothing in her mind now but her own thoughts. Her head felt very empty.

It was becoming too much for you, came Marhalt's thought. *Power or no, you are still of your world.*

Alexina shook her head. The shapes around her were solid, real—she saw the campfire, Loran and Gwynys, Taryn—but underneath, she could almost discern other shapes, the same yet different, the shapes of the world Marhalt had just shown her. Almost, she could feel it. She closed her eyes for a moment, and when she opened them the illusion was gone.

Do you understand now, Alexina? Marhalt asked.

Yes. She met his golden eyes without difficulty. *I understand. Thank you. Thank you for showing me.*

He inclined his head gravely and then, suddenly, he smiled. It transformed his face. Alexina found herself smiling back. *You are uniquely privileged, Alexina,* he thought. *You are the first and only one of your people who will ever hear the Tale of the Worlds.*

Marhalt, there was something else, something I felt just at the end, something inside the Fortress. What was it?

There was a pause. Alexina saw that Loran and

Gwynys glanced at one another, then at Marhalt. *That was the Stone, Alexina.*

The Stone?

Yes. He paused for a moment. *The Stone is . . . a very powerful object. It has guided life in our world for more than a thousand years.*

Alexina frowned. *A stone?*

Not a stone, the *Stone. It has powers quite beyond the conception of one who is handpower-born. There is nothing even remotely like it in your world. It possesses the power to know anything, anywhere, at any moment. It has been our guide for centuries. It is the essence of mindpower. It is the most precious thing in our world.*

Alexina digested this. *Is it alive somehow?*

Marhalt held up his hand, and she understood that it was a warning. *I can tell you no more, Alexina. The Stone is a great mystery. Even we who tend it do not fully know it. The Stone is our charge. As Guardians we guard what is most precious in our world—not simply the powers of the mind, but also the Power of the Stone. It is the heart of our order and the center of our world. For centuries we have held it safe, free from harm and the avarice of men, a sacred trust for our people.*

Alexina felt something behind the thought, and suddenly she put it all together. She knew now why the sense of the Stone seemed familiar. She had felt it before, on the ledge as the dark man passed below her. *That's what the man stole. Your Stone.*

Marhalt nodded slowly. *Yes. In spite of our efforts, it still sometimes happens that people of our world choose handpower. Even among ourselves, for he was once one of us. We do not know how he became corrupt. We know only the depths of his corruption and the road he chose. He is much worse than a criminal. He is . . . monstrous.*

Alexina shivered. Behind Marhalt's thoughts lay an image of something hardly human, a brooding malignancy reaching out like a cancer to infect all it touched. And she had nearly met this man face-to-face; he had inhabited her dreams.

We must find the Stone as soon as possible, Marhalt thought. *We don't know how long it can stay in your world unharmed.*

Does this man want to harm it?

It is your world that will harm it. Passage through the Gates brings change. Whatever goes through begins to fall prey to the forces of the world it enters. Each world contains . . . currents, you could say, just as the ocean does. The currents of your world are handpower currents. They surround you constantly, and they bombard anything coming through the Gates. We are only able to survive here because we are protected by our barriers. Unprotected, we would eventually lose our power, succumb, become just like your people. That's why Taryn became ill—it was the beginning of that change.

And you think the Stone will lose its power?

We fear it may be destroyed. You cannot understand how alien the Stone is to your world, how dreadful an effect your world-currents could have upon it. No barriers are strong enough to protect the Stone, not even the barriers of the man we seek, though he is powerful. Inevitably the currents will penetrate, and the change will begin. But it will take time. We hope we can rescue it before the damage is irreversible.

He leaned forward. *Alexina, that is why we need you and what you have seen. You see that time is short. Every clue is vital. We need you to tell us everything, every fact, any detail that might enlighten us about his direction, his actions. You must understand the urgency of this mission. Without the Stone, our world has no center. Without the Stone, we fear our world may die.*

His steady eyes held the urgency of which he spoke, and something else—an appeal. An appeal to her for help. How strange it was that she had the power to help these powerful people. Without hesitation now, she recounted all she had seen and felt, as well as the two dreams that had come to her later, including every detail she could recall. At last she finished, her head aching slightly from the prolonged transmission of thought. Silence fell.

What does it all mean? she asked at last. *What were those things I felt?*

Marhalt's eyes met hers. Alexina had the sudden impression that he regarded her from across a great gulf.

What you felt initially was the opening of the Gate. That is not surprising in one of general psychic ability. On the ledge, you contacted the barriers of this man. But— here he exchanged a glance with the other Guardians—*you seem also to have formed a link with him. Taryn did tell us, but we thought he might have exaggerated.*

A link? Is that bad?

In the moment when your minds touched, a psychic thread was spun, linking mind to mind. It is a rare occurrence, a connection that is usually established only with the volition of at least one of the people involved. Though his barriers are closed, that tie must still be there. That is why you had the two dreams you describe. Your mind, freed in sleep from the constrictions of your handpower concepts, went out along the thread and followed him.

Alexina put her hand to her head. A link? A link that bound her to the monster Marhalt had described . . .

Does it work both ways? Can he reach me with it?

Yes.

But then—but then how do I know I'm not in danger from him?

The thread is not physical, Alexina. Even if he did reach back along it he could do you no harm. You might have a nightmare, or he might try to use the link to call you. But it's possible to resist these things.

Alexina shook her head, with a feeling close to panic. That tugging feeling in her dreams . . . She imagined she could feel it now, evil and coldly alien within her mind. *Can it be broken?*

It can. There are two ways. The first is attrition. When we conquer this man we will take away his barriers; he will succumb to the forces and lose his powers, and the link with them. It will happen naturally, inevitably. You will be free of it then.

What's the other way?

That is more difficult. Face-to-face, mind-to-mind, in a struggle of wills. He is a powerful man, Alexina; that is not the way for you.

His eyes were steady. She took a breath to calm herself. Not physical, she thought. It *would* be broken. But in the meantime it would be there within her, like a parasite, alive with a life separate from her own and beyond her control. She shuddered.

There remains one more matter, Alexina. The price. The payment for the knowledge I've given you tonight.

But I thought . . . I assumed my telling you . . .

Marhalt shook his head. *You should not have assumed. There is something else we need from you, and it is mine to ask it now.*

The catch, she thought. It's the catch. And suddenly she was afraid, really afraid.

We will be traveling through your land, among your people. We will need to be able to communicate. We need your language.

My language? She looked at him blankly. Her initial fear had vanished. *I suppose I could teach you,* she thought doubtfully, *but it would take an awfully long time—*

No, we would not learn as you think. I can link my mind

with yours and take the language from your mind all in one piece. The others will acquire it too, through me. His amber eyes met hers without faltering. *Alexina, we cannot force you. Remember, we are forbidden to enter your mind without your permission. But we need your help, and we are asking you to honor our bargain and help us in this way.*

Alexina was aware of tension. They were all watching her, shadowy in the firelight. They were waiting for her answer . . . almost as if it were a test of some kind. She believed Marhalt when he said they would not force her. It was her own fault she had made assumptions, not asked questions. Yet what Marhalt asked required a great deal of courage. She had held his thoughts in her mind, and given him her own, but this was much more. It was to place herself wholly in the hands of another, to trust him with what was more precious than possessions or even her own body. She looked at Marhalt, at the tawny eyes which did not waver from her own. Why had he not asked this at the beginning? But then, would she have understood before he told her the truth about the two worlds? Probably not; perhaps it had been necessary to wait. Marhalt had been honest with her, patient; he had answered all she asked. She remembered the strength with which he had held her above his world; she had trusted herself to him then, and he had not betrayed her. She took a deep breath.

All right, she thought.

Marhalt's serious, waiting face broke again into his rare smile. The warmth of it was formidable.

He got to his feet, moved around the fire and knelt in front of her. He held out his hands, and she understood that she was to put hers into them. His grip was light and cool. There was silence, a silence strangely alive, filled with pulsing currents, and

Alexina knew that she was experiencing the mindlink. She looked into Marhalt's eyes. For an instant, the barest breath, she felt an electric touch, a crackling current that filled her mind and raced through her body—then it was gone. She felt quite calm. Far off across the lake, a loon called once.

Marhalt let go of her hands. "How do you feel?"

"Fine. Aren't you going to—" She stopped abruptly. He had spoken, out loud, in English. She had answered him before she was aware of it.

"Is it over?" she said. Her voice sounded odd after the prolonged silence of mindspeech. "Do you know English now?"

"Yes. The others too, even Taryn."

His voice was deep, and there was a slight oddness to his pronunciation. Alexina put her hand to her head. At the very least she had expected to lose consciousness for a moment, or somehow to feel the passage of knowledge out of her mind and into theirs. It had been so brief.

"We thank you, Alexina. You have discharged your part of the bargain well." He got to his feet. "I must return you to your home before you are missed."

Looking around, Alexina saw that it was almost dawn. A faint line of light lay on the horizon beyond the mountains. The trees were visible now, and the lake. She was surprised to find it so close, no more than fifteen paces away past a final stand of trees. She knew where she was now—this was the lake that was visible from her cave. She looked at the others around the fire.

"Good-bye," she said. "And thank you."

Gravely, Loran and Gwynys nodded in response. She looked at Taryn. He grinned quickly, the remote expression he had worn during the night slipping aside like a too-large garment.

"See ya," he said.

"Taryn!" It was Marhalt, his voice as sharp as the crack of a whip. Taryn's smile vanished and his gaze dropped. Puzzled, Alexina turned to Marhalt. He was holding out his hands.

"Come, Alexina."

He carried her through the forest with the same disorienting swiftness as before, and soon they were standing at the edge of the pine forest around the farm. He set her gently on her feet.

"Good-bye, Alexina," he said. And then he reached out and laid his fingers on her forehead, very gently, so that she could scarcely feel them. They conveyed a slight shock, a fleeting echo of the electric feeling of the language transfer; Alexina could not prevent herself from flinching, for it took her unawares and the removal of her memory, forgotten during most of the night, was vivid again. But when Marhalt took his hand away she found that nothing had changed. Her memory was intact.

"You . . . you're not going to take my memory this time?"

He shook his head.

"Thank you. Oh, thank you, Marhalt."

"Don't thank me." His expression was unreadable. "Everything serves a purpose."

And before she could absorb these enigmatic words, he had turned and was gone. He just seemed to vanish. For a moment, the spot where he had stood glowed brighter than the air around it, as if the power of his presence had left a trace of itself behind. Alexina felt bereft. There was a chilly breeze. With the dawn had come the dew, and her feet were damp in their sneakers.

She turned and looked at the farm. It was quite light now—it must be about five o'clock—and she could see it clearly, the buildings shabby even from this distance. She felt, suddenly, a moment of complete disbelief. She could not be going back there. Last night she had traveled into another world. How could she return to this one? Never, not even in the first moment she saw the farm, had it held quite such constricting ugliness. She stood on the border between meadow and mountain, feeling like Cinderella at the stroke of twelve, poised between the hours as the things she most desired slid from her grasp. Three times wonders had entered her life; three times they had departed. What was left for her now?

Alexina picked up her unwilling feet and began to descend slowly to the house. The atmosphere seemed to thicken as she walked, dark despite the growing dawn. Her head ached; her mind swam with foreign concepts and ideas received too quickly. She felt incapable of thinking one more thought, of absorbing one more image. She slipped through the kitchen door and tiptoed upstairs to her room. Dropping her clothes on the floor, she curled up in bed, and fell immediately into a dreamless sleep.

8

Alexina's alarm rang at seven o'clock. She shut it off and sat up slowly, feeling as if she had just woken from an incredible and complicated dream. But it hadn't been a dream. Last night she had sat with people from another world, learned things which went beyond all her imaginings. Her memory was vivid with the experience, her mind suffused with the wonders of Marhalt's Tale. Though she had had barely an hour and a half's sleep, the muddy bemusement of last night had vanished, and her mind felt sharp and clear.

But the farm-feeling was still there. Usually it assailed her only after she had been away, or after she turned out the light at night. But now . . . She looked around the room. How threadbare the quilt was, how muddy the brown-painted floor, how cracked and lopsided the wardrobe. The damp stain on the ceiling seemed to leer. The windows framed the meadow and a portion of the mountain, an azure blue sky and a world irradiated with intense golden sunshine—a world as vivid and beautiful as her room was blurred and hideous. The odd clarity of her senses made it all the more painful. Alexina rested her head in her hands for a moment. Surely this was the dream.

She got out of bed, dressed, and went downstairs.

In the kitchen she ate mechanically, and then went out to the long fields to gather produce. She was aware, with the acuteness which had woken her and which would not soften, of how much she hated this work. She loathed it all—the burning sun on her back, the sweat rolling down her cheeks and stinging her eyes, the unpleasant damp feel of the vegetables as she picked them.

She was quiet during lunch, picking at her food. Julia put a hand on her forehead and wondered aloud if she had a touch of heat exhaustion.

"You'd better take the produce booth this afternoon, Alexina. You can be in the shade there. Becky Miller was going to do it, but I can send her out to the berries instead. I don't want you getting sick again."

Alexina looked at Julia. Inexplicably, she felt a rush of sadness. "Thanks, Julia," she said.

She sat in the shade of the trees by the booth, unable to read the book she had brought with her. The wind played among the trees, rustling faintly as it moved over the grass of the meadow. About halfway through the afternoon it dropped. In the silence Alexina looked around her. She saw the produce booth, its metal sides rusty and its painted shelves peeling. A little distance away was the rutted dirt road leading to the farm. As if she were actually walking it, Alexina's mind moved toward the crest of the hill. The house and buildings rose up in her mind; she saw them entire in their barren loneliness, their poverty and shabbiness.

Her whole soul revolted. It was wrong, wrong. She thought with horror of the next year and a half, of the work that never ended, of Toby's teasing, of the boredom of school. If she managed to endure it, she would go back to New York with Jessica. But for the first time that did not seem like deliverance—only, in some strange way, more of the same. Loneliness, isolation, never quite fitting in, possessing bleakly and forever the burden of her solitary gift and the knowledge that the world she lived in contained no one else like herself. It was unbearable.

Everything came together at once in her mind. That could be her future. But it did not have to be. She could choose another path. She could follow the Guardians on their Quest.

The idea was so astounding that for a moment she ceased to think. But as the seconds passed she realized that this was the only possible action. Moreover, the decision had not been made just then. It had been there all along, in the wonderful acuteness of her mind and the power with which the ugliness around her attacked her senses. Perhaps it had been made the night before in her sleep, or even in the moment when she looked down at the farm. It didn't matter. She only knew she could not let this chance slip away. It was this for which she had been waiting—she was certain of it. The Guardians were people of power. They were her own kind. With them she would, finally, be at home.

Later, much later, she would wonder how she could have missed the strangeness of that day. It was as if part of her were slipping away—the familiar Alexina who endured, who went to school and did chores—leaving only the secret part of herself, the part she did not really know, the part that *waited.* Even the waiting was not quite familiar. Beneath it a coldness stirred, a splinter of ice at her very heart. The small strain of the thing that had hooked into her mind had become constant, so constant she had almost ceased to be aware of it as something separate from herself.

At five o'clock she closed the produce booth and walked slowly back to the farm. Oddly, as soon as she had made her decision, the farm-feeling vanished. For the first time, cresting the hill, she did not feel that sinking sense of desperation. She stopped for a moment, looking at the shabby house, the decaying outbuildings. *I'm leaving,* she thought to it, *I'm getting away. You can't touch me any more.*

Alexina sat through dinner, her resolve wrapping her like a blanket. The dining room seemed very far away—the faded wallpaper, the threadbare carpet, the oak table with the everyday placemats, the family around it. It could not touch her either; its shabbiness provoked no reaction.

Toward the end of the meal, Julia glanced at her. "You're pale, Alexina. Do you feel all right?"

"Yes. Yes, I'm fine."

"You've been working pretty hard lately. I think you need a day off. As a matter of fact, so do I. We could go into Bradenton, do a little shopping and have lunch, maybe go to a movie. What do you say?"

Alexina looked at her. She had a sudden vision of Julia discovering she was gone. Julia would be very upset. She felt a rush of guilt and dropped her eyes. "Yes, that sounds good," she said with an effort.

"Great. We can take the station wagon into town, and catch the bus from there."

* * * *

After dinner, Alexina went up to her room. Slowly she filled a backpack with extra jeans and shirts, socks, underwear, everything she thought she might need on a Quest. Finished, she looked at her watch. It was only six-thirty. Turning off her light, she lay down on her bed.

Charles would be concerned at her absence, of course, for he was responsible for her. But she knew Julia's concern would go deeper. She wished she could tell her somehow, provide some reassurance so she would not worry. Of course she could not, for Julia would try to stop her from going. Oddly, she felt that Toby, if his memory were intact, would be a good person to tell. He might be able to set his natural skepticism against what he had seen the other night.

Perhaps she should make peace with Toby before she left. She considered the thought. It seemed right; she wanted very much to have a clean break with at least one person. She looked at her watch. With luck, he wouldn't have left for work yet.

She tiptoed down the hall and rapped at Toby's door. She heard a muffled "Come in," and entered. Alexina stood awkwardly, not knowing exactly how to begin. Toby sat on his bed tying his shoes.

"Um, Toby . . . there's something I want to talk to you about. About . . . well, about the quarrel we had."

Silence. He was watching her now. She could not interpret his expression, but it was clear he was not going to make it easy for her. She fought down a surge of resentment.

"I guess—I guess you were right, in some of the things you said. I guess I do act kind of stuck-up sometimes. It's just that sometimes I don't know *how* to act. And the farm, everything here, it's so—so different from everything I was used to." She paused again. Still silence. Did he want more? "And I guess you didn't mean it all the time when you teased me." This was harder to admit. "I know I took it a bit too personally. But no one ever teased me before. Maybe

I overreacted, but you have to admit you were hard on me."

A series of expressions crossed his face; Alexina felt dispirited. What a dumb impulse, she thought. He's just going to be self-righteous and rub it in.

"I guess I *was* kind of hard on you," he said.

Alexina was startled. He avoided her eyes.

"I'm used to my family. I know it's a bad habit, but it just kind of slips out. You may not believe me, but I'm always sorry afterward. And . . . and I'm sorry about what I said the other day, about seeing you go into the woods and all that. I think I really knew you wouldn't tell. But I panicked when I woke up that morning, and I spoke without thinking."

By now Alexina was thoroughly taken aback. She had wanted to clear the slate and had expected at least some acknowledgment, but so complete an about-face was really a surprise. She eyed Toby warily. She saw he was eyeing her too. She realized that each was waiting for the other to make the first move, and all at once the whole situation struck her as funny. She felt a laugh tugging at the corners of her mouth and, giving in to the impulse, let out a giggle. For a moment Toby looked surprised and then he smiled too.

"You did kind of ask for it, you know," he said. "Remember the first time Ma showed you the chicken house? You looked like someone had dropped manure on your head."

Alexina started to feel defensive, but then, recalling herself picking her way gingerly through the chicken yard trying to preserve the pristine whiteness of her sneakers, she had to smile back—if reluctantly.

"*You* have to admit you were a real jerk about it. I'd never even seen a live chicken before, except on

T.V. You made me feel so embarrassed I didn't know what to do."

"Yeah. I guess so." He looked down. "We kind of fanned each other's flame, huh."

"I guess so."

"Actually, I was thinking about telling you this. I've definitely decided I'm going to college in the fall. I can't let the chance slip away, no matter what the consequences are."

"Oh, Toby! I'm glad. I think you're doing the right thing."

"Thanks." He pushed himself off his bed and held out a hand. "So, what do you say? Truce? I'll try not to tease you so much if you'll try not to look down your nose so much."

Alexina regarded him for a moment. Then she returned his smile. "Okay," she said. "Truce." She crossed the room and took his hand, and they shook. He held her hand for a second and she saw that look come over his face again, the searching-for-a-memory look. It was a combination of this, what he had told her, and her own desire to let someone know what she was going to do that motivated her next words.

"Toby, I'll be leaving too."

He looked startled. "You will?"

"Yes. Tonight. I can't tell you where I'm going or why, just that I have to go. It's really important."

There was a pause. "Do Mom and Dad know?"

"Are you kidding? They wouldn't let me go if they did."

"Are you coming back?"

Alexina took a breath to reply and then stopped short. Not until this moment had that question occurred to her. Toby looked at her closely. "Of course!" she said. "It's just for a few days. No big deal."

"I don't know about that. It's not like me. I'll write them as soon as I get to Binghamton, and anyway I think Ma already knows. They're going to be awfully worried about you."

The nagging guilt was back. "I know. I'm sorry, but it can't be helped. I just can't tell anyone where I'm going."

"You aren't in some kind of trouble, are you?"

"No. It's just something . . . something I have to do. I'll be perfectly all right." Alarmed by his intent scrutiny, she said, "You wouldn't tell, would you?"

He shook his head. "No. You kept my secret, and I'll keep yours." He hesitated. "You know, I have the weirdest feeling I should know what this is about."

"No," said Alexina firmly. "I'd tell you if I could, but I just can't."

"All right. I'll have to take your word for it. Good luck to you, whatever it is."

"Thanks. Good luck to you too. I hope you do really well at college. Your father will come around eventually."

"I hope so." He sighed. "I sure hope so. He's going to be awfully mad, though."

Back in her room, Alexina turned off her light and settled by the window to wait. The question Toby had asked her flashed across her mind, but it was the end of the adventure, and she did not wish to think about an end.

Now that she had carried out her one remaining impulse, the last of her obligations slipped away; she could feel it happening, the farm and its people and her old life dropping from her like a heavy garment falling to the floor. Her mind turned toward what lay ahead. At last she was conscious only of *waiting*, an expectant sense of purpose that felt—almost—like an actual physical pull. She gazed out the window as the sun set and purple twilight fell over the meadow, streaking the sky dull rose over navy blue. She watched as the stars came out and an enormous orange moon climbed toward its zenith. The squares of light thrown on the grass by the bedroom windows blinked out one by one, and stillness enfolded the world.

interlude

The dark man waited. He meditated, building his strength for what lay ahead. And he walked, pacing the rich hallways of his home, surveying the silent candlelit rooms and the multitude of his possessions, his dark robe whispering as he moved and his black hair loose upon his shoulders.

So far, he was pleased at the way things had gone. His theories about this world had been substantially correct; he had adjusted well, and now had no difficulty on the rare occasions when he left his domain. His first observation had been borne out: Parallelism was, as far as he could tell, absolute. Allowing for man-made changes, the geological features of the worlds were virtually identical. Towns and even specific buildings were often located in precisely the same places. He had yet to deduce the reasons for this, but it had given him a real advantage. He had grown up in the north, traveling widely about his homeland when young, and in the equivalent land of this world, despite the changes wrought by handpower, he usually knew exactly where he was. The place he chose as a refuge had long been a place of power in his own world, and by the time he reached it he was not surprised to find a building located there. Badly dilapidated as it was, he purchased it, and refurbished and fortified it. Now, drawing from the well of power that lay beneath the worlds, it was virtually impregnable.

The heart of the house, the heart of his plans, lay in the basement. Often he thought, with amusement, of the horror with which the Guardians would have viewed it. He was proud of his achievement: It had not been easy. The forces and disciplines of this world were incredibly complex; it had taken time, selective mindlinking, and extensive reading, to build the base of knowledge he required. The mindlinking had been the simplest part for, unfamiliar with mindpower, these people had no barriers against it and were not even aware of what he was doing. Gradally he grew to understand the context of this world and learned what there was that had to be learned. Finally he sought out a person who possessed the specific information he needed. He left him with only a slight bewilderment during the few moments it took for transmission. With his new expertise, he set about assembling the complex in the basement. It was complete now, needing only a touch to awaken it. But he let it sleep. He wished first to dispose of the Guardians.

He had believed they would never trouble him again. Unassisted they would never have found him, for he was invisible to them when he chose. But somehow, incredibly, a link had been formed between himself and someone of this world. They had located it. Now they were using it to track him down.

It was hard to accept, that link. He had been aware of something unreeling behind him as he moved away from the Gate, though he had dismissed it at first, thinking such things impossible here. But that night, and for a few days thereafter, a power visited him and he knew for certain a linking had taken place. The linker was a young girl, with dark hair and a fine, serious face. He could feel her fear; she withdrew almost as soon as she contacted. It was clear she had not linked deliberately. She did not even understand what had happened.

The link-sense faded. Perhaps, motivated by her fear, she had blocked it away from her conscious mind, cutting it off just as she had established it. But one day it came again, and clearly within the fear he felt purpose. She was seeking him out deliberately—but not of her own will. Behind her stood the Guardians. He felt anger, a brief explosion of fury and frustration. They must find him now, for the link was infallible. A battle would ensue. It would mean wasted days, wasted power, delayed plans. He regarded the dim richness around him with blazing, unseeing eyes. Would he never be free of the limitations of the world he had left? Yes, he thought, and breathed deeply to calm himself. He *would* be free. Not as soon as he had expected, perhaps, but in time. He would destroy them. And he would destroy the link, so that all connection to him would be severed.

But she visited him again, and this time he recognized the nature of her gift. Almost, he doubted his own insight. It was incredible; as yet, he had sensed only the smallest vestiges of power in this place. He realized that she did not understand herself or what she was. They had not told her. Or perhaps they themselves did not—could not—see it. Unwillingly, he began to admire her courage, her determination, the way she held herself firm against her terrible fear. At the heart of that fear lay curiosity: about him, about herself, about power. He sensed the questions she did not yet know how to ask.

It was in this that he began at last to envision a new direction, a new plan. It would offer difficulties, but it would also offer enormous possibilities. It meant that succcess could be doubled. And it meant that violence, which he abhorred, would not be necessary.

And so the dark man paced the rooms of his house, waiting. He was aware of the march of power through this world, of time drawing in, of the narrowing path that led them to this place. Most of all, he was aware of *her*—not just her power, but her selfhood, all her fears and fascinations and wishes. He became convincd that it had not been chance that spun the link. He need not destroy it now, for the success of his plan would ensure that it could never betray him. As for the Guardians—they would be spared too, and they would be used. But first . . . first he would teach them a lesson they would never forget. Once and forever, they would know who stood against them.

9

It was after eleven o'clock when the last square of light winked out on the ground behind the house. Waiting fifteen minutes for safety, Alexina shouldered her backpack and crept stealthily out of her room. She took care to move softly through the backyard, breaking into a run when she reached the meadow. Gaining the safety of the pines, she paused for a moment to adjust her backpack and to gain her bearings.

She felt it suddenly: a slight shock, an electric tingle that for an instant catapulted her back to the night before. Ahead, one of the spindly pines seemed unnaturally thick. As she watched, the trunk divided itself in two, and a tall shape moved toward her. Alexina clapped her hands to her mouth to stifle a scream. It was a moment before she realized what—or who—it was. Marhalt.

He came to stand before her, a dark figure without detail. His presence was astonishing. Yet, at the same time, it was almost as if she had expected it.

"I'm coming with you," she said lamely.

Marhalt nodded. "We know."

"But, I didn't know myself until this afternoon."

"You weren't aware of your intention until then, but it was taking shape in your mind last night, even as we spoke. Power calls to power. It communicated itself to me through the language transfer."

"Oh." Alexina could think of nothing else to say. She had been gearing herself to offer arguments in favor of her presence on the Quest. She felt slightly disoriented, the kind of feeling that comes from stepping off a stairway, in darkness, and finding flat ground instead of another step.

"It is not an easy task we have before us," Marhalt said now. His voice was grave. "The Quest brings with it many rigors, not the least of which is the traveling itself. We will protect you and help you as much as we can, but it will be difficult for you. Do you understand?"

Alexina nodded. "I understand."

"There is one thing more, a condition to your presence with us. We will accept you in our midst, even though you are handpower-born. But because you are handpower-born, you will not be able to fully understand the things we do—or the thing we seek. You must always do precisely as you are told, Alexina. You must follow any order I give you, at once, without question, and without fail. If you say yes to the Quest, you say yes to this condition, and you must never forget it."

Alexina could sense his power. She felt a brief prickling along her spine. What he asked was no more than what she had intended to do anyway, yet he was asking as if it were far more. Was there a meaning here she had not grasped? What did she really know of them, she thought—of the Quest, of the Stone, or even of their world?

"Well, Alexina?"

She took a deep breath, and the strange dislocating uncertainty was gone. "Yes," she said.

He inclined his head. Then he lifted her in his arms as he had done last night, and in no time at all they had reached the camp. He set her on her feet.

The campfire had been extinguished and the Guardians wore bundles strapped to their backs. Marhalt bent to shoulder a bundle of his own. He spoke to the others for a moment in their own language, and then turned to Alexina.

"We must travel on foot, Alexina, because we cannot be in contact with your handpower conveyances," he said. "But our way of travel is not yours, and we move much faster than your people can. Loran and Gwynys will help you to move at our pace. Just relax, and trust them. Walk as you would normally. They will do the rest."

Loran and Gwynys came forward and positioned themselves on either side of Alexina. She felt her hands clasped in theirs, their grip cool and confident. It was difficult to breathe. This was the moment in which the action she had taken would become irrevocable. Images—the farm, Julia, Jessica, Toby—rushed jumbled through her mind. Then Marhalt made a gesture. "Let the journey begin," he said.

There was a tug on her arms and the world around her disappeared.

Alexina's mind went blank. When she began to think again, she was aware only that they were traveling at great speed. The landscape was a dark blur, like the view from the window of a train. Yet her legs moved at an ordinary walking pace, and she could feel the ground beneath her feet. She stumbled frequently, unable to accustom herself to the sensation of covering immense distances with each stride. She cowered each time she sensed something approaching, afraid Loran or Gwynys would let go of her hands and send her flying, or that they would misjudge and crash into a tree. How on earth could they tell where they were going? But they never faltered and their grip on her hands remained firm.

At last Alexina's fear began to lessen. She was beginning to feel the rhythm. It was possible to fall into it almost naturally for a moment or two, but then she would become aware of herself and her muscles would tense, and she would stumble again.

They stopped once during the night for a brief rest. Alexina was glad of the chance to sit, for she was tired and her feet were beginning to hurt. She had never imagined she would be thankful for the hard farm labor that had toughened her muscles and increased her endurance. Marhalt, amazingly, was no more fatigued than if he had gone for an afternoon stroll, and Gwynys and Loran, even with the additional burden of Alexina, appeared only slightly tired. Taryn, however, had fared less well. He sat with his head bowed on his knees, breathing heavily. For a while they all sat silently in the moonlight. Too soon, Loran and Gwynys clasped Alexina's hands again and they were off.

When at last they halted to make camp, dawn was a gray wash over the sky to the east and the rest of the world was still nightbound. Gratefully, Alexina sat down and removed her shoes from her aching feet. To her left she could hear Taryn. They were in a small clearing in the midst of a substantial stand of trees. Heavy undergrowth and shrubbery matted the ground. Except for the fact that there were no pines, she might have believed they had not moved at all during the night.

Loran and Gwynys took off their packs and stood facing each other, their hands joined and their eyes closed. They looked odd, as if they had gone to sleep standing up. Alexina became aware of an electric current in the air, the same feeling she had sensed during the language transfer. The softly increasing light seemed to tremble, and all around the clearing the vegetation quivered. There was something—not a sound exactly, more of a subliminal pulsing that vibrated in the bones, mounting in a slow crescendo until it peaked and then, abruptly, was gone. Loran and Gwynys stepped apart and opened their eyes. Alexina saw that at the edges of the clearing the air seemed to have thickened. It shimmered, like the heat waves rising from the surface of the road back at the farm, forming a translucent curtain that ran without a break around the camp. She could see through it, yet she had the feeling that, like a two-way mirror, it formed the back side of an illusion. Should anyone happen into these woods they would see only empty forest where the camp lay.

Again Loran and Gwynys joined hands, kneeling this time. A curl of smoke sprang from the ground between them, and a little flame began to burn, growing until it became a good-sized campfire. Prosaically, they busied themselves with pots and provisions. Soon Loran handed around bowls of a thick, nutty-tasting porridge sweetened with aromatic honey, chunks of dried jerky, and cups of a pleasant tealike liquid to wash it all down.

Alexina ate slowly. She felt a sense of awe. These great forces, called up as if it were something done every day—was it as ordinary an occurrence as they made it seem? She doubted if she would ever be able to take such things for granted.

It was all too much to absorb at once. Alexina let her thoughts drift. The rest of the world seemed very far away, pressed back by the barrier that enclosed the camp. She could just hear the soft sound of the Guardians' language as they conversed together. Taryn was sitting apart from them, his back against a tree and his eyes closed. Alexina moved over to sit beside him.

"Are you all right, Taryn?" she asked quietly.

His eyes flew open. She could see the dark circles beneath them. "Yes. I'm all right."

"It's tough going. I'm lucky to have help." A pause. "You look terrible," she said frankly. "You're not still sick, are you?"

He shook his head. "No. I'm all right, I told you."

His tone was brusque. Alexina could feel his fatigue, but there was more than that: There was a distance in him, as if . . . as if he did not want her there. She thought of the night before, and the impersonal expression he had worn.

"Well, I think I'll go to sleep now," he said curtly. "Good night."

And he turned away. Alexina sat where she was, not quite believing that he had snubbed her. But he was readying his blankets and removing his shoes, behaving as if she were not there at all.

Angry, Alexina lifted her chin and unpacked her own blankets with her back to Taryn. She chose a carpet of leaves, the softest place she could find, but as she rolled up in her covers she was aware of the ground beneath her, bumpy and uncomfortable. I'll never be able to rest on this, she thought—but even as she thought it, exhaustion overwhelmed her and she slept.

* * * *

Alexina awoke abruptly, confused. There was a canopy of leaves above her where there should have been a cracked ceiling. And the light was wrong. Her heart pounding, she bolted upright. It was an instant before everything flooded back, and she remembered: the Quest. She was not at the farm, she was on the Quest.

She sighed and let her breathing become normal.

She was rested, but her feet were sore and her back ached from the unyielding ground. It was late afternoon; the sun was just beginning to sink below the tops of the trees. Taryn lay nearby, wrapped in blankets, only his fair hair visible. The others were sitting crosslegged around the fire. Their eyes were closed and their faces wore smooth, sleeping expressions. Yet somehow Alexina knew it was not sleep—it was colder, more remote. In their strange, dull-colored clothing they looked like waxworks, as if their souls had flown away and left behind only stiff semblances of Guardians.

Alexina could hear the rustle of the wind in the leaves and grasses outside the shimmering curtain that surrounded their camp, but within its boundaries everything was still. In the silence not even the breathing of her companions was audible. It was as if she were completely alone, cut off from all living things inside a wall of air. Her own breathing harshened. She tensed, ready to leap to her feet, to shout, anything to bring them back, to reanimate those closed, blank faces.

Marhalt opened his eyes. The panic vanished. Alexina relaxed, feeling a little silly. Marhalt stretched, speaking to the others in their language. They too opened their eyes and began to unfold from their stiff poses. It was hard to recapture the strange way they had looked a moment ago. Marhalt came over to sit by Alexina.

"How are you feeling, Alexina? Not too tired?"

"A little tired. But not as much as I'd expected."

He nodded. "You did well last night. In a day or two you will be used to it."

Alexina hesitated. "Marhalt, when I woke up you were all sitting there with your eyes closed. You looked so . . . so strange."

"That was meditation. It is part of our discipline, a way of turning inward, of slowing the body and tapping the power sources within us. We must do it for an hour or so each day to build and conserve our strength, and to maintain our barriers against your world."

"Oh." Alexina glanced at Taryn, just beginning to stir in his blankets. "Shouldn't Taryn be doing it too?"

Marhalt looked at Taryn. "Yes, but he does not need as much time. He is only an apprentice and besides, we protect him." He got to his feet. "Come with me now, Alexina. There is something we must do."

Alexina hung back as they reached the edge of the camp.

"Just step through it," Marhalt said. "It is not a physical barrier."

She took a deep breath and walked forward. She felt a tingling sensation and briefly her vision swam. Then she had passed through the barrier, and everything was normal. She turned and looked behind her. She saw nothing but trees and underbrush. She stretched her arm out into the area she had just crossed, and saw it disappear to her elbow. Her skin crawling, she pulled quickly back.

They walked through the trees for a little way until, quite unexpectedly, they emerged on the rocky shore of a large lake. In the distance to their right Alexina could see a group of picnickers. They raised their heads and looked at Marhalt and Alexina, briefly at first, and then with more curiosity as Marhalt's odd costume registered. Marhalt glanced at them, and Alexina felt the subliminal pulse that marked the use of power. The picnickers turned away, back to their meal.

"Their attention is elsewhere now," said Marhalt. "They will no longer notice us."

He seated himself on a large stone and motioned for Alexina to sit down also. She obeyed.

"Now, Alexina," said Marhalt. "I must ask for your help."

"My help?"

"Yes. You may find it frightening, but I assure you there is no danger. I would like you to use the link."

"The link?" Alexina felt cold. "I'm not sure . . . I'm not sure I understand."

"Do you remember what I told you about it, that your mind could follow it to *him?*" Alexina nodded. "That is what I wish you to do. I want you to follow it voluntarily, to find him and tell us where we must go."

Voluntarily? Open her mind voluntarily to that awful tugging, approach of her own accord a man they had told her was evil, mad . . . "I can't," she said. Her voice was unsteady. "Marhalt, please don't make me do that."

"I *ask* you to do it." Marhalt's voice was gentle. "We need your help, Alexina. You see, it is difficult for us to sense him here. Your world-forces impede us. We could find him, but it would take a good deal of time, and sap us of much power. You, on the other hand, are tied to him directly. You can use the link to reach him and see where he is hiding from us." His face was very serious now. "Time is of the essence, Alexina. I explained that to you before. We must reach the Stone before it is damaged, perhaps destroyed. You understand the importance of our Quest. Your presence with us is proof of that. That is why I ask your help."

Yes, Alexina thought, she understood the importance of the Quest; she understood the urgency he spoke of. And it was awesome that she, untrained and without power until recently, could truly help them. She knew that should she refuse, Marhalt would not compel her. She wanted not to do it. She was afraid, terribly afraid of the link and the dark man and his icy power. Yet she sensed that what Marhalt asked was not just a request that could be simply refused: it was binding. Everything he said carried shades of meaning she could not quite grasp. She felt claustrophobic, caught between her fear and what he asked of her. She looked up and met his eyes. She remembered his strength, with which he had held her over his world.

"You'll be right here?" she said.

He nodded. "I will be beside you the entire time. Remember, Alexina, it is not a physical link. He will not harm you, just as you cannot harm him. It is mind contact only. You will be quite safe."

"You're sure? You're *sure* he can't hurt me?"

"No matter how much he should wish to, he will not harm you in any way. It is one of the conditions of the link."

There was a pause, and then Alexina nodded. "All right. What . . . what do I do?"

"You must open your mind. It is your handpower concepts that keep the link away from you now. You must try to let them fall away, open yourself to what is beyond them so the link can surface. Empty yourself of thoughts and feelings; let the world flow through you like a river beneath a bridge, passing by but leaving nothing behind. When the link grips you, let your mind go out along it. You will see it before you; follow it. It will lead you to him."

Alexina swallowed. "And you'll be here? You won't move?"

"I will not move."

She looked at Marhalt one last time. Then, feeling as if she were plunging off a precipice, she closed her eyes and tried to relax. It was difficult. Her mind was like a clenched fist. She forced herself to do as Marhalt had described, to let go, to open up. Her arms and legs began to feel heavy: She could feel her body loosen, muscle by muscle. Slowly her mind loosened also, spreading outward. She was aware of the sounds of water and wind, of faint voices down the beach, of the cry of a bird. Gradually the sounds lessened, faded away entirely. Images pulsed behind her eyes like static on a television screen. She was expanding, losing touch with the beach and with her heavy limbs. . . .

It began as something very small at the edge of consciousness; rapidly it built into the tugging of her dreams. She tensed, her mind withdrawing like a leaf curling in on itself. Her eyes flew open. She saw the lake and the sky and the beach and Marhalt. She tried to move and found she could not. Her leaden arms and legs felt anchored to the ground.

"Slowly now." Marhalt had moved to her; his hands were on her shoulders, bringing calmness. "Don't try to move just yet. You're in deep relaxation from the meditation." There was a pause. Then: "You felt it, didn't you?"

"Yes." It came out as a kind of croak.

"What happened?"

"I lost it. It . . . it startled me."

He took his hands away and knelt before her where she could see his face. "You're too afraid, Alexina. I understand. You are handpower-born, after all. It is natural for one of your world to fear power." He lifted her chin so she looked right into his topaz eyes. "But *you* have power. You mustn't give in to fear. You're a brave girl—you've proved that already.

You wouldn't be here if you weren't able to overcome obstacles. Now you must overcome yourself. You must follow the pull, you must conquer your fear. Do you understand me, Alexina?"

His fingers still cupped her chin. More than anything she wanted to give in to her panic, to burst into tears and say she could not do it; yet something in Marhalt stopped her. She was not sure what it was—a trace of hardness in his eyes? The tension of his face? His eyes held her, compelled her toward this thing. Alexina felt her throat constrict with fear, and in that instant she was not sure if she were afraid of Marhalt or of the link.

Marhalt removed his hand, and Alexina took a deep breath to calm herself. He was right; she must not let fear overcome her. She took several more breaths, and then nodded.

"I'm all right now. I'll try again."

Once more she closed her eyes. His words—you must overcome yourself, you must overcome yourself—ran over and over in her mind as she began the process of letting go, fading back and back until all sound and thought were lost, all sensation gone. Open, her mind floated somewhere in darkness, waiting. At the first tug she tensed reflexively. But it was not quite so bad this time, and grimly she held on as the tugging strengthened, became a wrenching that strained to pull her mind away. She gathered her strength; and then she yielded.

There was a moment of dislocating terror as her mind raced forward, and then everything was swallowed in the blur of speed. Images flowed beneath her, gradually focusing until she could see. She was skimming over treetops and meadows, over hills and lakes, almost too fast to take them in. It would have been exhilarating but for the nature of her mission.

The landscape looked . . . northern, definitely northern, though considerably west of their present camp. It was cold and growing colder. She crested a last hill and saw a wood. In the middle of the wood was a huge, tumble-down house. It looked as if it had been abandoned for some time: Its planks were bare of paint, its doors closed and its windows boarded. Vines rioted over the walls and grass grew between the porch slats. The house and clearing were encircled by an enormous hedge. She could see no opening.

There was just time to take all this in before she became aware that there was life here, a stirring awareness that was alert to her presence. It was moving, unfolding, reaching up. The cold increased, hard and searing. It was *him.*

Instinctively, Alexina pulled back and fled. She could see the path she must follow—it was a luminous trail leading over the hills—and she was aware that the questing intelligence followed too along the same line, reaching out as if to stop her. Over an expanse of water she flew, to a rocky beach; there was an instant of panorama, a flash of two small figures sitting on the shore and the oddest sensation of seeing her body from the outside. Then, with a jolt, mind and body came together. Alexina's eyes flew open. Her heart was hammering. The pursuer was gone.

Marhalt's hands were there again, massaging her shoulders, and at last her shivering lessened. "You were successful this time," he said.

Alexina nodded. Her neck was stiff.

"What did you see?"

She cleared her throat. "A house. A house in the woods. It looked as if it hadn't been lived in for years. It was cold." She turned to Marhalt. "That's where he is. I felt him. Marhalt, he followed me. He followed me to this lake. He knows where I am now."

Marhalt removed his hands and sat again on his rock. "Of course he does. Possibly he has known all along."

"What—"

Marhalt made a little gesture, almost of impatience. "I told you that he can reach you just as you can reach him. It's as important for him to know as it is for us."

"But . . ." Of course she should have deduced this for herself, but somehow she had not. Alexina felt something terrible rising in her, something worse than panic. "Then he might already have come to me? And he could do it anytime!"

"While you are awake you can guard against him. Use your barriers."

"But when I'm asleep. . . ." Alexina stopped. She was aware that his voice was less warm, that his golden eyes seemed hooded. It was her fear. Overcome yourself, he had said. A Guardian would not yield to fear, she knew, the fear of the handpower-born. She thought of the pity and contempt with which he had spoken of her people when he told the Tale, the sting in his use of that phrase, "handpower-born." She did not wish to bring that contempt upon herself. No, she thought. Handpower-born she might be, but she was not like the rest of her people. She was a person of power, like the Guardians. She *would* overcome herself. She gripped her emotions, fought for control of the cold and the terror, forced consciousness of the link down until it no longer threatened.

"Yes," she said, and her voice was calm. "I will use my barriers."

Marhalt nodded. "Now, Alexina, could you tell where his house was?"

She had fled too quickly to grasp anything definite about its location. She frowned, trying to pinpoint her vague impressions. "It was north of here, I'm sure of that, but farther west than we are now. Oh, yes—I forgot. There was this enormous hedge around the house. All the way around in a circle. I couldn't see any way in."

"A hedge? A real one, or an illusion?"

"I couldn't tell. Just a hedge."

Marhalt frowned. "That's odd," he said. "It's hard to believe he would squander his power so. Can you be more definite, Alexina? How far north must we go?"

"I'm sorry. I . . . I guess I ran away too fast. I just know west, and north."

"Very well. It will have to do for this time." His face was neutral, but Alexina knew she had not done as well as she might have. She must do it again, and then again perhaps, over and over until she got it right.

Marhalt got to his feet, and held out a hand. "Come, Alexina. We'll go back now and have our meal." He pulled her to her feet. The heaviness in her limbs was gone, but she felt deeply tired. Marhalt looked down at her, and then lifted his hand and touched her lightly on the forehead. He smiled. "You've done very well today, Alexina. I am proud of you."

Alexina felt as if the sun had just come out. The last lingering traces of link-chill were dispersed by the warmth of his face; her worry and fatigue were gone. They moved back toward the trees. Down the beach, the picnickers did not even look up.

Dusk was beginning to close in. Alexina had forgotten the curtain around the camp, and it was a shock when Marhalt, slightly ahead of her, disappeared into thin air—not all at once, but progressively, like a drop of water absorbed by a sponge. Then she was through as well, her vision distorting and righting itself to show her the others, visible where an instant ago there had been only trees. She stopped, put her hand to her head, and stood still for a moment. The small campfire burned brightly, and she could smell food cooking.

Loran and Gwynys took no notice of their arrival; Taryn, however, looked up. There was something odd and sullen in his expression. Abruptly he turned away and began staring at his knees. Alexina saw that Marhalt's eyes were on Taryn, and that his expression was once again hooded. She had a sense that something had passed between them in that swift exchange of glances.

Alexina had not forgotten Taryn's behavior the night before, but he looked so forlorn that she went again to sit beside him. It might have been just his fatigue; after all, he did have a harder time of it than the others. But despite her attempts at conversation, he would not be drawn out. He did not snub her outright, but he managed to make his monosyllabic replies as discouraging as possible. At last, getting angry again, more hurt than she wanted to acknowledge, Alexina moved away and sat by herself to finish her meal.

Dinner over, Loran and Gwynys packed up the camp. They joined hands briefly to remove the curtain. Then they placed themselves on either side of Alexina, and the little group set off once more into the night.

10

Alexina woke earlier than usual on the fourth day of the journey. She lay sleepily under her blankets for a while, gazing up at the blue afternoon sky. They were camped on the edge of a meadow not yet mowed for hay. The tall grass, waist-high, was visible through the shimmering protective barrier, distorted like waterweed at the bottom of a lake.

The landscape through which they traveled had changed, mountains and forests replaced by farms and flat open fields. Alexina thought they might be somewhere in the Midwest, but she could not be sure, for she had no idea how far they went during the night. She had asked Marhalt, but he told her unsatisfactorily that his world measured distance in a different way. For all she knew, they might be anywhere.

Like the landscape, the character of time had altered. No longer was it composed of minutes and hours strung together like beads; it had become flat and featureless like the fields, hour blending into hour until it was difficult to tell one from the next. It was often hard to remember that they had been moving for only three days. The Guardians had an uncanny ability to avoid encountering other people, and since the first afternoon Alexina had seen no living soul but her companions, not even through the curtain, although the country they passed through was not sparsely inhabited. Each day, closed inside the barriers of their illusion, they ate and slept and ate again within a little pocket of their own space.

Most of the time, Alexina did not even think of the days before the Quest, when she had existed in a world barren of power. The curtain around the camp and the fire that sprang from the ground itself had become as much a normal part of life as her blankets or the pots Loran tied to his pack. She had felt her old life slipping from her as she waited by her window that first night; it had done so with finality. Though images of Jessica and New York or the farm and its people remained, they were curiously far away, like books or playthings left behind in growing up, and sometimes Alexina felt that only the moments she was living now were truly real. It was as if all the other things she had ever done had simply been preparation for the path down which she now walked, each step carrying her closer to the moment of confrontation. What lay in that moment was a mystery—a power and a presence, a blind house in the heart of a wood, the Stone and the dark man and the destruction of the link—and each day drew toward it with increasing strength.

The link too was stronger. As the distance between herself and the dark man diminished, its icy hold on her increased. Though it had been present before the journey, it had been intermittent, ignorable. Now, though she could pretend it was not there, she was conscious of its waiting presence at all times. It threatened today, uncoiling malignantly beneath the sunny afternoon, and determinedly she shut it away.

Alexina sat up. The Guardians were nearby, immobile in meditation. She had become accustomed to the way they looked at these times, but she still did not like to watch them for long. To her left, Taryn's blankets were empty. That was odd. Normally Taryn slept until just before the Guardians broke their meditation for the evening meal, meditating himself for about half an hour on awakening.

She got to her feet and stretched. Through the shimmering curtain, she could see that it was a beautiful afternoon. The sky was indigo blue, the wind stirred the grasses, and in the distance she could hear the faint sound of running water. It was hot and still inside the camp, and the thought of the breeze was inviting.

Passing through the barrier, she stood for a moment as her vision normalized, and then looked around her to fix the camp's location in her mind. A trail of crushed grass extended across the meadow to the crest of a little hill, and she struck off along this ready-made path. She had reached the top of the hill and was descending when she saw that someone had preceded her. Taryn. He was leaning against a fence, his shoulders slumping wearily. His back was turned.

Alexina stopped. Should she ignore him and go on, or should she go back? Over the past days, Taryn's unfriendly behavior had not changed. He seemed to want nothing to do with her. It was baffling. Try as she might she could think of nothing she had done to offend him. She was angry, but it was more than that—she had thought they were friends. She had felt a bond with him, and thought he felt one with her. But it was clear she had been wrong.

Before she could make up her mind what to do, he had sensed her presence and turned. He looked surprised and not very welcoming, but his face, momentarily unguarded, was also forlorn. Alexina was reminded of his struggle to keep up every night, and she felt some of her anger slip away. On impulse, she came forward and joined him at the fence. On its other side the land was planted in clover, a stippled mass of green and lavender, bordered by a dusty dirt road. Here and there huddled clusters of houses and buildings, dwarfed by the great, unrelieved flatness of the land.

"Shouldn't you be asleep?" she asked.

"My foot hurts. It woke me up."

"Are you all right?"

He shrugged. "It's just a blister."

Silence fell, quickly becoming oppressive. Alexina stole a glance at Taryn; inwardly she sighed. It was like the other times.

"Aren't you even going to talk to me?" she asked.

Again he shrugged. "We can talk if you want."

"I *do* want." All at once she was determined to have it out. "Why are you ignoring me, Taryn? Why are you acting like such a *jerk?* Did I do something to make you mad?"

"No."

"Well, what is it then? You can't deny how incredibly rude you've been since the day we started out. Is it that you don't want me along or something?"

He shook his head.

"Well, what then?"

He glanced at her quickly, then away. "It's not rudeness, exactly. It's just that I have to keep to myself. Stay away from everyone."

"Why?"

"I'm not supposed to be here at all, you know."

"Oh. You mean you're being punished. So it's not just me?"

"But it's not a punishment, exactly." He paused. "And it *is* you."

"I thought you just said—"

"I didn't say anything." He made a strange noise,

halfway between a snort and a laugh. Alexina felt a rush of frustration.

"I don't understand *what* you're saying," she burst out. "All I wanted to know was why you're ignoring me. If you don't want to tell me, just say so, instead of dropping hints and making cryptic remarks. Let's at least be honest with each other. I mean, I thought we were friends! I thought . . . that is, I thought you liked me."

No answer. He was staring stonily off into the distance. Alexina was furious. The beauty of the afternoon was gone. Let him suffer all by himself if he wants to then, she thought. She began to turn away from the fence, but Taryn reached out and caught her arm. His face had unfrozen, and Alexina was shocked by the desperation in it.

"Alexina, I'm sorry." His voice sounded strangled. "Don't go away, please don't."

He let go of her arm and turned back to the field, grasping the top rail of the fence, his knuckles white from the intensity of his grip. Baffled at the sudden change, Alexina waited. After a moment his hands relaxed.

"You're right." His voice was calm now. "I do owe you an explanation. You saved my life, after all." He turned and met her eyes fully for the first time. "You see, Marhalt has put me under obedience."

"So you *are* being punished."

"Well . . . it's more like a test."

"A test?"

"Being under obedience means you have to meet certain conditions and follow certain orders, no matter how hard they are or what temptations you encounter. My obedience is to do everything alone, as if I were a full Guardian, without any allowance made for my incomplete training. Also, I must do it in solitude. I must hold myself apart from the solace of companionship."

"Oh, Taryn! It sounds awful!"

"But I was disobedient. Disobedience is the worst crime an apprentice can commit, short of misusing the power, of course."

"I should think there were much worse things you could do," Alexina objected.

"Not really. Obedience is one of the most important parts of our training. It develops strength of character. It helps you control your ego so that it doesn't interfere with the power inside you. Only if you can conquer yourself can you become truly powerful. Apprentices must be obedient to all masters, without question, no matter what is asked or who asks it. It's the first thing you learn. You must never, never, disobey. That's the whole point of the obedience exercises. Disobedience shows unfitness to be a Guardian. The obedience exercise allows you the chance to become worthy again. If I succeed in keeping my obediences, it'll show I'm still fit to be a Guardian, despite what I did. If I fail, well . . . my Guardianship will probably be forfeit. They might even leave me behind, here in this world. And my barriers aren't strong enough to protect me, they know that."

"Taryn, I . . . I can't believe . . . Did they actually say that? That they'd leave you?"

He nodded. Alexina was silent. She could not imagine they had meant it literally—it was the sort of thing a parent might say to put a scare into a child.

"But I will keep my obedience." Taryn's voice was grim. "I *will.* When we return and I stand before them in the Great Hall to receive my punishment, they'll all know I'm fit."

"You mean you'll still be punished? Even if you keep your obedience?"

"Of course."

There was a pause. "It seems . . . unfair, Taryn," Alexina ventured after a moment. "All for coming along without asking? That doesn't seem so very awful. After all, I did it. Marhalt wasn't angry with me."

He threw her a look. "You're not a Guardian. Anyway, I did something much worse than that. You see, I'm not supposed to know the Stone is gone."

"Why not?"

"Because it's a secret. Only full Guardians know it's been stolen."

"You mean your people don't know?" Taryn shook his head. "But how can they be kept from finding out? If the Stone is so important to your world, wouldn't people guess?"

"Yes, of course. That's part of the reason why it's so important for us to act quickly. Think of the panic and fear if the knowledge got out! It's much better to keep it a secret, even I can see that. Even from the others in the Fortress."

"How do *you* know, then?"

"It was an accident." He looked away, evasive. "But it doesn't matter how I found out. Once I knew, there was no going back. I didn't care what rules I broke, or how they punished me. Any disobedience is bad, but finding out about the Stone was the worst disobedience you can imagine."

"You said it was an accident! How can you be disobedient if you don't know what you're doing?"

"It doesn't matter. Disobedience because you misheard an order is as bad as disobedience because you heard and didn't follow. You should have been paying enough attention to hear properly in the first place.

A good apprentice would have made himself forget he had ever heard the Stone was gone, because he would know it was something he wasn't supposed to hear."

"But, Taryn, that doesn't make sense. You can't just make yourself forget things."

"Yes, you can. But I didn't. And even worse, I acted on what I knew. So here I am."

"But that's so unfair! How could anyone think that something you did involuntarily was as bad as something you did on purpose? I can't believe Marhalt would . . ."

Her words faded as she saw the look on his face. "You don't know anything about Marhalt," he said after a moment, his voice low. "Marhalt would throw me out of the Order today if it were up to him. He would have left me behind already if he weren't required by tradition to give me the chance to prove myself through the obedience exercise. He knows—" He caught his breath and threw a glance over his shoulder, almost as if he expected somone to be watching. "It doesn't matter. I chose to do what I did, and so I chose the consequences too. But when something like this happens, something that's once in a millennium, the old rules just don't apply any more. I have to make Marhalt see that. I have to make him understand that this one time is different. So I'll keep my obediences. I'll do all he tells me, to the letter. Because I *am* fit to be a Guardian."

He turned back to the fence and rested his chin on his hands.

"Well," Alexina ventured after a while, "I guess I know now why you've been staying away from me."

He glanced at her, his eyes sliding away when they met hers. "There's a little more where you're concerned."

"What do you mean?"

"You see, there's two obediences. I've only told you the first. The second . . . the second is you. Marhalt wants me to avoid you as much as I can."

Alexina stared at him. "But why?"

"Well, he's afraid we'll . . . talk about things."

"What things? What do you mean?"

"Handpower things." His voice was almost inaudible.

"Handpower? Why on earth should we talk about that?"

"Well, you're handpower-born. It's what you know."

"That's a lousy reason. I may be handpower-born, but don't forget I have mindpower too!" Her cheeks were hot. How she loathed that label, and it was especially unbearable to be called that by Taryn. "Why does Marhalt think we'd talk about that?"

He shrugged. "He didn't explain it to me. He doesn't have to. Obediences don't have to be explained, just followed."

Alexina suspected that Marhalt had explained exactly why the obediences were what they were. She looked at Taryn. Still he would not meet her eyes.

"Anyway, Taryn, why would just talking about it be so bad? I know you have some kind of limits on it, but aren't they on specific tools and things?"

"Yes. But there's more to it." Taryn seemed to be struggling a little with his words. "There's more to handpower than just tools, you see. There's a . . . a way of thinking—the way that led people to take up handpower in the old days before the split. If people never start thinking in that way, they won't be so easily tempted by handpower itself. So the Limits are to keep your thoughts in the right paths, as well as your hands. But your world is full of things that go so far beyond our Limits we can't even imagine them. Just hearing about that kind of handpower could trigger that wrong way of thinking. If you hear you can remember, if you remember you can begin to understand, if you understand you've already fallen into the trap. Do you see?"

Uncertainly, Alexina nodded.

"That's why we're traveling this way. So we can avoid the handpower things of your world, avoid the corruption they might work in us. I'm lucky in a way that I got so sick—I don't remember anything about the places I was in."

Silence fell. What a lot of Limits there must be, Alexina thought. Limits on thought as well as action. She understood what he meant about the handpower way of thinking, yet it all sounded so rigid.

The sun was setting on the world beyond the fence, creating great shadows on the flat green fields. The air was still and clear, and a cool breeze swept across the clover. Taryn's profile was sharply defined against the sky. For a moment Alexina looked at him as if for the first time. She saw the long hair, the strange clothes, the gleaming medallions around his neck. And she saw that behind Taryn, behind the obediences and the Limits, stood an entire world—a world of complex rules and customs, governed by its own complex power—a world about which she knew almost nothing. She thought of the vision Marhalt had offered through the medium of his mind. It was like the view from an airplane, panoramic but without detail. Suddenly it was not enough. She wanted more.

Taryn turned toward her, placing his hand on top of hers where it rested on the fence.

"Alexina," he said. "Alexina, will you be my friend?"

"I never stopped being your friend, Taryn," she said. "But what about the obedience? Won't it get you in trouble?"

He looked away again. "I told you about the obediences," he said after a moment. "I didn't tell you that some of them are cruel. Even pointless." His eyes were fixed on the horizon. "I never liked being rude to you, Alexina. I hated it. But I had no way to explain it to you, and I did it because I had to. I'll still have to. That won't change. You must see that I have to obey Marhalt. But deep down, below the surface, I'd know you were my friend. And it would help. It would help to know you understood and weren't angry with me."

"I'm your friend, Taryn. I'll be your friend for as long as you want me to be."

He turned to her and smiled for the first time that day. "Good," he said. "Good."

"Taryn, can I ask you a question?"

He nodded.

"Why did you do it? Why did you follow if you knew the consequences would be so awful?"

"Because of the Quest, of course." He leaned against the fence. "You see, the Stone is . . . like air, I suppose, or water—something you take for granted. Something you can't live without, but you don't realize that until it's gone. When I heard it *was* gone, it seemed too terrible to be true. For a while I just walked around in a daze. But when I woke up, I knew that there would have to be a Quest to get it back, like in the olden days when the worlds were one."

"The Stone was in the world before it split?"

"Oh, yes. The Stone has been in the world since before history began."

"Really? Were there a lot of Quests?"

"Yes. People recognized its power from the very beginning, and evil men were always plotting to steal it and use it for their own gain. A king or warlord or wizard would take it and try to keep it for himself, and then righteous men would regain it and give it back to the people of the world. The Quest is the most glorious thing a person can ever do."

"So the Guardians haven't always had the Stone."

"No. It passed from hand to hand for centuries before it came to us. One of the reasons the Guardians were established was to stop that from happening. You see, just before the worlds began to split apart, an especially evil lord stole the Stone and hid it in his fortress, using his powers to make it impossible to find. The Stone disappeared from the world for more than two hundred years. Many Quests were mounted to find it, but all failed. Eventually the Stone came to the lord's great-great-grandson. He was not strong enough to hold it. One Quest was finally successful, and the Stone was rescued by a man named Percival. He vowed the Stone would never be stolen again, that it would never fall prey to handpower. He carried the Stone into our world and founded the Order of Guardians. We measure time from that day. We are in the one thousand, five hundred and sixty-first Year of the Stone."

"That's . . . fifteen hundred years!"

"Yes. And now the Stone has been stolen again. I remember when I was little, and listened to the Quest stories, I would wish the Stone would be taken so I'd get the chance to experience the Quest. Of course, I never really thought it could happen. But it has. I didn't find out about it by accident, Alexina. I'm sure this chance has been given to me for a reason. I was *meant* to know. I was *meant* to be part of this Quest."

"Do you ever regret following?"

"No." His voice was firm. "Not for a moment. I knew it would be hard. A Quest is a trial of spirit, after all. No matter what happens, I'll know I've passed that trial." He glanced at her. "I don't know if it's easy for you to understand that."

"I understand," said Alexina. "I understand very well. That's a lot like my reason for coming."

"How could it be?" He seemed to bite off his words. "I mean—"

"I suppose you think that because I'm handpower-born I don't know about these things," Alexina said, stung. "But I do. What you said about things not happening by accident. I had to come, just as you did: I've always felt as if I were waiting for something. I never knew what, but now I do—it was this. All of it—the Quest, finding out about your world and your people and the Stone, even about myself. I always felt different from everyone I knew. I don't any more, because I know there are others like me. Marhalt said something that first night—power calls to power. That's what happened to me."

Taryn was watching her with a strange expression on his face. Abruptly, he dropped his eyes. His face had closed again, the grimness returning like a curtain falling.

"Taryn? Did I say something wrong?"

"No. You didn't say anything wrong." He pushed himself away from the fence, tucking a piece of unruly hair behind one ear. "It's getting late. I haven't meditated yet." Alexina made a move to follow, but he held up his hand. "No, you mustn't come with me. Stay here for a while. Marhalt mustn't see us together."

"Oh. The obediences."

"Yes. And whatever you do, don't let on you know about them. Do you promise? He's just looking for a good reason to decide I've failed."

"I won't say anything. I should think you wouldn't even need to ask."

"I'm sorry." For a moment he looked at her, and she thought he would say something more, but he just lifted his hand in farewell. He turned and moved off along the fence, limping slightly on his blistered foot, and disappeared among the nearby trees.

11

Alexina lingered for some time after Taryn had gone, staring out over the fields. She was troubled. For a little while Taryn and she had really talked, but just the mention of Marhalt's name had made him retreat, back into the grimness and the oppression of his obediences. It was natural, she supposed, to resent the person who imposed penalties on you. But Taryn seemed to hate Marhalt. She found the thought distressing. And the obediences now seemed to hang over her head as much as Taryn's. Despite what he had told her, she was aware that she did not really understand the principle behind them.

Absently, she rubbed her forehead. There was a lot she did not understand. She had meant to ask him to tell her more about the Stone. There was so much she wanted to know.

It was getting late. The light had deepened, and the blue sky to the west held the green tinge that precedes twilight. Alexina began to climb the hill, following the trail of flattened grass. She passed through the curtain, from the fields gilded with the setting sun into the shadow of the trees. Taryn was sitting apart from the others, his eyes closed in meditation. Dinner was almost ready.

Marhalt looked up as she appeared. Later, as she was eating, he came over to her.

"We missed you this afternoon, Alexina."

"I woke up and couldn't get back to sleep. I went for a walk." She was glad of the darkness that hid her face.

"Taryn also walked this afternoon. You did not meet, by any chance?"

Alexina thought rapidly. "I did see him. But he ignored me. He's been very rude to me lately."

Marhalt nodded. "I must ask you not to stray away from camp in future, Alexina. You might . . . endanger us if you met with any of your own people. We must maintain our secrecy. You understand?"

"Yes." She looked down at her half-finished bowl of porridge. She felt him get to his feet and move away.

Mechanically she ate the rest of her food. She hated having to lie, especially to Marhalt. In fact, she felt terrible, almost as if it were she who had been disobedient. She glanced toward Taryn, his head bowed over his bowl. He had given her his trust. She would not betray it.

* * * *

The next day, just before sunset, Marhalt again led Alexina away from the others to follow the link. She felt slightly uneasy in his presence and was silent at first, guarding her thoughts.

She did not flinch from contact with the link this time, or allow herself to drop the connection, and she forced herself to notice details of landscape and atmosphere. She hovered over the clearing, feeling the stirring coldness of his presence. She felt him rising up to meet her, closer, almost visible . . . . She turned and fled, as fast as she was able. He did not follow her this time. But she could feel him stationary behind her, watching her go.

She came back to the world weak and icy. Marhalt's hands on her shoulders were a lifeline of warmth and calm to which she clung until she was able to speak. She told him what she had observed. It was time now to turn north. The house was near a small town called Pinehurst, by the shore of a great lake she thought might be Lake Michigan. They were very close now, only a few nights' journey.

It was difficult to push the link-feeling away today, and Alexina had to brace herself, as if she might be sucked under again. She was terrified that the polarity might reverse, that inadvertently she might draw him toward her. She wondered about him, about this being to whom she was tied, about the cold, fierce consciousness linked with hers. What would it have been like if she had waited, if she had allowed him to confront her? Would his power have been too bright, too terrible? Would it, like Medusa's glare, have turned her inexperienced awareness to stone? Her curiosity acted as a small goad within her fear. She had never seen his face. She found herself wondering if he were young or old, if his features were deceptively bland or marked with evil. His power confused her. Though it was cold, it was bright like fire, not dark like ice.

"We should be returning, Alexina." Marhalt's voice broke through her thoughts. He was looking up at the darkening sky.

"Marhalt . . ."

"Yes?"

"Marhalt, what made him do it?"

He watched her for a moment, his face grave, and she began to think he would not answer. "He is mad, Alexina. He is quite insane."

"Was he born that way?"

"Once, he must have been like the rest of us. It was handpower that drove him mad, and that is a sickness which must be acquired. What caused it cannot be known, or when it took root. But it had time to grow to monstrous proportions."

"I thought your Limits made it hard for that to happen."

"They do. Yet sometimes it happens even so. Greedy or evil or mad people come to love handpower too well, or to use it too often. Usually we discover it before it is too late. But somehow he managed to hide it from us until the end. It was not until he had gone that we discovered his secret place. It was filled with tools." Even through the controlled tone of his voice, she could sense his revulsion. "He had developed and fabricated hundreds of them, all quite beyond comprehension. Some were weapons and instruments of torture." He shook his head. "There is some purpose in his actions. I am sure of it. I believe he has some twisted plan for the Stone."

"You mean here? In this world?"

"It does not matter, Alexina. His plans will come to nothing. The Stone cannot function here. We wish only to take it from him before it is destroyed."

"What will happen when we get there?"

"There will be a battle. Not a physical battle, but a battle of power. When it is won, we will remove his barriers and give him to this world. His ability will leave him forever."

Alexina thought of the force she had sensed three times now, of the strength and the strange brilliance of it. "He is very powerful, isn't he? I can feel it."

"Yes, he is. But he is one and we are three. He must lose in the end, the Stone and his power and everything else."

"Are you really sure? I mean, can you be *sure* the world-forces will take his power away?"

Marhalt's expression did not change, but Alexina was aware of his disapproval. "Alexina," he said. A rebuke underlay the gentleness of his tone. "Alexina, I think you still find it difficult to accept what I have told you about yourself and your own power. You must simply accept that we know things you do not. Somehow the power in you has adapted to your world-forces. But for one of us, one from our world, that is impossible. We know this to be true. We know it beyond the possibility of a doubt."

Alexina kept her eyes on the ground. He had not used the phrase she hated so, but she could hear it in his voice.

"He *will* become as your people are," Marhalt said. "Of course, we will make sure that it is truly done before we leave him. You will be free of him then. And we will have the Stone."

"Marhalt." Alexina took a deep breath. "Marhalt, when you have it again, can I see it?"

For a moment he was very still. When he spoke, his voice was neutral. "Why?"

Because it's an object straight out of a legend, she thought, because it has a power that goes beyond magic. . . . But she knew she could not say that. She must answer in a way that would point up neither her ignorance nor her background, and at the same time would indicate that she was capable of understanding.

"It's the purpose of this journey," she said at last, carefully. "It's why you're here, in danger and risking your lives. So in a way it's why I'm here. I want to see it once. I sensed it, you know—on the ledge, and inside your mind. I felt some of its power, and it was like nothing I've ever felt before."

His topaz eyes met hers coolly. "Do you really think you could understand, Alexina? The Stone is as alien to your world as if it really did come from another planet. Do you think you are capable of going beyond the limitations of your world, your upbringing, your entire life?"

Frustration welled up inside her, so sharp she could have bitten down on it. "I know I'm handpower-born. I can't help that." She paused for a moment to steady her voice. "But I'm not like the others. I'm *different.* I've understood what you've told me so far, and I can understand more. Oh, Marhalt, there's so much I want to know. Not just about the Stone—about you. About myself."

"You want answers, Alexina," he said at last. As usual, she could not read his expression. "Yet even we don't possess all of them. The Stone, for instance. The Guardians have held it safe for centuries, but what we know most fully is that it is a mystery. Where it came from, the source of its power—all these things are hidden from us. Even we must accept certain things on faith."

"But you told me that first night that it was a guide for your world!"

"And so it is. You see, the Stone is like a mirror, a mirror turned always on the world, the whole world and all its people. Only it is a mirror that reflects not just the surface of things, but inside them too, to their very heart. The Stone is linked with the world and its people in much the same way, actually, as you are linked to the man we seek. It can know, at any time and any moment, precisely what is going on in any place or any person or any thing. It has memory, and retains full knowledge of all that has occurred. It is a vast storehouse of knowledge and wisdom."

"Does it speak to you?"

"In a way. It is possible to link our minds with it, and to direct the link in such a way that specific questions can be answered. Only Guardians can do this. But anyone can ask a question, through us, and receive an answer. Thousands come each year to our Fortress. We screen each questioner to be sure there is no evil intent, of course; beyond that, any question is allowed. The Stone belongs to the people of our world. We are its Guardians only, the conscience of our world and the keepers of what is most precious in it."

"Have *you* communicated with the Stone?"

"I have."

"Can you tell me what it was like?"

"I cannot. The experience of communication is never discussed. Loran and Gwynys, for instance, are as ignorant of it as you. They are Journeyers, on the second level. Only Speakers, on the first level, can communicate."

Silence fell. Without meaning to, Alexina sighed.

"It is difficult for you, I know," Marhalt said gently. She looked at him.

"I'm not sure what you mean."

"To possess power in this place. It struggles in you always, straining against the forces that hold it captive, against the ignorance that tries to crush it. I am not unaware of the suffering this must have brought you."

Alexina thought about that. Had she suffered? "I'm not sure," she said slowly. "I always felt different from other people around me, though I didn't know just how. And there was this kind of reaching out that I did with my mind ever since I was small. But I never connected the two. I never dreamed I had power at all until I met Taryn."

"And but for that accident, you would never have known."

"Marhalt, I want to learn." The words were there before she knew she had said them. She plunged on. "I want to be able to use my power. I know I could never do what you do, or Loran and Gwynys. But . . . but maybe I could do a little. If you'd teach me, I'd have something to hold onto after all of you were gone. I could even help other people, people in my world, to believe in mindpower again. I'm sure that would be a good thing. There's so much I could do here, if you would only teach me."

There was a silence. "Do you know what you are saying?" said Marhalt at last.

An impulsive yes sprang to Alexina's lips, but then, looking at him, she did not say it. His eyes, darkened with the gathering evening, were fixed on hers. Suddenly the uneasiness she had forgotten returned in force. It was as if he could see right through her, down into the smallest crevices of her mind, down to her doubts and her hidden fears and her guilty knowledge of Taryn's second obedience. She felt a hot flush begin at the base of her throat and rise slowly into her cheeks. Marhalt spoke, and his voice was terrible.

"No, you do not know. You do not know what it means to learn the ways of power; you do not know the burden and the responsibility it brings. You do not understand your world, its darkness and perversion, the hideousness of the notion that power can be exercised in this place, or penetrate the quagmire of handpower consciousness. Power exhausts itself upon the currents of this world, exhausts itself and dies. Away from us you could not exercise it at all."

Alexina felt tears in her eyes, and struggled not to

shed them. She tore her gaze away from his, away from his brutal words, and stared out over the flat farmland. The sun was setting and twilight descended, blue and heavy, blotting out details.

"But I understand that it is your power that asks this question." His voice had softened. "I must forgive you the ignorance of it, for you are the victim of the limitations your world has bred in you. You do not possess the knowledge to think rightly, and for that you cannot be blamed."

There was a short silence. Marhalt got to his feet. "Come, Alexina. Enough talk for today."

Slowly Alexina rose, stiff from sitting crosslegged. The air around her seemed murky with more than the coming night, and she could still feel the heaviness of the link. Marhalt watched her. Then, as if he sensed her feelings, he moved over and gently brushed a stray strand of hair from her forehead. His fingers lingered for a moment on her brow, very warm. She could just see his eyes. They held kindness.

"Don't worry, Alexina," he said, and his voice, too, was kind. "You have done well on this journey. You have been brave and obedient. All the signs are there. It remains only to gain the conclusion. And one day . . . one day you may have the answers you seek."

He turned, and led the way back to camp. Alexina followed. Her mood had reversed itself, and now instead of depression, she felt a spreading warmth. He had rebuked her, but he had also seen and appreciated her effort to fit in, to do as she was told; he had called her obedient, and she knew now the premium the Guardians placed upon obedience. Perhaps he would teach her after all. He had not said so, but his strange words seemed to allow the possibility. Oh, let it happen, she prayed. More than ever, she was determined to show him she was worthy of knowledge, to erase once and for all the shadow of her world that stood between them.

12

Alexina was dreaming. In her dream she was enclosed by a fog so dense she could not see anything around her. She seemed to be standing in a space just large enough for her body, with billowing pale gray walls. Through the fog something began to glow, a luminous cord that stretched away from where she stood until it became a silvery blur and was lost from view.

Something was approaching, moving toward her along the cord. With certainty, she knew that it was *him.* Terror rushed through her like a great wind, and she tried to pull away; but the polarity had reversed at last, and she was helpless against it. She was aware also that within her fear lay a kernel of horrible fascination—for at long last she would see his face.

There was a blur, darker than the fog, darkening. At last he stood before her. The link was no longer a cord but a clear, brilliant light that enclosed them both, so that he stood within a nimbus of mist touched silver at its edges like cold fire. He was a tall, slender man in his early thirties, with irregular features and full lips. His hair was black, tied back from his face and braided at his neck, and he wore a thin beard. His eyes were long and narrow, as black as his hair. They held a look that was neither threatening nor hostile. They were . . . interested, that was it. He was interested in her. For a moment he watched her. Then he smiled.

Hello, Alexina.

His lips did not move, but his voice was there in her mind, not like the impersonal flow of mindspeech, but exactly as if he had spoken. His smile was like his eyes, interested, even friendly: There was no threat in it. It struck terror into the very core of Alexina's soul.

Don't be afraid.

Alexina closed her eyes, but this was a dream, and she could still see him. *Go away,* she thought miserably. *Please, please, leave me alone. Oh, why can't I shut you out?*

I couldn't shut you out, he replied to her thought. *Why should you be able to shut me out?*

I'm sorry. I didn't want to come to you. I had to do it—you must understand. . . .

But it doesn't matter how you came, or why. The link makes it inevitable that it will happen somehow. Even if you had never met the Guardians, you would have found your way to me.

No. No, I never would.

Alexina, I won't hurt you. Don't you know that people who are linked can't harm one another? What befalls one befalls the other in equal measure. The link is not merely spiritual. It is physical as well.

No, she thought. *No.*

There is much they *have not told you, Alexina. I am not like them. I will tell you everything you wish to know—save, perhaps, one thing. Don't you want to know the answers? You will soon be where I am. Come to me then, and I will tell you everything.*

No. I don't believe you. You want to find out about the Guardians. And we won't be linked much longer. When we reach you, the Guardians will defeat you and the link will be broken.

He smiled again, briefly. *We shall see. Remember my invitation when you arrive. Look to the hedge, and you will see the way inside.*

He paused a moment longer, regarding her with his dark eyes. Then he turned and began to recede, a black figure growing more and more indistinct until he was finally gone. The link was once again a cord, glowing fainter and fainter until it was only the smallest glimmer in the mist. At last it was extinguished altogether. The fog closed around, damp and lightless, and suddenly Alexina was awake.

It was midafternoon. The sun slanted through the trees in great shafts of light that seemed almost solid, enclosing the meditating Guardians in warm gold as the dark man had been wrapped in cold silver. Inside the camp all was still, though a restless wind stirred the woods outside the shimmering barrier. It could shut out air currents and make them invisible to passersby, but it could provide no defense against the link.

Alexina shook with the cold of her dream. She felt as if she were falling into an abyss; she was alone, utterly alone. Tears filled her eyes. She could still feel the hateful link crouched within her like a living thing, falling once more into sleep but always ready to wake and render her helpless. She put her hands to her throat as if she could grasp the link itself, feeling her pulse beat against her palms.

Only a few more days, she thought, breathing deeply to calm herself. A few more days; it would all be over then, and the link would be gone forever. But two days of this fear would be a lifetime. She could still see his smile, his narrow eyes, the face she had dreaded and wondered about in equal measure. It was wrong that he should be just a man, a handsome man, unravaged by time and unmarked by any obvious evil. He should be old, ugly, branded somehow with whatever terrible thing had caused him to steal the Stone.

The Guardians were rousing themselves from meditation. Alexina watched as Marhalt glanced around the camp, then got to his feet and approached her. She opened her mouth to tell him about what had happened—hiding the worst of her fear, of course—but he spoke first.

"Alexina, do you know where Taryn is?"

Surprised, she looked toward Taryn's blankets. They were empty. She shook her head.

"Did you see him go?"

"No. I . . . I didn't notice. Marhalt, I've something to tell you—

"Later, Alexina."

Marhalt gestured to Loran and Gwynys, and they spoke for a few moments in their own language. Then Marhalt and Loran strode quickly off into the woods. Alone with her fear, Alexina huddled in her blankets and watched the shadows solidify into darkness as night fell.

When at last they returned, Taryn was walking a little in front, his eyes on the ground and his hair falling over his face. In silence they seated themselves—Taryn, as usual, apart from the others. Marhalt and Loran served themselves from the pot on the fire. Taryn made no move to do so, nor was he given anything. Trying not to be obvious, Alexina cast glances at him now and then. He was sitting crosslegged, his head bowed and his back and shoulders rigid. The others, conversing softly together, behaved as if nothing were amiss. Clearly, Taryn was in renewed disgrace.

* * * *

They began their journey that night as usual, and during the rest period Alexina was aware of Taryn's breathing somewhere in the darkness. But when they stopped to make camp, she realized he was no longer with them. She was imagining it, she told herself, or he was hidden in the half-light of the coming dawn. A terrible dread began to take shape. She remembered what he had told her about failing, about being left behind.

Marhalt knelt not far away, unrolling his blankets. He looked up as Alexina approached.

"Marhalt." She swallowed. "Marhalt, where's Taryn?"

He sat back on his heels. "He's being punished, Alexina. There was . . . an incident yesterday."

"You aren't going to leave him behind, are you?"

"Now why would you think that?" He looked at her, and Alexina dropped her eyes, afraid she had revealed too much of what she knew. "No, Alexina, we won't leave him behind. He will be punished, that's all. He will stay apart from us until tonight, without food or drink."

"Oh." She had been wrong to fear, she thought. But her relief was still tremendous. "Will he be all right? Away from your protection, I mean?"

"He is still under our protection. He is only a small distance away. You seem very concerned about him."

"Well, I . . . I suppose I am."

"You like him, I know. Taryn *is* likeable. But he is also impulsive, and that is not a good quality in a Guardian. It is necessary to think before one acts, and often Taryn does not do so." He looked at her searchingly. "You don't look well. Is something wrong?"

Alexina could not control a shiver. "Yes," she said.

"Tell me. What is it?"

"He came to me, Marhalt." Her voice trembled. "The dark man. In a dream. Only it wasn't a dream, it was the link—I could feel it pulling. He spoke to me."

"What did he say?" Marhalt's voice was sharp.

"Not very much, really, just that he wanted me to come to him. That he'd tell me things. He said if I looked in the hedge, I'd see a way inside."

"Did he say what he would tell you?"

"No. I didn't want to know."

"Did he say anything about the link?"

"Only that he couldn't harm me through it, that he would be harmed himself if he tried, or something like that. I don't remember. Oh, Marhalt, I know I should be braver, but he frightened me so."

For a moment Marhalt did not reply. "He may come to you again, Alexina," he said at last. "With the same invitation. You must refuse him if he does."

She shivered again. "Of course. I don't understand why he did it at all. Surely he knew I wouldn't say yes."

"He is trying to lure you to him through some illusion wrought by his power. You must be very much on your guard against this, Alexina."

"But why should he want me? What use could I be to him?"

"It is the link. He feels we have power over him while we have you, and by taking you himself he would no longer need to fear. Remember, this is a madman. There is no telling how his mind may work, or what he intends to do."

He had not seemed mad in her dream. He had seemed perfectly rational, even reasonable. Perhaps that was what had made him so horrifying, the contrast between what he was and what he seemed.

"What can I do?" She tried to keep her voice steady. "Is there anything that can help me be on guard against him?"

Marhalt shook his head. "Nothing outside can help you. Your guard must come from within, from your own power and your own strength. He can reach you through the link and you cannot control that, but he cannot mislead you unless, somehow, you want him to."

"No! I would never want that!"

"We will concentrate our own barriers, and perhaps this will provide some protection for you."

Alexina nodded.

"Alexina." His voice had changed. He was watching her with great intensity. "Until now I have avoided giving you a direct order, even though your obedience was one of the conditions for this journey. But now I must. You must not go to him, no matter what he says, no matter what he threatens or promises. I lay this obedience on you through the power, Alexina, the power which we both possess. Do you understand?"

Something was there suddenly, charging the air around them: a humming just beyond hearing, an invisible electricity against the skin, a showering of sparks at the edge of vision. It was his power; and inside Alexina something stirred in response, as if his meaning had reached a place far below the threshold of thought. "I understand," she whispered. "I will obey."

"Good." Briefly he smiled, and his face was transformed; then he was serious again, even somber. "Eat now, Alexina, and sleep. We must follow the link again today."

Alexina picked at her bowl of food. She had no appetite, and anyway, she was going to take it to Taryn. She had known she would go to him as soon as Marhalt told her of his punishment. He was alone, tired, and hungry, and facing a night of exhausting travel on an empty stomach. She knew, of course, that she should not do it; she should not interfere, or further jeopardize Taryn's obediences. But it did not change her determination. The Guardians would be asleep and she would not stay very long. She could not think about sleeping herself. She knew that if she closed her eyes the image of the dark man would rise up behind them, the clear light of the link burning all around him.

She waited for a time after the Guardians had finished their meal and stretched themselves in their blankets. Then, noiselessly, she gathered up her unfinished breakfast and passed through the curtain. She took careful note of landmarks and struck off through the trees. Though she moved almost at random, it took her only a little while to find Taryn. He was huddled in his blankets among the trees, a lonely shape with his head bowed on his knees. Alexina's foot snapped a twig as she approached, and he jerked up abruptly, wide-eyed. An expression of amazement spread over his face, followed quickly by one of pleasure.

"Alexina! What are you doing here?"

"Sh. I snuck away when they were all asleep. Here—I've brought you some food."

He took it and began to eat ravenously, mumbling through mouthfuls. "You shouldn't have done it.

He'd be furious—you can't imagine. You must go back right away."

"I know, the obedience. But I'll stay until you're finished."

At last he put down the empty bowl and wiped his mouth with the back of his hand. "Thank you, Alexina," he said. "I don't know how I'd have made it through tonight without something to eat."

"What did you do yesterday? Marhalt made it sound like something bad."

He looked away. "I couldn't sleep again. There was this stream nearby and I wanted to wade in it. But I wandered off a little too far and got lost. I came out into a field, and suddenly this man—one of your people—was asking how I got there, who I was and so on. I think he wanted to take me away and question me. Luckily Marhalt and Loran came along, and Marhalt made the man forget he had seen me."

"That's it? That's all you did?"

"Well, I endangered the mission. If the man had taken me off somewhere, Marhalt would've had to find me and bring me back. It was . . . it was irresponsible of me. And Marhalt did tell me not to go away from the group. It wasn't an obedience, but I did wrong in disobeying." He shrugged. "Anyway, Marhalt's glad to have an excuse to punish me. He wants to remind me I'm not supposed to be here and that there's worse waiting for me when we get back."

"Taryn," said Alexina, and then stopped. Taryn looked at her. "Taryn, is there something between you and Marhalt? I mean, it seems like you hate him."

Taryn hesitated. "Sort of."

"I just can't . . . I just find it very hard to believe that he'd do the things yo say he would, or that he'd punish you just in order to punish you. He doesn't seem like that kind of person."

"You don't see that side of him." Taryn looked at her darkly. "You're different, you see."

"What do you mean, I'm different?"

"You have the link. You get special treatment."

Alexina flushed. "Yes, I get special treatment. I get to do something I'm terrified of, I get to initiate contact with an insane criminal, I get to live in fear that he'll come to me and pervert my mind or something. Personally, I'd rather sit by myself out in the woods every day."

"I'm sorry. I didn't mean that the way it sounded."

"I know."

"Alexina, you've done so much for me. You saved my life. You brought me food. I'm so much in your debt."

"It's all right." She felt uncomfortable. "I know you'd do the same for me."

For a moment he looked at her, and there was something in his expression; she could almost see words struggling behind his green eyes. Then he dropped them, and the moment was gone. Silence fell.

"Well." Alexina picked up the bowl. "I'd better be going back."

Taryn raised his head, and his face was full of resolve. "Don't go just yet. There's something I want to talk about."

"What?"

"I've never done anything for you, Alexina. And I've been lying to you—" he broke off abruptly. "But there is some truth I can tell you. About myself."

Alexina sat back a little, instinctively pulling away from the intensity of his words. "Are you sure you should?"

"Yes. I'm sure. I feel you should know something, even if it's only the kind of person I am. Besides, I *want* to tell you. Even if there were no debt between us, I'd want you to know the truth about me. So that perhaps one day things can be . . . clean between us."

"I'm not sure I understand," Alexina said hesitantly. "You make it sound terrible."

"It is."

"I can't imagine anything terrible about you."

"Yes, but you see, that's it. You're handpower-born."

Alexina clutched her head in both hands. "If I hear those words again, I'll scream. Why does everything have to come back to that?"

"I'm sorry. But it does come back to that. To handpower. Because of me."

"You?"

He took a deep breath and seemed to brace himself. "I didn't tell you everything when we talked before. I didn't tell you how I found out about the Stone."

"You said it was an accident."

"Well, yes, in a way it was. I happened to be in a hidden gallery in one of the meeting rooms when they were holding a conference about it. It was just by chance I was there at that particular time."

"A hidden gallery?"

"Yes. The Fortress is full of secret passageways, tunnels, false walls, peepholes—things like that. We didn't build it, you know, and before us it was owned by a king who was famous for his spies. When we came to the Fortress the Guardians had no reason to use them, and gradually their existence was forgotten. I only found out about them because I was doing research for one of the Masters in one of the oldest record books, and I came across a reference to the passages and their mode of construction. That book was covered with dust—it might have been a century or even more since someone had read it. Well, as soon as I saw it, I knew I had to find the passages and explore them. The trouble was I couldn't stop once I started. I kept on, even though I knew how dreadfully I'd be punished if they found out. I've been exploring for years."

"Why would they punish you so severely?"

"Because what I'm doing says something about the kind of person I am."

"I don't understand."

"Well, you remember what I told you about the handpower state of mind. Some types of people are more prone to that sort of thinking than others. There's a whole section of Limits on the handpower-prone personality and how to identify it."

"Is that really so important?"

"Yes, because people like that are the ones who are more likely to succumb to temptation if they encounter it. Well, you see . . ." His voice trailed off again, his eyes avoiding hers, and when he spoke his tone was hesitant. "My personality fits some aspects of the handpower personality pattern. I've always been too interested in tools. I can use them easily, understand them quickly. I'm very good with my hands, at making and building things." He paused. "I can't help the way I am. I was born with it. It's something that's always been there inside me, ever since I can remember. Just little things, you understand—nothing *really* wrong. Things are looser in the outside world. In the Fortress, though, everything is very strict. It was hard for me at first, and I made mistakes. They beat me a lot. There were a lot of obedience exercises. But all the apprentices make mistakes—it's expected. Eventually I stopped making them, and they thought the training had bred the bad habits out of me. I thought so too—I really believed I'd killed it in myself. But those tunnels . . . it was like being addicted to something. I couldn't stop. And I was *good* at it, at following clues, figuring out the location of rooms and passages from the architecture of parts of the building, unlocking complicated secret catches and spotting hidden doors. It was different from the small things. It was . . . it could be . . . proof."

He had picked up a twig and was breaking it into tiny pieces. Alexina felt a little bewildered. "Proof of what?"

"Don't you see?" He let the pieces of twig trickle from his hand onto the ground. "Proof of the fact that I'm handpower-prone. In the beginning, they thought I just had bad habits, like anyone could have. But this—it has all the marks of the handpower personality pattern. And knowing it and doing it anyway—well, that's even worse. It shows . . . well, someone could interpret it to mean I've been corrupted. And that's what is between me and Marhalt."

Alexina hesitated, trying to grasp the connection between handpower and hidden passages.

"So Marhalt found out about the passages?"

"Oh, no, he doesn't know about that. Of course, I had to tell him how I found out about the Stone, but I said I fell against a tile one day and it was a secret catch on a door opening into a passage, which just happened to lead to that particular conference room."

"What is it then? Does he know something else?"

"Yes. Marhalt is very powerful, you know. When I first came to the Fortress I was brought before him—I can still remember it. He looked at me. He looked right through me to my other side, and he saw everything that was wrong, every thought I had and every action I'd performed that was forbidden. He made it his business then to know about my mistakes, about all the obediences I was given. And when I stopped making mistakes, when even I thought the bad habits were gone, he still suspected something. He looked at me, and he didn't believe I'd just outgrown it. He can't prove it. But he'd like to. He's always looking for a way."

Alexina frowned. "So he suspects you're doing things you shouldn't be."

"He doesn't suspect, he knows!" Taryn's voice vibrated with intensity. "He knows, I tell you. That's why he's so hard on me. He's just waiting for me to slip up and betray myself to the entire Fortress, so he can prove to everyone I should be thrown out of the Order."

Alexina was silent for a moment, thinking. "Taryn," she said at last, slowly, "are you telling me you've done things that someone would interpret in a negative way if they found out for sure? Or are you saying that you actually *are* handpower-prone?"

He did not meet her eyes, and there was a long pause. Finally he ran his hand through his already disheveled hair, and turned his face toward her. It was bleak but determined. "Yes. I can't deny it anymore."

Alexina could begin at last to understand what he was trying to tell her. The magnitude of his trust was enormous—he had shared with her his innermost secret. He still looked at her, and now his face was vulnerable.

"Alexina. You don't hate me, do you?"

Astonished, she stared at him. "*Hate* you? Why should I?"

"Because . . . because of handpower. It's terrible, I know. I just don't want you to hate me for . . . for what I am."

"Taryn . . ." Alexina groped for words. There was a gulf between them, she saw, made up of all each did not understand about the other's world. She had heard what he said and understood it, but in a way she could not truly know what it meant to him, just as he could not truly know how little handpower mattered to her. "I don't hate you," she said at last. "You mustn't worry about that."

He sighed, and she realized he had been holding his breath. "I hoped you'd feel that way. I wasn't sure, but I had to take the risk."

"Taryn, why did you follow Marhalt? Why didn't you choose one of the other search groups?"

"It had to be him. Only Marhalt could find the Stone."

"And you still want to be a Guardian? Even with being . . . the way you are?"

"Yes." His voice was firm. "I've always wanted to be a Guardian, ever since I was old enough to understand. It's the greatest honor in the world, to serve the Stone and to serve the people."

"But it'll be awfully difficult for you, won't it? You'll always have to keep part of yourself secret."

"Yes, it will be difficult." Taryn sounded strained. He took another twig and began to trace a design in the earth beside him. Then, abruptly, he snapped it in two and threw the pieces away into the woods.

"I just feel that some interest in handpower isn't wrong. You have to know the thing that threatens you in order to deal with it properly. It's not enough to shut it away, to ignore it as if it didn't exist." He paused for a moment; when he went on his voice was hushed and his words hurried, almost furtive. "Perhaps there's even something to be learned from handpower. After all, it existed in the original world, and people used both powers, yet kept the balance. I'm not saying handpower wouldn't have to be subordinate to mindpower, or that it should be just allowed to develop without control. But maybe . . . maybe if the Limits were loosened we could learn something."

"But handpower did terrible things. It destroyed the original world. It ripped everything apart."

"I know that." Taryn took a deep breath. "But maybe it's not the tools themselves that are wrong, but the way they were used back then or the attitudes of the people who used them. That's where your world could have made its mistake. Perhaps there's a right way to use them, a way so they could do good instead of evil." He shook his head. "There are so many things in my world that could be changed. I saw my mother die when I was eight years old. She was just . . . worn out, with bearing children and working in the fields and keeping house for us all. Where is the good in living like that? What harm could it do to help people, as long as the world didn't go mad with tools the way it did in the past? There's so much that could be done with only the smallest relaxation of the Limits. Sometimes . . . sometimes—"

He stopped, cutting himself off sharply, as if pulling back from the edge of a precipice. He drew in a breath and closed his eyes briefly.

"Don't think I don't know how dangerous these thoughts are," he went on after a moment. "But I can't help myself, I can't help what I am. I can't help wondering about handpower, being curious about handpower things. Like that thing you wear, that thing on your wrist."

"You mean my watch? This?"

He nodded.

"It's just a watch. It's not that interesting. Everyone has them."

"Everyone?" His eyes were wide in wonder.

"Yes, it's the most common thing you can imagine. There are millions of things like that in my world, everywhere. But compared with power, they're nothing. Anything your people can do makes handpower look small. Like mindspeech and creating fire and—and—"

"And becoming invisible and flying and moving things from afar." He shrugged. "It's just a matter of training. If you have power, you can learn to use it. There's nothing wonderful about that."

Alexina was silent. He had reeled it off as if he were reciting a grocery list. How could you reduce such things to a matter of training? She understood Taryn's curiosity about objects in her world, but not his wonder. Wonder belonged to his world, to everything her world had lost forever, to everything of which handpower had deprived her.

"It doesn't matter anyway," Taryn said. "The Limits will never change. I'll never be able to do the things I want to do or know the things I want to know, or reveal my thoughts without being called corrupt. I may never get the chance to become a Guardian now." He leaned toward Alexina, his eyes fierce, almost as if he were accusing her. "Can you imagine what it's like for all the things you long for to be out of reach? Do you know what it's like never to have a moment in which you don't feel alone? If only I could be myself, my real self, for just a little while. If only there were someone else like me. But there isn't. And you know, I probably wouldn't know if I met them. Because even I don't know who I am."

Instinctively she had drawn away from him; all at once his face was anguished. He reached out and placed his hand on her arm. "Alexina, I'm sorry. I shouldn't have said all of that. I'm so confused sometimes. It's like there's something terrible inside me I can't control. I'm weak, I should be able to fight it, I should be able to stop thinking these things." He buried his face in his hands. "Maybe I *am* corrupt. Maybe Marhalt's right."

His turmoil was like a haze around him. After a moment he raised his head. His eyes were dry, his face very pale. They looked at each other.

"You're . . . different, aren't you," said Alexina slowly. "You're really different from the others."

He did not reply. And for the first time Alexina saw that he must feel as isolated in his world as she in hers. He too must dream of powers, of knowledge somewhere out of reach. But she felt no comfort, only a sharp and spreading loneliness. She had a heavy sense of things that should not have been said, thoughts which should not have been revealed, a secrecy that had just deepened into something dangerous.

She looked away. She saw the sunlight breaking through the leaves overhead, and suddenly she realized how much time had passed. It must be nearly noon.

"I'd better go right away," she said. "I didn't know it was so late."

He nodded.

She got up and stood for a moment, awkwardly. "Well, good-bye. I'm sorry I won't be able to come back."

"It's all right." He did not look at her. "Good-bye."

She made her way through the trees back to camp, praying she had not stayed too long. When she crept through the curtain they were all asleep, as she had hoped. Her presence had not been missed. She rolled into her blankets and, without thinking even once of the dark man, closed her eyes and drifted into sleep.

13

Alexina woke abruptly, as she had on the first day of the journey, aware that something was wrong. She opened her eyes. It was already growing dark; she had slept much longer than usual. The campfire was burning in its circle of stones, surrounded by packs and bedrolls, but the Guardians were nowhere to be seen.

It took her a moment or two to become aware that the barrier, usually close around the camp, was not there. She could see off in all directions without a break. They were camped in a field; close-by rose the beginning of a grove of pines. Into the wood ran a road that was no more than a track, disappearing into darkness down the avenue of trees. The ground on which she sat was scattered with their needles. She could smell the faint aromatic scent. It had still been dark when they made camp this morning, too dark to see the trees. But now recognition began to dawn. She had seen this place yesterday, in the link-vision. They were here. The path into the woods was the path to *him.* They had arrived.

Alexina stared at the pines, swept with a feeling of unreality. A hand seemed to have closed around her heart, and it had become difficult to breathe. Journey's end, she thought; the moment of decision. Deep within that wood was his house, with its peeling boards and blank windows, and the massive hedge that walled it in. Inside, he waited for confrontation. Inside, the Stone waited for release. There would be no more traveling, only battle.

It was odd: Even though they could be no more than an hour's walk from him, she could not feel the link at all. She was aware of a pervasive chill that seemed to breathe from the dark depths of the pines themselves, but it was clearly outside her. The link had been there yesterday, crouching evilly within her, when Marhalt woke her to follow it one last time. She had been terrified that when she reached his house he would rise up again to confront her, that this time she would be unable to escape. But he had not. Now she could feel nothing. It was better not to think about it, she told herself. She must not allow herself to hope that for some reason it had gone. She must remember Marhalt's warning.

Where were the Guardians? She could see only Taryn, preparing food by the fire. She stirred in her blankets, and he looked around.

"Hello," he said. "I was starting to think you'd never wake up."

Alexina got to her feet. "Where is everyone?"

He looked back at the pot he was stirring. "They've gone into the wood."

"Into the wood?" she echoed.

"To *him.* The battle begins tonight."

Alexina looked around her, at the dark trees, the dimming sky. "But why are we here? Shouldn't we be with them?"

Taryn shook his head. "Great forces will be at work tonight, and if I'm not strong enough to withstand them, you're certainly not. We'll be safe here. We wouldn't be safe there."

"Oh." The disappointment was sharp and immediate. She was aware that it did make sense, for Taryn's training was incomplete and she had no training at all. Yet somehow she had always assumed that she would be there for the battle itself. She hated that any of the Quest should take place in her absence.

"Where's the barrier?" she asked after a moment.

"They can't fight and maintain it at the same time. They need all their strength for tonight."

When the food was ready they ate it without speaking. Alexina glanced at Taryn's closed face. Oddly, she felt a slight constraint after yesterday. He seemed to feel it too. She wondered if perhaps he regretted having told her so much.

Night fell and the absence of the barrier became less noticeable. The fire cast an uncertain illumination, making the night seem blacker by contrast. Shadows writhed with the fluctuation of the flames, as if half-seen forms danced at the perimeter of the light. The wind sighed among the branches.

Alexina was not sure at what point she became aware of something more than the wind—a whispering, like the sound of a distant ocean.

"Do you hear it?" she breathed. It was mounting even as she spoke.

Taryn nodded. "It's the power, the forces. They must be fighting now. Don't listen. Try to shut it out."

But she could not. Her bones vibrated with it; sparks and colors flashed at the edges of her vision. It was building, growing greater and greater: a roaring as if of a mighty wind or tremendous breakers, a shaking as if the earth were wrenching itself apart. And yet it was not really like any of these things. Deep in the woods where the Guardians were the earth would be firm, the trees would not tremble, the air would be still. The sound she heard was not sound at all for the cataclysm was not material.

Now something more was added: a series of concussions, a rhythmic pounding, as if far away some great beast threw itself against an unyielding obstruction. It went on and on. Alexina could not tell the power of the Guardians from that of the dark man, nor could she gauge the course of the battle. All that could be grasped was the conflict itself, the elemental fury of those distant powers clashing in the night. Unable to shut off her senses, she could only endure. Taryn too could not completely shield himself. They sat together, their hands locked, waiting for it to be over.

At last, at long last, it was. The raging forces fell away. The shock of cessation spread through the world in widening circles, blanketing everything in silence.

Slowly Alexina raised her head. The quiet was unreal, echoing in her ears and through all the spaces of her body. It was dawn. The just risen sun cast long shadows over the land, and the sky was a pale but perfect blue. Small voices of ordinary reality were audible again. Alexina could hear the cry of birds, the stirring of leaves and grass, the crackle of the fire. The world was beautiful and quite unchanged; it was as if the battle had never happened. Was it over? Had the dark man been vanquished?

Beside her, Taryn had opened his eyes. She looked at him, but he shook his head. He did not know either. She felt his hand slip from hers, and he moved away to start preparing breakfast over the fire.

It was about an hour before the Guardians appeared. As they approached, Alexina could only stare. They seemed to have aged ten years in a single night. Their faces were gray and haggard, and they walked as if they could barely place one foot before another. This was not the bearing of victors. Even Marhalt was slumped and worn. Alexina was shocked beyond speech.

The Guardians entered the camp and sank to the ground. Taryn handed around bowls of food, and as they ate they seemed to regain some of their strength. At last Marhalt glanced at Alexina. He nodded, and she understood that she was to approach.

"We fought last night, Alexina," he said. His voice was low. "It may take more time than we had thought to finish him."

Alexina caught her breath. "You mean it isn't over?"

He shook his head. "Did you think it would be decided in one meeting? No, there will be many more before he is vanquished."

He passed his hand over his eyes in an absent gesture that frightened Alexina even more than the way he looked.

"Are . . . are you all right?" she said, hearing the urgency in her voice. "You look so tired."

"We *are* tired." He met her eyes, and she saw that in their topaz depths his intensity was undimmed. "Of course we are tired. But so is he. Great forces were conjured up last night, and he stood alone against our united power. He did not even come out to meet us; he is not strong enough for direct engagement. He stayed hidden behind his barriers. We could not break them down last night, but over time we will. Each night it will take him longer to replenish his power. When we do break through to him, he will be helpless."

"So he *will* lose."

"Yes. I should not need to tell you that. You must be on your guard, Alexina. I do not know if he will be strong enough to use the link, but you must be careful even so. When he realizes he is losing, he may try to trick you through it."

The hand was there again, compressing her chest. She nodded. "Yes. I'll be very careful."

"Good. Now we must all sleep to be ready for the night."

He spoke a few words to Loran and Gwynys. The three rose to their feet. They joined hands, and Alexina felt the pulse of power that accompanied the creation of the barrier. It seemed to take a very long time. Complete, it seemed too thin, less substantial than it ought to be.

The Guardians rolled themselves in their blankets and fell at once into sleep. Taryn, too, slept. Only Alexina remained awake, afraid to close her eyes lest the dark man come to her and work some treachery in her dreams. She stared at the barrier it had taken three of them to bring into existence, at the pale worn faces that showed above the blankets. She supposed she *had* thought it would be over quickly. She had thought they could move in and vanquish him, without effort, as they performed every other act of power. She had not imagined they could ever be drained. It was profoundly disturbing to see them look so . . . so human.

She sighed. She felt disoriented and depressed. The effect of the terrible night was still with her. In her imagination she could still hear the concussion as the power of the Guardians hurled itself against the dark man's barriers, again and again.

She must not sleep . . . but her eyes were so very dry and heavy. She would close them, just for a moment. Just for a moment . . .

* * * *

A hand brushed gently across Alexina's face, bringing her up from unconsciousness. Just before she opened her eyes she thought she heard someone call her name.

She sat up, shaking herself awake. It must have been the end of a dream: The Guardians and Taryn were still asleep. She had not meant to fall asleep herself, but somehow the sun had deepened toward afternoon.

She looked around her. The light was still and golden, and she could hear the monotonous sound of crickets in the grass beyond the barrier. The air was hot. Not a breeze stirred its stifling weight. It was as if the whole world were asleep, except for herself.

Then, as clearly as if she had actually seen it happen, she felt something: a trembling of motion in the silence, a transformation somewhere in the distance, the opening of a door. It took her only an instant to know what it meant. The way in—it was there. It waited for her now.

She did not hesitate. Noiselessly, she got to her feet, lacing up her shoes with swift, sure fingers. Then, quietly, she passed through the curtain. She could feel as she did so that it *was* thinner. Looking back for a moment, she could just see the shapes of the people inside the camp, superimposed on the empty field like images on a scrim.

There was a vague flurry of motion, and Taryn emerged. For a moment they stood in silence, staring at each other.

"I'm coming with you," he whispered at last.

She could see in his eyes that he knew where she must go. She understood that she was meant to go alone. Yet she was not sorry to have Taryn with her.

There was no time to stand about, anyway. The door would not stay open for very long. She nodded.

He stepped forward, and together they set off along the track, into the shadow of the great trees. The sunlight and the sound of the crickets faded away behind them, so that they seemed to be entering another world. It was very dark; the branches met in an almost solid canopy over their heads, and fallen pine needles cushioned their feet so they made no sound. It was a long way, but Alexina was not conscious of the passage of time. She was drawn by an urgency that blocked out thought, a physical imperative that drew her, almost running, like an arrow through the woods. She was almost unaware of Taryn by her side, following doggedly where she led.

Abruptly, the trees thinned and the light increased. The track ended, running up against a solid barrier that rose toward the sky. The hedge.

At least twenty feet high, it was regular and unbroken like a man-made wall. Yet it was not a wall. It was a living tangle of vegetation, a net of thick and sinuous branches twined together as closely as the warp and woof of a loom. The branches were studded with small green leaves, and wicked thorns, at least six inches long, pointed outward like sharp steel spikes. Large roselike flowers nodded on the ends of long stems, their pale pink petals deepening to red at their hearts. The ground was dusted faintly golden with their pollen. The flowers breathed out a strong fragrance, a sweet and somehow somnolent perfume.

Directly ahead, rather small and so neat it looked as if someone had sculpted it into the body of the hedge, was a rectangular opening. A swatch of grass was visible beyond it, bright with sun. The song of the crickets was audible again, rising and falling with hypnotic regularity.

Alexina stood still only for a moment. Not running now but moving slowly, as if her feet were weighted, she stepped forward through the little door. She was aware of branches to her right and left, of the thorns that spiked them, of the intensification of the heady flower scent, of Taryn just behind her.

The clearing was large. There were signs it had once been planted as a formal garden, for flowers and rosebushes were everywhere gone wild, and pocked stone steps, overgrown with grass and moss, led upward in a series of barely discernible terraces to the house. It was a mansion built in the Gothic style, three stories high with a turret rising a fourth. The tall windows were crudely boarded up, and haphazard planking revealed the ruins of elaborate woodwork. The decay she had seen in the link-vision was overwhelming face-to-face. The boards were warping, parts of the roof had fallen in, weeds thrust up between the porch steps, and the foundation was sinking slowly to one side. A wisteria vine had gone amok, distorting the wood to which it clung. Alexina could imagine the collapsing floors inside, the plaster ceilings dispersing themselves in drifts upon the rooms below.

An extraordinary drowsy peace hung over everything. The afternoon sun streamed down, stupefying. The only sound was the pulsing rasp of the crickets, joined now by the hum of bees at work among the flowers, and the occasional whine of a fly. Alexina could still smell the perfume of the hedge, mingled now with other flower scents. Amid all the sleepy heat, there was not the smallest sense of chill. The house and garden held no more menace than an open summer field.

She felt a hand on her arm. Taryn was pointing back the way they had come.

"Look," he whispered.

She turned. The hedge was closing itself. The branches writhed, twining around one another like snakes, weaving themselves together to restore the impenetrability of the barrier. It took only a moment. The slight trembling of the flowers was the only sign there had ever been an opening.

Taryn looked alarmed. "We're trapped," he whispered.

He was right, perhaps. Yet it had all been inevitable anyway. The urge to go forward was reasserting itself. Alexina's feet itched to move across the soft grass, to step onto the sloping porch and inside the house itself.

She started forward. Taryn followed, his eyes darting to right and left, his body tense. But Alexina was no longer aware of him; her entire being was absorbed in the path before her, the tiers of uneven steps that led to the house. Through the dreaming garden they moved, the sound of their footsteps absorbed by moss, the sun hot on their backs. At last they reached the crooked porch. Ahead of them stood immense double doors, massive slabs of dark wood set in a framework of elaborate curlicues. The right one hung slightly ajar. Alexina placed her hand on it, pushing it open wide enough to let them through.

Neither of them could have anticipated what was inside. Alexina stopped short, so suddenly that Taryn ran up against her. Before them lay the richly furnished hall of a palace. The walls were covered with flocked burgundy wallpaper. The floors were of softly polished oak, strewn with narrow Oriental rugs. A stairway, its oaken balusters rubbed to a dark gloss, curved up from the hallway to the second floor. The steps were covered with more rich carpeting and secured with gleaming brass rods. A chandelier descended from the central well of the ceiling, a crystal confection crammed with burning candles. More candelabra hung on the walls, their candles also lit. The myriad glinting points of light cast a soft glow over the hall, blurring outlines and deepening colors. It was very quiet. There was not a trace, in this elaborately appointed place, of the dilapidation that gripped the exterior of the house. Alexina felt as if she had suddenly stepped onto a stage set or into a movie.

Taryn let out his breath in a long sigh that sounded disproportionately loud. "What—," he began, but Alexina held up her hand.

"Don't talk," she whispered. She felt very strongly that they must not break the silence that held them. Taryn cast his eyes around the hallway, and said nothing more.

To the right was a large doorway. Alexina moved over to it, drawing Taryn with her. Instinctively, their hands had locked in a tight and clammy grip. This room was as rich as the hall, an incredible expanse of polished floorboards and heavy carpeting, with ceilings at least fifteen feet high. Small islands of furniture—little groups of sofas, chairs, and tables—were scattered through it. Heavy red velvet draperies hid the tall windows. Rows of bookcases contained leather-bound books; dark oil paintings hung in the spaces between them, each with its own pair of sconces. Like the hall, this room was taper-lit and silent, cool but not cold.

It was like a dream; like dreamers, Taryn and Alexina drifted slowly from room to room. The silence and dimness of the house formed a little universe of its own. The sounds and smells of the world outside were no longer perceptible, and time stood still. There was no longer any urge to move forward, any compulsion toward haste—only a suspension, in which it was possible to do anything at all and have all the time in the world to do it.

On the other side of the hall was a dining room with a great mahogany table that looked as if it could seat twenty people. Upstairs, there were smaller rooms—bedrooms with embroidered spreads and brocaded chairs, studies with massive desks and more bookcases, bathrooms with brass plumbing and sumptuous tubs. The house was mazelike; it seemed possible to wander through it forever without coming to the same place twice. Each curve, each stairway, each hall seemed to lead deeper inside, farther away from the starting point. In all the rooms candles were lit, flickering from wall sconces, from candelabra, from chandeliers. The heavy rugs absorbed sound so that the only noise Alexina could hear was of their breathing, and the occasional rustle of their clothes. It was as if the house were enchanted, lying sleeping for a century, waiting for the spell that would wake it.

Eventually they found themselves downstairs again. At the back of the house was a kitchen arrayed with armies of gleaming pots and pans. Off the kitchen, behind the back stairs, was a door. It was the only one in the house that had been closed. Alexina went over to it and pulled it open. She could just see a narrow stairway leading down into darkness. Visible at the bottom was a thin line of light. Even from here, it was obvious that it was a good deal brighter than anywhere else in the house. Alexina began to descend the steps, drawing Taryn after her.

A different kind of dream awaited them, but in its way as great a shock as the first. For this was modern light, from fluorescent tubes, and what it illuminated was a fully equipped computer complex. The walls were lined with banks of disk drives, crystal storage, and magnetic tape units. There was a large console with screen and keyboard. In the center of the room was a scaffold of polished metal that supported a confused-looking web of circuitry, unlike anything Alexina had seen before. It seemed to be central to the complex: Heavy twisted cables ran from various points of this structure, connecting it with the banks of equipment. The floor, walls, and ceiling were of antiseptic white tile, intensifying the glare from the polished metal surfaces. Like the rest of the house this place was eerily silent. Though the complex looked fully operational, it was not running.

Alexina heard an intake of breath—she was not sure if it were hers or Taryn's. It was beyond strangeness, descending from the enchanted house into this garish science fiction setup. Beside her, Taryn was spellbound.

"What is it?" he finally breathed.

"A computer."

"What is that?"

"It's a kind of machine, a machine that thinks. A thinking tool."

"A *thinking tool?*" His eyes were bemused. "How can that be?"

"It's just technology. It's not that different from the way a person thinks, only it can think much faster and retain much more knowledge. It can do complicated calculations that would take days for people to do. It can store information—all you have to do is ask it a question to get the information back."

There was an expression of almost comical wonder on his face. "It's . . . I can hardly believe it. I knew there were great wonders in your world, but this. . . ."

His voice trailed off. But Alexina was waking up. The overpowering incongruity of the room was acting on her; the dissonance of it was bringing her at last out of the waking dream in which she had been lost. Too late, her sharpening senses told her that some strange constraint had been laid upon her, lulling her into forgetfulness of the danger that existed here. The link, she thought. It must have been the link, from the moment she woke this afternoon. Somehow he must have activated it as she slept. Oh, why had she allowed herself to close her eyes? Why had she not recognized it as it dragged her through the woods, why had she not distrusted this deceptive peace? Yet never, not once, had she felt the chill—not yesterday, not when she woke this afternoon, not even now.

They must get out, with all possible speed. They might have a chance. Perhaps he had not realized she would recognize what he had done to her. She grasped Taryn's arm.

"Come on," she whispered. "We've got to go."

He was alert at once. "Why? Do you feel something?"

"I'll explain later. We have to go. *Now.*"

She led the way up the stairs. She held up her hand, and they stood still for a moment as she searched for any sense of his presence. She could feel nothing but the cool atmosphere of the house, the velvety silence that now seemed stifling. She began to move toward the front doors. The hallway stretched out under her feet, impossibly long. The doors were closed. Had she closed them as they entered? She took hold of one, then the other. They were locked, or stuck. In any case, they refused to open.

There was no sound behind her, no chill, no sense of him at all—yet suddenly, with solid certainty, Alexina knew he was there. She stood, rooted to the spot, paralyzed as she had been in the link-dream. She was caught, a rabbit in his trap, a foolish, willing quarry. She clenched her fists. Marhalt had warned her. But she had forgotten and, dismayed, she remembered not only his warning, but his order. She had disobeyed. It had not been her fault, and yet it had, for she had somehow failed to be on her guard.

Slowly, she turned to face him. He was standing at the foot of the stairs, dark against the rich red walls, blotting out the tapers. Truly face-to-face now, she saw in the flesh the features of her dream—the expressive eyes and mouth, the neat jawline beard, the dark hair loose upon his shoulders. He came forward now, holding her in his black gaze. He was smiling a little. It was the same friendly, interested, somehow knowledgeable smile he had worn in her dream. Alexina could not take her eyes off him.

"Welcome to my home," he said in his pleasant voice. Powerful as his presence had been in the dream, it was a good deal more so in actuality. He radiated energy and vitality. He showed no signs of battle or weariness. This was not a man who needed to replenish himself. Alexina thought of Marhalt's haggard face and felt a terrible dread stir within her.

"Your friend was not invited," he said. "Never mind. We'll fit him in." He clapped his hands, twice. Alexina and Taryn both jumped. "Fico!"

There was a pause, and then the sound of feet on the stairs. A stocky man appeared and Alexina recognized him as the other one she had seen on that ledge, so long ago.

"Take them to their rooms," said the dark man. "Lock them in."

"Wait a minute," said Alexina, finding her voice in a moment of bravado. "You invited me here, remember? You said I'd be your guest. You don't have to lock us up!"

"You *are* my guests. But I want to be sure you enjoy my hospitality."

Fico came up behind them and took an elbow in each hand. His grip was firm, just short of painful.

"I shall see you at dinner," said the dark man.

"This won't do you any good," said Taryn breathlessly. "The Guardians will get us out, you'll see. You'll see!"

The dark man looked at him. "To them, you are already dead."

Fico turned Taryn and Alexina about and began to march them up the stairs. As they rounded the first curve, Alexina looked down. She saw his back, his long robe just touching the floor, his black hair on his shoulders, as he moved slowly toward the dining room.

14

Fico locked Alexina into one of the rooms on the second floor. She heard the turn of the key, the receding sound of footsteps, then silence, the deep, almost textured silence of this house.

She turned to look at the room. The omnipresent candlelight showed her a high double bed with posts, a canopy and curtains, massive and archaic like something out of the Middle Ages. It was covered with a brocaded spread of a delicate rose color. The floor was muffled with thick carpeting, the windows with velvet drapes, both of a slightly darker rose, and there were two comfortable looking easy chairs. There was a mirror surrounded by sconces; on the dressing table beneath it brushes and combs and little jars and boxes were set out. The door of the heavy carved wardrobe stood slightly ajar, and Alexina could just see the corner of something trailing out. Investigating, she found several floor-length dresses in vivid colors and unfamiliar styles, a long nightdress, and a quilted dressing gown. The jars on the dressing table contained creams and perfumes, and the boxes held ribbons, a couple of pretty necklaces, and a selection of earrings.

It was an opulent room, seductively lovely; it invited her to sink into it, to surrender to the sensuous dimness of its atmosphere. Deliberately, she went to the windows and pulled back the soft velvet drapes. The haphazard planking became visible. She felt a small welcome jolt of reality, as if she had glimpsed the ropes holding up a theater set. She stared at the afternoon sun slanting through gaps in the boards, at the little chinks of the outside world they showed her.

When she had turned to face him, she had felt fear and a futile, impotent rage; now she felt only a sort of passive helplessness. Like a character in a Greek play, she had been seized by a flow of events which no action of hers could change. She clenched her fists, hating herself for succumbing. She looked again at the room—the colors, the trinkets, the fairy princess dresses. It was as if it had been created especially for her. She thought of that knowledgeable smile, and shuddered. Could it really be that he had stood against the Guardians last night and emerged unscathed? She could still see their faces when they returned from the woods, worn with struggle. Soon they would wake. Soon Marhalt would know she had failed to obey.

Alexina dropped the curtain back over the window and was enclosed again in the universe of the room. The candles, she noted with fascination, burned without ever diminishing in length. She was tired from lack of sleep and self-disgust. Opening off the bedroom was a bathroom. She ran a tub of steaming water and, shucking off her grubby jeans and shirt, soaked clean. Afterwards she dried on one of the soft towels, and put on the quilted robe. It was a petfect fit. She looked at the bed, at its thick coverlet and fat pillows. Well, she thought, she need no longer fear sleep, for all the treachery he could work through her dreams had already been done. The link could pull her no farther.

Some time later the rasp of a key woke her, and Fico entered. He made gestures, pantomiming eating and drinking, pointing at the wardrobe, to indicate that she should get dressed for dinner. Alexina nodded at him to show she understood. Satisfied, he nodded back. He left the room, closing the door softly, and she heard the *snick* of the lock.

She lay on her bed, making no effort to rise. She felt a little as if she were not awake at all. In a little while she would be in that magnificent dining room, at the table with *him,* in close physical proximity with the power to which she was tied with bonds stronger than flesh. . . . She shuddered. Her fear felt like a premonition. She remembered that in her dream he had spoken of wishing to tell her things.

Yet beneath fear ran a darker current, difficult to define. Around her lay the room, the house, the fathomless silence, the shifting, dreamlike illumination of the candles that never consumed themselves. All of it called her, urged her to give in, to abandon resistance. What's the difference? the flicker of the tapers and the dance of the shadows seemed to ask. You're here. You can't escape. For you, there is nothing outside.

Without willing it, Alexina found herself on her feet, moving across the soft carpet toward the wardrobe. She saw her hand reach out, hover for a moment above the rich dresses, then select the simplest. It was of deep garnet velvet. The heavy fabric was gathered into an Italian Renaissance style, with a high waist and flowing skirts. There were shoes to match. At the dressing table, she brushed out her still damp hair and braided it into a long rope down her back. She tied it with a garnet ribbon. Opening several small boxes, she selected one of the gold necklaces and a pair of small garnet earrings.

She stared at herself in the mirror. She saw her own face; yet the clothing and the candlelight made it unfamiliar. She looked now as if she belonged in the house—one of those dim oil paintings come to life. She had the oddest feeling that she was actually receding into the house, becoming part of it, another piece of luxurious furnishing like the rich fabrics and the soft rugs. She pushed quickly away from the mirror and went to sit again on the bed.

After a while the door swung open, and Fico beckoned from the threshold. When Alexina reached the hall she saw that Taryn too had been included in the dinner invitation. Like her, he had changed his clothes. He wore a sober, floor-length robe of deep, brilliant blue, gathered into an ornate belt of worked silver disks set with blue stones. He had tied back his hair. His expression was serious and, combined with his clothing, made him look older than he was.

Fico led the way down the hall and, behind his back, Taryn looked at Alexina. "You look beautiful," he whispered.

Alexina felt herself flush. "Thank you."

"I'm four doors down from you, on the other side of the hall. Has he tried to do anything else to you? Through the link, I mean."

Alexina shook her head. "What can he do? I'm here now." She glanced at him. "Did you know it was the link all along?"

He nodded.

"Then why didn't you *do* something? Why didn't you stop me? Why did you just let me come here?"

"I couldn't have stopped you, Alexina. It's the way the link works. The only thing I could do was to come along to protect you." He took her hand possessively. "Don't worry. I won't let him hurt you." He lowered his voice even more. "I have a plan."

Alexina looked at him in alarm, but they were starting to descend the stairs, and she had no time to speak before they saw the dark man standing below. When they reached him, he gestured toward the dining room.

"Please seat yourselves," he said pleasantly.

They obeyed. As she sat down, arranging the unfamiliar weight of her long velvet skirts, Alexina tried to catch Taryn's eye. He would not look at her. She was afraid he was planning to do something foolish during dinner, something that could not possibly succeed. The dark man gestured to his servant, who disappeared into the kitchen, and came to sit with them.

The table had been set at one gleaming mahogany end. Thin white porcelain plates, rimmed with gold, were flanked by snowy napkins and a formidable array of silverware. Two crystal goblets stood at each place, their twisted stems and rounded bowls duplicated in the table's mirrorlike surface. Two large silver vessels, one piled with roses, another with fruit, stood in the center. Twin candelabras of worked gold provided the only illumination. The table sat in a small oasis of light, the rest of the room in indistinct shadow.

The dark man behaved as if this were a dinner party, as if they were really guests. He poured wine from a bottle that had been breathing in a silver bucket by the side of the table. He poured water from a crystal pitcher. He even made small talk: How did they find their rooms, was everything to their liking, did they require any further comforts? Taryn said nothing, his eyes downcast, his face taut. Alexina managed nods and monosyllables. The combination was bemusing: the incredible richness of the elaborate dinner party setting and the banality of the dark man's conversation. He had changed his robe—he wore deep rich red, the color of darkest burgundy wine.

Fico appeared with a large silver tureen; it contained a hot, creamy soup, savory and delicious. Alexina found that her appetite was not impaired by the situation, and she ate appreciatively. Across from her, Taryn did the same. Next came a fish roasted in butter and almonds. A fowl followed, elaborately prepared in a nest of wild rice, and after that a tender cut of beef. Each course was expertly prepared and presented, accompanied by appropriate vegetables and breads. Conversation ceased entirely as they ate. Alexina had never seen so much food at one time in her life, nor food so elaborately laid out. It seemed impossible that anything less than an entire army of chefs could have coordinated this magnificent meal. Plates were changed for each course, and for each a different wine was poured. Alexina, wary, drank only a sip or two; Taryn, however, was less cautious. Alexina could feel the dark man's power like a net over the three of them.

The beef disappeared, the plates were whisked away yet again, and a salad of mixed greens was brought in. Alexina's hunger was more than sated by this time and she could eat only a few mouthfuls. She glanced at Taryn. He was not eating either. He watched the dark man, his brows drawn into an expression of anger so intense it was almost like a mark. Pressure was building around them, like water flowing into a container without an outlet.

"You think you have us penned in here," Taryn said at last. His voice was quiet, but behind it tension strained. His words were very slightly slurred. "The Guardians will get us out, you'll see."

The dark man simply smiled.

"You can't win, you know. You don't stand a chance. They know all about you."

The dark man turned to regard Alexina. "You're a sensible girl, Alexina," he said. "What do you think?"

Alexina looked down at her half-finished plate of salad. "I don't know."

"Surely you have some opinion, based on all this." He made a gesture that included the house and everything in it. "What do you think? Do I seem affected by the first encounter?"

Alexina looked at him. The dark eyes met her own. "No. You don't. But how can I really tell? I don't know anything about you."

"Nor, as should be becoming clear, do the Guardians." He flicked a glance at Taryn. "It's comforting to know they are still underestimating me."

"You're bluffing," Taryn's face was flushed. "You're lying. You're holding us so you can get us to tell you something you want to know."

"Not necessary," said the dark man pleasantly. "I know everything already."

"And you want to use *her!*" Taryn gestured at Alexina. "You've worked out some way of using her through the link. Well, I won't let you do it."

"And just how do you think you can stop me?"

Taryn glared murderously from beneath his brows.

"I suppose that is why you came here—to protect her."

"Of course."

"The only reason."

"Of course!"

The dark man's voice was suddenly serious, the light tone gone. "I remember you, Taryn. From the Fortress."

Taryn's face twisted. He was coiled like a spring, his knuckles white on the carved arms of his chair.

Alarmed, Alexina projected her force into one word: "Taryn!" He hesitated, looked at her, then at the dark man. Slowly, he relaxed.

The dark man turned to smile at Alexina. "It's all right. He's just angry; it's perfectly natural. There's rather more to Taryn than meets the eye."

Alexina stared at her plate.

The dark man clapped his hands, twice. Fico removed the salad, and soon the table was set with dessert plates and coffee cups, a platter of assorted cheeses and biscuits, and a tray of pastries. The dark man took a green apple from the bowl of fruit and deftly peeled and cored it. Cutting it into quarters, he set it on Alexina's plate.

"Come now," he said. "Have an apple. It helps settle the stomach after a large meal."

He poured coffee for the three of them and sat back in his chair. Alexina could feel him watching her. She could imagine the look on his face: amused, tolerant. After a moment she glanced up and there it was, just as she had thought. She felt a sudden rush of anger.

"Why are we here?" she said. "What do you want with us?"

"I only wanted you."

Taryn glowered.

"*Why* did you want me?"

"Taryn knows. At least in part. You're the only one with access to me. I had to get you away before they used you against me."

"Used me against you? How?"

"Through the link. Once they knew they could not win, they would have forced you to activate it and, while we were connected, cast you into mind-sleep. I would have been cast under at the same time, and they could have come in here unimpeded."

"Mindsleep?"

"Paralysis of the cognitive functions of the brain. It's a last resort—very dangerous. There is a strong chance you would never have woken up again."

"I don't believe you." He did not answer, watching her instead with a pleasant expression on his face. Accusingly, she said: "You used the link on me to get me to come. You used it to hypnotize me."

He shook his head. "No. The link itself uses those it binds, draws them of their own accord. I just gave it a push, that's all. You would have come by yourself sooner or later. If that weren't so, I would never have been able to compel you."

Alexina stared at her plate, at the symmetrical pale green slices of apple. You're lying, she thought. I would never, never have done it of my own will.

"Do you remember the dream, Alexina?" he said. "There are things I wish to tell you. I'm sure *they* told you a great many unpleasant stories."

"Actually, very little," said Alexina defiantly. "I don't even know your name."

"My name is Bron."

Alexina shook her head. "Why should you want to tell me anything?"

"You must trust me," he said with surprising gentleness. "Let's just say that it's to our mutual benefit, you to listen and me to talk. What do you say?"

Alexina looked at the dark eyes, the mobile features, the strong throat above the severe collar of his rich red robe, the black hair falling over his shoulders. She could not deny that, despite her fear, despite what her intellect told her about his motives, something in her wanted to trust him. It's the link, she thought; it's working on me, even now when I can't feel it. I can't trust my own mind. It seemed terrifyingly easy just to give in. Desperately, Alexina clung to the last shreds of her determination. She must keep her barriers up. Whatever else occurred, he must not use her against the Guardians if she could prevent it.

"Go ahead," she said, not meeting his eyes. "I know I can't stop you."

"It's another trick, Alexina." Taryn's voice was urgent. "He's trying to use you."

Alexina looked at him. "I'll be all right."

Bron smiled. "Very well, then. I think that first I will tell you that I am the direct descendant, in a line that stretches unbroken for more than a thousand years, of the man from whom the first Guardian stole the Stone."

Taryn's eyes widened. "Bron!" he exclaimed. "So that's why you have that name."

"It's my real name. The one I held at the Fortress was false, for obvious reasons."

Taryn looked at Alexina. "Bron is the name of the man the first Guardian *rescued* the Stone from."

Bron ignored him. "You see, Alexina, in the distant past when the worlds were still one, my ancestors gained the Stone in battle. For generations we held it. Many came on quests to take it for themselves, though none succeeded. Its great power was widely known, and many greedy people coveted it. Even your world remembers it—not as it really was, of course, but masked in legend."

"What legend?"

"Are you familiar with the stories of King Artos of the Misty Isles?"

"Yes," said Alexina. Then, slowly: "Are you saying that the Stone is in the Arthurian legends?"

"It appears as the object called the Holy Grail."

"But the Holy Grail was the chalice from the Last Supper, a big gold cup, not a stone."

"In some of your legends it does take that guise," said Bron. "But there are other legends, and they portray it more accurately, as a magical object of one kind or another. By the time these legends were written down the worlds were almost completely split, and your people had forgotten the true nature of the Stone. All they could remember about it was its power. That is what the legends portray, no matter what form they give it. The Stone is connected with Artos, I think, because of all those who sought it he was the most persistent. In the minds of the people he came to stand for all who coveted the Stone, and his failure came to represent theirs. You see, your world is not as cut off from its past as some would have you believe. Myth, legend, fairy tale—all are ways of remembering."

Could it be true? Alexina told herself that she could not trust Bron or what he said. It did fit with what Taryn had told her: Percival, the Quest, the powerful talisman held in a place whose whereabouts were not quite known. . . . But she had barely time to take it in as Bron continued.

"The man whose name I bear was the great-great-grandson of the one who gained the Stone for my family. This man saw the splitting of the worlds, so the story goes, and felt that the emerging world of handpower was unfit for the nature of the Stone. He determined to pass into the world of mindpower with his family, all his worldly goods, and the Stone; but before he could do so Percival, the first Guardian, breached his stronghold. Percival murdered my ancestor's people and burned all his goods, and then, with the Stone, crossed into the world of mindpower. By sheer happenstance, the newborn son of my ancestor and his nursemaid were elsewhere at the time. They escaped the slaughter. The nursemaid too crossed into the other world and gave the baby into the care of friends loyal to my ancestor. For all practical purposes his lineage disappeared. But the boy was not allowed to forget, and he did not allow his descendants to forget. The tale has been passed through my family for more than a thousand years, a tale of a special destiny—for the ending is that eventually one with the power would come from among us, one who would be able to win back the Stone and avenge that ancient wrong." He placed both hands on his breast. "Myself."

Taryn's face was red. "You forgot to mention the fact that your ancestor murdered and slaughtered seekers of the Stone, as well as anyone who gave even one hint of knowing where the Stone was! You also forgot to say that he used the Stone for his own personal gain, to become fabulously rich. And he kept it away from the people, who are its rightful owners!"

Bron shrugged. "I won't deny it. There's little to choose between my ancestors and the first Guardians in terms of greed and bloodthirstiness. But for the Guardians, it became a tradition. I don't suppose they told you"—he had turned to Alexina—"that the Stone is kept in a mountain fortress so inaccessible that hundreds of people are killed each year trying to get to it. Many don't even attempt the journey because it's so difficult. The exact location of the Fortress is secret—does that sound familiar?—so that people must apply to one of the Journeyers, the Guardians who live outside the Fortress, to get permission to come there at all. All this is done so that iron control can be exerted by the Guardians over who questions and what is asked."

"You're a liar!" Taryn burst out. "We're not murderers like your ancestor! There are those who die, but they're the ones who try to get there on their own without knowing the way! Of course people have to apply to the Journeyers—you don't suppose we could have every thief and criminal asking whatever he liked, do you? Power like the Stone's has to be . . . regulated. Access to it must be controlled."

"We could spend weeks arguing over it," said Bron reasonably. "In any case, it is the consequences of ownership that have made the real difference. The Guardians used the Stone not simply for their own personal purposes, but also to gain control over an entire world. Percival and his men made up their minds that it was the pursuit of handpower that had caused the split so they set out to outlaw handpower completely, or at least as much as was possible. Of course some tools were necessary, for tilling the earth, for building, and so on. But they put their heads together and cooked up a lot of limits and prohibitions on even those. Book after book of Limits they wrote, and endless appendixes to each book.

"The world of mindpower was just emerging from the split. It was a world fragmented, confused, incomplete—the people were frightened and did not understand what was occurring. It was not difficult for a group that seemed to have the answers to gain trust and influence—and power. All they had to do was to win the powerful ones, or those who seemed likely to become powerful, to their side. And that is what Percival and his successors did. It was the Stone that really made it possible. They used its power to legitimize theirs, asserting that their possession of it made them the chosen ones. They built up its reputation, of course, proclaiming its power throughout the world. They made it accessible, so people could see it wasn't just a legend, yet they controlled all access to it so awkward questions couldn't be asked.

In your world, you would call it a very successful public relations campaign."

"You may have stolen the Stone." Taryn's voice was shocked. "But it's obvious you don't understand it. The Stone is the most powerful thing of its kind that has ever existed. How can you hold it and not know that?"

"The plan worked." Bron continued as if he had not been interrupted. "People willingly accepted the Guardians' authority and their view of the world. As for any who disagreed—well. That's another story. At any rate, by the time our world was complete the Guardians controlled it, to all intents and purposes. And to ensure that this order remained stable, they created their own safety net: the suborder of Journeyers. Each Journeyer is trained in some worldly skill and sent out into the world to act as advisor, teacher, librarian, administrator, and so on. Journeyers are everywhere. They are sworn to watch for any violation of the Limits, however small, and to report back to the Fortress. So the Guardians have not only the support of the ruling class, but a reliable organ of intelligence. They are able to control an entire world while still remaining behind the scenes. Do you see?"

He paused, as if waiting for an answer. Alexina compressed her lips. This is hatred speaking, she thought. He hates the Guardians. Perhaps by discrediting them he hopes to win me to his side, making me a willing tool against them. I won't answer him, she thought. I won't.

He seemed to sense her feelings. A look of amusement passed over his face, and Alexina could feel herself flush. "Ah, well," he said. "I can't expect you to absorb it all at once. Suffice it to say that it has been this way through all the centuries. There is no change—the Limits see to that—and so the power of the Guardians is never insecure. The Guardians do believe they are holding off the possibility of another split: They're sincere in that at least. But what they're really doing is holding back progress and, in the process, inflicting incredible suffering." Abruptly, he was completely serious. "Can you imagine a world in which people work themselves to death before they are thirty years old? Can you imagine a world in which disease is free to kill off entire populations in the space of one winter? Can you imagine a world in which people aren't allowed to develop ways of farming that would provide adequate food, so that millions starve to death each year?" He turned to Taryn, pinning him with his black gaze. "And you," he said, with focused intensity. "Can you imagine a world in which all these things are *not* so? In which people live to be fed, to be healthy, to be old? Answer me, Taryn. Can you?"

Taryn sounded breathless. "It's . . . it's the sacrifice that must be made. To preserve the precious powers of the mind. What does it profit to gain comfort and wealth if the powers of the mind are forfeit?"

"You sound like a proper little Guardian." Bron's tone was deadly. "Reciting your lessons by rote. Marhalt would be proud to hear you. But do you really believe those words you parrot at me?"

"Of course I do!"

"Come, come, Taryn. You were punished a great deal at the Fortress—do you think I don't know why? It's because you, too, ask questions."

"No!" The anger in Taryn's face was not matched by his voice, which seemed curiously weak. "Questions are one thing, but what you've said is another. I never in my life thought such things!"

Why was he denying it? His eyes caught Alexina's, slid away almost immediately, but she had time to glimpse what lay behind them. It was a revelation. Taryn's anger was a mask for fear: He was deathly afraid of Bron, perhaps even more than she. But for very different reasons, she sensed. There was something intensely vulnerable in his eyes.

"Were the Guardians wrong about handpower, then?" she asked, saying the first thing that came into her head, anything to take Bron's attention from Taryn. "That it caused the split?"

He transferred his gaze to her. "I didn't say that. But it's a matter of degree, of attitude. The split situation is not a necessary consequence." He was silent for a moment, his eyes slightly narrowed. Then he shook his head. "But that's all too technical for you. For me too at first, of course. When I first became a Guardian I knew nothing. I wished only to recover the Stone for my murdered ancestor—I, alone of my family to possess the power. I saw only that one ancient injustice, and I believed the legend as if I had actually been there and seen my ancestor murdered. Once I was apprenticed, however, my view widened. I came to know the Guardians' narrow-mindedness, their fanaticism and rigidity, their lust for power. I began to see the Limits for what they were. And I left the legend behind. I saw that a bloody theft in ancient times was trivial compared to a slavery imposed on an entire people and maintained over hundreds of years. I started experimenting on my own to see what could be done outside the Limits, building tools, modifying them. Farming implements, mostly."

"Marhalt said they were weapons."

"Did he." Bron seemed amused. "Well, I suppose it's a natural assumption, given his lack of imagination. They *were* farming implements. At any rate, it became clear to me that with only the smallest change of the Limits, much good could be done. And I thought, if the Limits were gone altogether, who knew what a wonderful world might be created? I realized then that I must indeed take the Stone back, as the legend dictated, but for very different reasons. Your world has proved me right." He stopped for a moment. "It wasn't until I came here, until I read and observed, that I truly understood how backward was my world, how enslaved. I gained much knowledge from your people. You have seen the fruits of that here in this house."

"You mean the computer complex?"

"In part."

"Marhalt was right about you. About your feelings about handpower."

Again he appeared amused. "And I can imagine what he said—that I am mad, or corrupt, or evil beyond the power of words to express. But it is Marhalt's own limitations that make him think this, Alexina, and his beliefs say more about him than they do about me. Your world is overflowing with things of value, things of power. The evil is a result of the use, not of the things used."

"You seem to think my world is so wonderful," Alexina said, "but don't you value mindpower at all? Tools don't automatically bring good. People starve and die here too, in spite of all our tools."

"True. But you cannot conceive the scale on which people starve and die in my world. As I said before, the loss of mindpower is not a necessary consequence of technology, if the change is made in the right way. After all, you have power, here in this world where it's not supposed to exist. Why do you think that's so?"

Alexina was silent, refusing to give him the satisfaction of knowing his words had struck a chord. She did not believe him, not a word. Yet she could not ignore the strength of his own belief, the disturbing force of his conviction.

"How did you keep all of it a secret?" she asked. "Weren't you afraid they would find out how you felt?"

Bron took a sip of coffee before replying, setting down the thin porcelain cup with a small clink. "I had my barriers, and I was careful with them. Believe me, I asked myself that very question more times than you would think. For a while I feared discovery hourly, daily. It wasn't until after the tests that I discovered the true strength of my barriers."

"The tests?"

"The Guardians impose a three-year preliminary apprenticeship, after which tests are given to determine whether apprentices are fit to continue training, and if so, what branch of Guardianship they are most suited for. The tests are designed to ferret out flaws in character and power, and most of all, to identify unsuitable interest in, or aptitude for, handpower. I used my barriers to pass the tests. If you know what they are testing for, you can project the sort of person they want you to be." He looked suddenly at Taryn. "Taryn is familiar with all that."

Taryn flinched involuntarily as Bron's eyes met his. "I don't know what you mean."

"Of course you do."

"No."

"Oh, Taryn." Bron sounded suddenly very weary. "Can't you admit we have something in common? It's not that terrible if you let yourself think about it. Can't you admit you came here because you wanted to see for yourself what I have been able to accomplish?"

"It's a lie! I came here for her!" Dangerous tensions sounded in Taryn's tone. "We have nothing in common. I may have a few interests, and I may have been disobedient. But I haven't done anything like you did. Whatever I thought, I never did anything. I could never be like you, never!"

"Yes. I did the unspeakable—I acted on what I thought." Bron shook his head slowly, and his voice seemed to hold genuine regret. "I am sorry for you, Taryn. You are a self-deceiver. You are too weak to act, too afraid to admit, and you will hide all your life behind the faint protection your barriers give you. There are many like you, you know. Because you passed the tests there is no proof, and they can't throw you out of the Order. But because they suspect you, they'll stick you in some primitive backwater where you can do no harm, and you'll live out the futile passing years until you are all dried up, your power and your questions wasted. That is your future, Taryn. Do you like it? Or can you still make a choice?"

For a moment Taryn stared at him. His eyes were open wide, the green completely swallowed by his dilated pupils. Then he tore his gaze free and turned his face away. He seemed overcome with lassitude, as if all at once he had become drunk again. Bron leaned back. He picked up his cup and sipped at his coffee, his face thoughtful.

"We were speaking of my true strength," Bron continued after a moment. "I realized very early that the power I had was different. It wasn't until the rigorous posttest training that I discovered how different. I found I could maintain feats of power they could hold only for instants. I found that I could do without training things it took them months to master. I found that my barriers were so strong I could throw up a shield around myself that rendered me utterly invisible. They never suspected." He shook his head in what seemed to be genuine puzzlement. "Even now they think I am as they are, if a little greater. They don't yet understand that my power is no more like theirs than night is like day. Even fully revealed, fully present, I am still invisible to them. That is what made it possible for me to take the Stone so easily. All I had to do was to walk past them and their defenses, put the Stone into a bag, and walk out again. Just like that. It was ridiculously easy."

He laughed, a full, infectious laugh, shaking his head. How arrogant he is, Alexina thought. As if he believed himself invincible.

"And so I came to this world. It took a little time, of course. I needed to prepare myself for its stresses. I needed to get well away from the Guardians so they would not know which Gate I had used, and I needed to find out from the Stone just where the Gates were and how to activate them. Normally, only Speakers are privy to that knowledge."

"Weren't you afraid of what would happen to the Stone here? And to yourself?"

Bron watched her for a moment. "You aren't eating your apple," he said at last.

Automatically Alexina picked up an aromatic green quarter and took a small bite. It was refreshing, and she went on eating. Silence had fallen. She stole a worried look at Taryn. He was slumped in his chair, nursing the wine goblet from which he no longer drank. His face was withdrawn, but his eyes glittered and she could tell he was listening. Bron took up a pear and began to peel it with a small, sharp knife, the blade flashing with reflected candlelight. His hands, like the rest of him, were well-made: He had long, clever fingers and there was something hypnotic in the precise way they moved, deftly manipulating knife and fruit. He cored the pear and cut it into wafer-thin, symmetrical slices. He consumed one and wiped his fingers on his napkin.

"Yes," he said, as if the conversation had not lapsed. "But it was a risk I had to take. There is no place in my world where there are not Guardians and I had no desire to spend the rest of my life as a fugitive. So I decided to take my chances. I felt I could carry out my plans as well here as there—and given the other inadequacies of the Guardians' knowledge, there was a strong chance they were wrong about this world too. They imagine it as a dark, perverted place, full of people who have become monstrous from living so long with handpower, full of hideous forces created by handpower that will inevitably destroy those with mindpower. Isn't that in essence what you were told?"

"Yes," said Alexina reluctantly.

"Well, given my new grasp of handpower, I felt sure they had greatly exaggerated all of it. There was the added advantage, too, that it would be much more difficult for the Guardians to track me here. I thought I would be free to proceed unimpeded with my plans. And if not for you . . ." He let the sentence trail off, watching her, but without rancor.

"What *are* your plans?" Alexina asked. "What are you going to do with the Stone?"

"That must remain a secret."

"What difference can it make? We're your prisoners. If you're as powerful as you say, we can't possibly escape."

Bron smiled. "Even if I were disposed to tell you,

it's not something you could understand yet. Suffice it to say that I shall use the Stone for good, not for evil, much as you may not want to believe it. I've accomplished my first goal, but my plans are larger than that. There is much, much more that needs to be done. I've hidden the Stone well, never fear. It's in a place where none of your people would think to look. Indeed, if they stood right before it they would not see it."

"If you're using it for something good," said Alexina, "why should you hide it? Wouldn't the Guardians understand?"

His face darkened, but when he spoke his voice was not angry. "No. Don't you see? They're incapable of it, just as they're incapable of change. For to understand would be to change. They are too rigid, too narrow, bound by their Limits like fossils embedded in rock. The same philosophy, unquestioned and unembellished, has been passed down century after century. The Limits have become more than physical: They are mental, too. They don't even really understand them any more, since they have never had to think about them—really think, as I have had to do. And slowly, they are becoming corrupt. Many are Guardians not for belief, but for power or personal wealth. Mindpower tends to be hereditary: The families that have power interbreed to preserve it; but interbreeding produces weaklings, and great power is of no use to a weak mind and body. There are Speakers now who aren't fit to come near the Stone. Whatever else, in the old days their power was pure and true. Then, even I might not have been able to conquer them, and a mere Journeyer apprentice like Taryn would never have been able to outwit the tests."

"You know Marhalt and you can still say that?" said Alexina incredulously.

Bron shrugged. "There are exceptions." He reached out and grasped the stem of his wineglass, turning it round and round in his fingers. Light played within the twisted crystal, drawing ruby-colored flashes from the wine still remaining. "But Marhalt, perhaps most of all, could never understand. What I have done will bring the Guardians down. In the end, power is what matters most to him. Power and control. They will not survive the loss of the Stone, you know. It will discredit them utterly."

"They'll bring *you* down." It was Taryn, emerging from his abstraction. The force his body no longer seemed to possess was concentrated in his eyes. "They'll take your barriers and leave you to this world and *your* power will be gone."

Bron looked at him. "That's a fairy tale," he said. "Properly fortified, there is a period of acclimatization which results in adjustment, not loss of power. Do my powers seem impaired? Yet my barriers are no longer against this world at all, only against the Guardians."

"Now I know you're lying," said Taryn. "I felt the change myself when I first came to this world. My barriers weren't strong enough. I got sick, and I couldn't mindspeak. Isn't that so, Alexina?"

Alexina nodded. Bron shrugged slightly.

"Think what you wish. Certainly Taryn became sick, because, as he said, his barriers were not strong enough. But he would have recovered, and his power would have been intact."

"You're lying," said Taryn again, but the erosions of the evening showed clearly in his face and voice. He could not find the certainty he reached for, and he knew it. Silence fell. They sat in the little circle of light, the three of them: Bron watching his hands, which now lay motionless on each side of his plate, Alexina watching the reflection of the candles in the finish of the table, Taryn seeming to watch nothing at all, his eyes half-closed and blank. Around them the dim house seemed to breathe gently, like a sleeping animal.

"Why have you told me all this?" said Alexina at last, breaking the silence. "I'd use it to warn them if I could."

"But you can't. As you pointed out, you're my prisoner. Anyway, it's not that." He leaned forward, looking into her eyes, very serious now. "We're linked, you and I. I don't know how it happened or why, I just know that it *is*. I also know that you have power—great power, power like mine."

Alexina shook her head. "I don't understand."

"Haven't you grasped it yet? Haven't you *felt* it? Your power is like mine, the power that comes once in a century. It is to the power of the Guardians as gold is to lead. You can do things naturally that they can do only with months of training. Do you know that if you wish, you can close your mind to me? No one else is capable of that. Had you not been exhausted this morning, I could never have pushed the link as I did. If you're on guard you are invulnerable. We are equal, Alexina."

Alexina shook her head again. Bron reached out suddenly and grasped her hand, holding it so tightly she could not pull away.

"We are equals, and we are linked. Have you any conception of how powerful that could make us? You have infinite natural ability, but it is undisciplined. I could teach you to harness it. That is why I brought you here. That is why I have told you these things about myself."

His hand gripped hers and his dark eyes bored into her own. She was aware of him, of his physical self, of the texture of his skin, of the dark, silky hair swinging forward over one shoulder. I hate you, she thought. But there was no denying it: Everything about him attracted rather than repelled. Her feelings made no difference to the force that drew her toward him. He knew it, too. She saw the beginnings of a smile behind his eyes.

She was conscious of being cold, very cold. His hand covering hers was icy. The link! she thought. It's the link, he's using it on me! It shocked her back into a more normal awareness, and with it came the knowledge that she had again allowed him to beguile her. The entire evening had been designed to that end, to catch her up, to relax her barriers, to open her mind so he could use her somehow. She wrenched her hand away and at the same time, instinctively, slammed closed the doors of her mind. Bron started back against his chair as if struck. Across his face came an expression of anger. Alexina clutched the arms of her chair, waiting for whatever would come next. For a moment it was a tableau.

"Forgive me," Bron said at last. His voice was not angry, but it was very cold. "Perhaps I've overestimated you. Reason is not yet enough. It's clear you aren't ready yet."

He pushed back his chair and stood up. At once Fico materialized from the darkness.

"Fico will escort you to your rooms. Soon it will be time for me to do battle again. I must prepare myself."

Fico came forward. Strong and stolid, he urged them out of the dining room and into the hallway. Taryn staggered a little as he walked.

Halfway up the stairs Bron's voice brought them to a halt. "Alexina."

Alexina turned. From there she had a panoramic view of the hall: the softly polished floors, the scattered rugs, the myriad points of the tapers. Bron's red robe melted into the darkness behind him. Only his face stood out, very white, and his eyes, very dark.

"It won't do you any good, you know. The link will do its work. You'll come to me sooner or later."

"Won't you," said Alexina, knowing it would not help but compelled to ask, "won't you let me go? Keep me a prisoner if you want, but break the link?"

He looked at her for a moment, his eyes holes in his face. Then he turned, all black hair and dark robe, and disappeared into the dining room. He had not answered.

15

Fico locked Alexina in her room again. Not knowing what else to do, she sat on the bed. She was exhausted. Without meaning to, she dozed off.

She awoke some time later. Getting up, she went to peer out between the planks on the window. It was still dark; the sky was clear and studded with stars. The forest and hedge were a black, featureless sea surrounding the pale island of the moonlit garden. Out there in the darkness those titanic forces must once again be coursing through the night. Out there in the forest the Guardians threw their power against a force they did not understand. And she was helpless, a prisoner, able to do nothing at all.

She pushed away from the window and wandered aimlessly around the room. With sudden revulsion, she stripped off her finery: the heavy velvet gown, the shoes, the jewelry, the ribbon. She left them on the floor where they fell and pulled on her own grubby clothes. Feeling a little more like herself, she sat down on the bed, leaned against the piled-up pillows, and drew her knees to her chin. Around her, the room was perfectly still: luxurious, confining, the shadows shifting slightly with the flicker of the burning candles. Alexina felt expectant, slightly breathless, as if she were waiting for something approaching along a faraway line that had not yet brought it into view.

The evening began to replay itself in a series of vivid mental images, pictures that for an instant took her right out of herself. She saw again the elaborate table setting, the twisted candelabras, the circle of light in which they sat, the darkness of the room around them, Taryn's flushed face against his deep blue robe. She saw the incredible procession of food, the garnet flash of flames reflected in a glass of wine. She saw Bron leaning toward her, his robe the color of the wine when light was not on it, his dark hair falling forward; she felt him grasp her hand. She had no sense of the link now. Yet the . . . attraction was still there. Convulsively she squeezed her eyes shut, as if by doing so she could block out what she saw with the eyes of her mind.

Yet even when the image of him was gone, she could still hear his voice and remember the things he had said, the strange offer he had made. And despite the knowledge that he wanted to beguile her and put her off her guard, she could not deny what lay beyond that: the strength of his own belief, and the strength with which he had wanted her to believe him. She shuddered. Knowing Marhalt, how could he expect her to accept that the Guardians were weak and corrupt? How could he hope she would believe, on his word, that they were bloodthirsty fanatics working their will upon a helpless world? Well, maybe some of the things about the Limits were true—Taryn had said so himself. Yet the same injustices existed in her world, and her world possessed no mindpower. Perhaps their world had made a great sacrifice, but her world had thrown away reality itself.

There was only one thing it was not possible to

disbelieve. He was as powerful as he boasted. With sure instinct Alexina had sensed the enormity of that power, lying coldly behind his eyes and voice, hanging heavy over the house and all that was in it. The terrible fear which had only stirred this afternoon had grown over the course of the evening into certain knowledge. Somehow, incredibly, the Guardians did not realize it. If only there were some way she could warn them. But she was trapped, locked away like an animal. He probably thought it a good joke. She could imagine the look of amusement that might pass over his face at the thought.

Alexina clenched her fists, and her dry eyes burned. How arrogant he was. How proud of his power, of outwitting the Guardians, of stealing the Stone. She hated his arrogance, his words, *him*, despite the thing in her which urged her not to. She got up from the bed and began to pace back and forth across the room, ignoring the thick carpet that dragged at her feet, the soft chairs that called her to sit in them, and the high bed that urged her to give up the struggle and seek oblivion in sleep. It was hate that kept her going. She would go on hating him. She would never let him use her. She would never be his tool.

Back and forth she paced, back and forth. Persistently, her mind returned to the offer he had made. She knew it was just another way of using her, or perhaps of misleading her through vanity and greed when other methods had failed. Yet somehow she could not dismiss it. *Could* it be true? Marhalt had told her that her power was a fluke, that it could not be exercised away from the Guardians. No, she thought firmly. Bron was lying, trying to trick her. I don't have that kind of power. I couldn't have.

If I did, I could unlock that door right now and walk out of here.

The silence of the house seemed to have increased. Alexina stopped pacing and stared at the door, at the lock that had clicked as Fico shut it behind her. Well, why not? she thought, possessed suddenly by a strange defiance, but also by a hope, a desire she did not dare acknowledge, even to herself. Tentatively, she focused her eyes on the door and sent her mind forward in the way she had done with telepathy. In her head, she built up a picture of a psychic key, an unlocking lock. Nothing seemed to be happening. After a moment, still only half-serious but feeling compelled, she walked forward and tried the handle.

It turned. The door opened under her hand.

Alexina stood perfectly still, staring at the door-knob. Her heart and breath seemed to have stopped. Carefully she closed the door and went back to the bed, her feet silent on the thick carpet. It must have been unlocked all the time, she told herself with calm rationality. Yet with equal rationality, she was completely certain she had heard the turn of the key. I'll just try it one more time, she thought. Again, she sent out her mind, again she got up to try the door, again she turned the knob. This time it did not budge. Incredulously she sent out her mind a final time. Now, she heard a faint click. The door was open.

Alexina felt her legs disappear. She sat down where she was on the carpet, her hands clutching at its deep pile. It's true, she thought. It's true.

Her thoughts seemed to echo slightly, as if suddenly vast spaces had grown inside her mind, great vistas too far to see across. It was as if a curtain she had never known was there had tumbled to the ground. She understood that the place she had always been was only an antechamber, the person she had always thought herself only a fraction of her real self. Why had she never seen it before? Why had her power never manifested itself? Yet she would not have recognized it if it had. She had never understood what power was, not until she encountered the Guardians and learned what it could do . . . or until she encountered Bron and learned what it should not be. It was Bron, though, who had told her of it. She felt confused—how could it be that he had told the truth? And how could Marhalt not have known?

All questions fell away before the existence of power itself. Alexina felt it strong within her, flowing through her body with the rhythm of her blood, filling up the empty waiting spaces. The disguise was gone, the curtain torn asunder, and nothing could ever be the same. She was larger than life, more than human, completely beyond the range of ordinary action. New abilities marched away like mountain ranges. If she could unlock doors, she could knock down walls and reduce stones to rubble. No chain could bind her, no door could close her in. She could do anything. Anything at all. She could even find the Stone.

The power within her gave an answering pulse, sang to a stronger rhythm. Yes. That was what she must do. Alone, she could never have found it, but now, with her power . . . Yet she *was* alone, untried and untrained, power or no. Could she really hope to pit herself against Bron? The enormity of the task rose up before her like a mirage, and she pushed it away. She must at least try. Oh, if she really could do it—rescue the Stone, vanquish Bron, give victory to the Guardians . . . Marhalt would surely forgive her then for her one transgression. She could show him, so that it could never again be denied, that she was not one of the handpower-born. She could give him her power as a willing gift.

Alexina pressed her hands into the carpet to lift

herself to her feet. Now, for the first time, she became aware of something that had been hovering at the edge of her consciousness all the time she sat. There was something strange about the room and its contents. An insubstantiality, an opacity—as if, while still able to see them, she could look right through the velvet curtains and the rose-colored carpet and the papered walls. As if beneath or behind this room lay an entirely different room. This second room was empty, its floor warped and its ceiling rotten. Its walls were stone, its windows narrow slits through which moonlight slid to rest in long silver spears on the dusty floor.

Alexina stared around her, fighting disorientation. Could it be Bron, some illusion wrought through the link? But she could feel no trace of that. Might it be some aspect of her newly found power, then? She did not know why or how, but she was sure both images were real. Somehow she was standing in both rooms, though she herself was not double. Could two realities exist simultaneously in the same space? She felt as if she were dreaming. Yet her mind was very clear, very still, alert, listening.

She could hear silence, suffocating and complete, spreading out through both rooms, both houses. But deep below the silence was something else. She had not sensed it before—it was subliminal, imperceptible unless a certain kind of stillness descended. Perhaps it was only her power, a stillness of the self, that allowed her to sense it now. Strong and steady, it filled up the silence, was inseparable from it, like a river pouring through a subterranean cavern, or the pervasive throb of machinery hidden behind massive walls. It hummed, like a sound—but not quite. It tingled, like electricity—but not quite. It was . . . not corporeal, not something physical at all. A power of some kind. Some force or energy.

It was the Stone.

What Alexina felt now was very different from the muted pulse she had perceived on the ridge or within Marhalt's mind. Yet she recognized it; she knew it beyond the shadow of a doubt. It was as if the Stone were calling out to her, in a language only she could speak. She had not even had to try to find it; it had found her. She was *meant* to rescue it. All doubts and hesitations fell away. She thought of Bron and almost laughed aloud. She hoped she would be there to see his face when he found how utterly he had underestimated her.

Alexina got to her feet, each motion swift and sure. The duality pursued her into the hall. For a moment it brought her up short, for there was no light in that other place. Trying to focus on the tapers that were there in one image, she made her way to the door Taryn had told her was his. She sent out her mind and felt the lock yield.

Like hers, Taryn's room was double, and he too existed in both images. In one he sat on his bed, in the other, moonlit like the room beneath her own, he appeared to be sitting on air. He had changed back into his regular clothing. He looked exhausted. He stared at her stupidly, as if she were an apparition.

"Come on!" she whispered to him.

It took him a moment to respond, but then he rose eagerly to his feet. "How did you get out of your room?"

"Never mind. We can escape now. But first we've got to get the Stone."

"The Stone?" He looked at her as if she were mad. "But it's hidden."

"I know where it is."

"But . . ."

"I tell you, I *know!* I can feel it, all around me. There's no time to explain, Taryn. Just come with me."

There was a pause, and then he nodded slowly. "All right. If you're sure. But what about Bron? He won't let you take it, not just like that."

"Just trust me, Taryn."

He opened his mouth to protest again. But his usual vitality did not seem to be there. Instead, he said in a low voice: "Alexina, I'm sorry."

"What for?"

"For . . . for everything. For . . ." He seemed to be struggling for words. Giving it up, he shook his head. "For everything."

"It's all right, Taryn. You've nothing to be sorry for."

He glanced at her for a moment, then dropped his eyes. "Let's go," he said.

The sense of the Stone grew stronger as they approached the back of the house; it seemed to be focused somewhere near the kitchen. Alexina stopped and closed her eyes to concentrate. She started when Taryn laid his hand on her arm.

"Look." He was pointing to one of the walls. "Are those weapons of some kind?"

She could see past gleaming pots and pans and counters to a ravaged room where grass grew up between the stone flags of the floor. On the wall of the first kitchen hung a rack of guns.

"We need a weapon," said Taryn. He had started determinedly toward the rack.

"Taryn—" But there was no time to argue. Taryn had lifted one of the smaller guns down from the rack. There was authority in his grip, and he held it correctly; he seemed to know instinctively how it worked.

Alexina closed her eyes again, searching for the pulse of power lying below the threshold of thought and feeling. It was very strong now. She was close. The power was like a river, deep and swift, yet somehow less than its full self: There seemed to be a barrier that held it in check. Her mind went out, pushing against the barrier, trying for the starting point. And suddenly she was sure. It came from below, from the basement. She understood now why Bron had been so certain of his hiding place. Weirdly, incongruously, the Stone was somewhere in the computer complex. It would have been conceptually impossible for the Guardians to look there, and she herself would never have done so had it not been for the added dimension of her power.

She turned to Taryn. "Come on," she said. Her words came out slowly, like a record played at the wrong speed. "Downstairs."

"In the room of thinking tools?" he said, wide-eyed. There was skepticism in his face, but as he looked at her the resistance died. He gazed at her as if she were not quite human.

And Alexina no longer felt human. She felt doubled, like the house, though not on the physical plane. Her normal everyday self was there, but there was also another self. Her powerself, a self she neither knew nor understood, a self that was drawn to the source of that great power as a drop of water is drawn toward a sponge. She turned and moved toward the basement door, white-painted wood in one house, dark mildewed planks in the other. She began to descend the dark stairs. Opening the second door, she stood still, blinded by the brilliant white light of the room. For a moment she swayed and would have fallen if Taryn had not steadied her from behind.

"Are you all right?"

She did not answer. The force of the Stone, concentrated here, swallowed her. There was still that sense of blockage, of . . . dormancy, almost as if the Stone were asleep, its power dimmed. Alexina pulled away from Taryn. There were the banks of equipment, the console with its dark screen, the long fluorescent tubes. . . . She could see them, and through them into utter darkness. In the center of the room stood the metal scaffold and its burden of tangled circuitry. Here was the center of the power. Somewhere within that strange jumble lay the Stone.

She became aware that something restrained her: Taryn's hands on her arms, holding her back. He was speaking, shaking his head. He did not want her to do something. With fierce strength Alexina shook him off. The power grew as she approached the center of the room; she bent her body against its force. Gaining the gleaming scaffold she grasped it with both arms, pulling herself against it as if she might be swept away. She reached out and laid a hand on the circuitry. Abruptly, all resistance disappeared. It was like reaching into the eye of a hurricane.

The construction before her was asymmetrical, messy, complicated, like something built by a child. Tentatively, and then with more assurance, she began to pull it to pieces, unplugging circuits and detaching wires, working her way toward its heart.

In a cavity at the very center lay the Stone. It was a rough opaque globe about the size of a man's head, tourmaline green in color, faintly iridescent. Alexina looked at it, and as she did, an incredible thing happened. The duality disappeared. The Stone, present in both images, united them; the Stone, seen through the eyes of both her selves, united her. It was as simple as that. Alexina took a deep breath. She reached her hands carefully into the tunnel she had created, to lift the Stone from its prison.

As she touched it, the Stone awoke. It *had* been asleep, a sleep artificially induced. Released, its pent-up power burst free with enormous force. The torrent of its rising consciousness rolled over the room, inundating the house, rushing toward the far corners of the world. Alexina stood immobile, both hands on the Stone still encased in circuitry. Her mind was caught in the tide, swept up by the irresistible current of awakening. She seemed to see with the eyes of the Stone, to *be* the Stone as, rising toward full awareness, the tale of its existence unreeled before her.

It began in darkness, blankness, for even the Stone did not know its origin. Alexina saw it on the earth before the birth of man, alone but not lonely, unaware of time. It contemplated itself, the immutable range of its power, the totality of its knowledge, the rhythms of existence. In its nature it was like a still and bottomless lake into which poured thousands upon thousands of tributaries: perceptions, events, conditions, all the minutiae of the earth and everything in and on it. From this lake an immense river reached out again into the world, all the tributaries consolidated and combined into one titanic force of pure power. Flowing out and flowing in, in perfect balance and endless cycle, the Stone drew breath for the world and was its breathing. In its center all things existed, and of all existing things it was the center.

Now Alexina saw the rise of man, the addition of another tributary to the unceasing flow of all the others. She saw the birth and development of the two great powers through which the human race controlled and shaped the world into which it came. Mindpower and handpower were equal then, each supreme within its own sphere of knowledge, each used according to inclination and ability. Their interplay was a concrete expression of the great balance of existence, a unity of invisible and visible.

Eventually man discovered the Stone. He did not understand it, for no power on earth could compare to it, thouqh dimly he sensed its nature. Not realizing it could not be possessed, he appropriated it. The world grew, kings and kingdoms rose and crumbled into dust, the Stone passed from hand to hand; it became a cycle as regular and integral as all the others. In time man even found a way to use the Stone. Through his psychic abilities he learned to tap into the vast continuum of its knowledge and glean small bits of information useful to himself.

Through it all, the Stone contemplated, unaffected. These small incursions were no more than a fleabite on the hide of an elephant. Wherever it was placed, it was still the center; wherever it was hidden, the rhythms of being pulsed unbroken and the harmonies of existence joined to form the boundless song of wholeness. But a time came when this could no longer be so. Alexina saw the kingdom of Arthur, the last and greatest flowering of totality, the final breath of a world in which the two powers which had shaped existence for so long were held together. Already the strains which would tear the world apart were growing throughout the other lands. With Arthur's death, the seal of change was set forever. The order which had held for eons melted away like salt in a rainstorm.

Now Alexina saw the breaking apart, the anarchy, the confusion and chaos; she watched the descent of the dark ages upon both emerging worlds. She saw Percival wrest the Stone from Bron's ancestor and carry it into the world of mindpower. She saw him place it in the Fortress, walled amid the peaks of an inaccessible mountain range. There Percival and those of his men who survived the perilous passage set themselves to become Guardians. They reached out to their frightened people, bringing the answers, bringing the Stone, bringing the Limits.

More ages passed. As before, the Stone was used—in that, nothing had changed. But for the first time, reality itself was not the same. Still the motions of the living world flowed into the Stone, still they were consolidated, still they poured out again. Yet this was not the same world. A vital piece of the continuum was missing. The harmonies had lost their richness, the rhythms become sour and syncopated. Existence was diminished: The Stone knew itself diminished with it. And the splintering continued; once begun, it was a process that could not be stemmed. Even as the diversity of this world increased, portions of it dropped away. Man called it history, progress. The Stone knew it was only loss.

One day a man came and lifted the Stone from the place where it had lain for so long. He carried it through a Gate into another world. Through his great power, the man cast the Stone into sleep. But no power compared with the Stone's. Though this man imprisoned it, he could not neutralize it; though he took it from the waking state, the sleep into which it fell was not complete. The Stone was aware that it was now surrounded by a weblike superstructure, harnessed to strange devices that were dormant like itself. Dimly, it sensed that the currents of the world it now inhabited were different currents, the minds different minds. But this world too was only a thin and drifting portion of what had once been an ineffable whole.

Awakening, surrounded by the awakening devices, the Stone expanded to fill this new world; it could not do otherwise. But with awareness came the knowledge that at last the unthinkable had occurred. Expanding, awake, it was even now no longer free. The great river of its power had been dammed, blocked, channeled away from the world and into the devices to which it was harnessed. For the first time, after centuries of attempts, the Stone had been truly enslaved. There were no more rhythms at all, only the metallic and unlovely clattering of the prison-machines.

If the Stone had been human, it would have despaired. It was not human. Yet in its own way it lamented its imprisonment, the splintering of the worlds, the vanished tranquility. It yearned for the symmetry of its contemplation at the beginning of time, when all had been balanced and man had not yet learned to shape what was. It was tired. It wished to be left alone, to be free, to be whole. At the end of memory and experience lay only desolation and loss.

Knowledge of loss flooded into Alexina as she stood with her hands on the Stone, and she knew that what was gone was more valuable than all that remained. She *was* the Stone; she saw what it saw, and its sadness was her own. Yet in a strange split vision, she still saw with the eyes of her human self. She was still aware of the room around her, of the clattering machinery, of Taryn watching her from beside the open door. This part of her heard footsteps pound overhead, down the stairs; this part of her saw Bron arrive on the threshold. Taryn also saw. He swung around, the gun in his hands. He hesitated. It was only a fraction of a second, but it was enough for Bron to act. Catlike, he launched himself toward Taryn and wrenched the gun away, holding it by the barrel. Unbalanced, Taryn fell backward. Bron raised the gun and slashed it down; it bounced off Taryn's upraised arm and struck him a glancing blow on the neck. Only his fall saved him. The full force of the blow might have killed him, and even the deflection rendered him unconscious.

For a moment Bron was still, bent over Taryn, his black hair falling forward over his face. He was breathing hard. Then he straightened. He shook back his hair. He looked at Alexina.

"Come, Alexina." His voice was quiet, calm, borne to her ears on a tide of machine noise, piercing faintly through the roar of existence that flooded the senses of the Stone. He was advancing on her, still holding the gun, his steps slow and careful. "Take your hands away from the Stone. You're not strong enough yet. It will kill you. You must take your hands away, Alexina. You *must.*"

But Alexina's mind, fused to the awareness of the Stone, was expanding even as he spoke, her human self left ever farther behind. Into her, as into the Stone, poured the whole enormity of the living earth, the particulars of every human consciousness, the spark of every consciousness that was not human. It was her skin men blasted as they mined and built, her body they poisoned with waste, her eyes they blinded with fumes, her soul they divided with ignorance. With the eyes of the Stone she saw her own vulnerable human body, standing helpless in a basement room, frozen as Bron approached. Yet she saw not just this small room, but all the rooms and spaces that had ever existed. She saw not just one man, but billions upon billions of men. She saw not just one power, but all of the mighty rivers of power that inundated the world. And she knew, as the Stone knew, that in the endless chain of existence and eternity this moment was a single small flash; in the ceaseless interplay of being and time, she and Bron would meet and act and then exist no more.

She saw Bron's dark eyes, locked to the eyes of her frail human self. She saw him halt, abruptly, as if his feet had fixed themselves to the floor. He swayed slightly, as if straining to hold his own against a force which threatened to push him back. She saw his face pale with the dawning of knowledge, with the impact of vision. She knew that he could go no farther. And she knew why: Her eyes were no longer her own. They belonged to the Stone. When he looked into her eyes, Bron saw the great pattern of infinity. And against infinity, he was helpless.

The Stone had achieved complete consciousness at last. For an instant the balance held, the knife edge between the Stone's enormous vision and the small mind it held captive. But it was only an instant. Alexina's human self began to shake asunder, disintegrating under the stress of too great a perception. Dimly she was aware that she must break free if she were to survive, if her consciousness were not to fly apart and scatter itself like volcanic ash over the surface of the world. But it was too late. She was a piece of debris upon a river, caught up in a current that swept her toward the rapids and the final darkness that lay ahead. And even as her human self cried out in terror, her power-self surrendered. It did not wish to be free. It wished to be one with the Stone, to become forever a part of the wellspring of power.

With her dissolving human vision, Alexina saw a growing expression of horror on Bron's face. He wrenched himself forward, the gun no longer in his hands, reaching out for her, but now two great shapes materialized on either side of him, engulfing his arms. Too late he struggled, but he was held fast. A familiar figure grew larger, moving toward her . . . the last shreds of selfhood recognized Marhalt. She felt him grasp her wrists and lift her hands away from the Stone.

The mindlink broke. It was like the snapping of a straining rope, flinging her on a wide arc into unconsciousness. With her went the last image of all, Bron's dark eyes, bitter with defeat.

16

Alexina swam up through the murky waters of unconsciousness, like a diver who has gone too deep and no longer knows where to find air. For a while she drifted in and out, aware now and then of voices, lights, motion. Surfacing at last, she opened her eyes, squinting although the light was dim, not sure for a moment where she was. The computer room had disappeared. She was propped up on a couch in the huge parlor on the first floor. The duality of the house was no longer present, nor was the exalted state of mind in which she had perceived it. She was confused, her thoughts muddy and slow, and she ached all over in a strange nonphysical way, as if her very soul were bruised. What had happened? Painfully, she recalled sensing the Stone, following it down into the computer room. She remembered putting her hands on it. She had . . . merged with it then. She could remember very little of that, only a parade of pictures not her own, a horrifying feeling of hugeness and disintegration. . . .

Hearing voices, she turned her head, and her eyes came to rest on Marhalt. Marhalt? Vaguely, with a pain that knifed through her mind, she could recall his form emerging from the blur of disintegration. He had lifted her hands away, and freed her from the Stone. He had rescued her. Alexina felt peace flood through her, easing the pain, washing away the confusion and fear. It was all over. She was safe now.

Marhalt's back was turned; he was standing in front of a chair, obscuring its occupant. Close-by, Loran held the arms of Bron's servant Fico in a tight grip. Gwynys stood next to him. A little away from the group, Taryn lay against the arm of a couch. He seemed to be unconscious.

Marhalt moved, and Alexina saw that the occupant of the chair was Bron. He sat very still, his eyes closed, his head thrown against the high back of the seat. Against the dark fabric his skin looked supernaturally pale, almost translucent. His hands lay limply in his lap. Astonishingly, all his arrogance and vitality were gone. He looked not like himself at all, but like an ordinary man—a defeated man.

Marhalt was speaking in the Guardians' language, sharply, quickly. Bron replied, his eyes still closed, his voice soft and weary. He spoke for a time. The Guardians listened without expression, but Alexina could sense from their rigid bodies that they were appalled by what they heard. At length Marhalt spoke a word and made a gesture, cutting Bron off. Bron's eyes opened. For a moment he stared at Marhalt, and then his gaze shifted, moved beyond the Guardians. Alexina realized he was looking at her. For just an instant something flashed in his face. But Marhalt caught the look. He turned, and saw that Alexina was awake. At once he moved over to where she lay. She looked up at him, drawing in the strength of his presence.

"How are you?" he said gently in English.

"All right." Her voice was a croak. She cleared her throat. "What . . . what happened?"

"His power broke—it must have been as you

touched the Stone. We breached the hedge and entered the house. He was not aware of us, and when he was, it was too late."

"So . . . we've won. . . ."

"Yes, we have won. There's just one more thing left to do. Then we can leave this place."

There was something she should be remembering . . . "Wait, the link—what about the link?"

"It will go. Rest now, Alexina."

He rose and crossed the room. Alexina watched him. He had been gentle, yet there was something. She did not know why, but she was afraid again.

Marhalt spoke to Bron. Alexina felt ice in his tone, as deep as a long winter. In response Bron smiled slightly, but with infinite scorn. He said something. Alexina received the impression that had Marhalt not been who he was, he would have struck him. Being Marhalt, however, he merely stood very still for a moment. Flatly, he spoke again. He gestured to Gwynys and Loran, who came forward and blocked Bron from Alexina's view. They joined hands. She heard Marhalt's voice again, and their voices answering in unison. They bent their heads. The air around them trembled slightly—they were linking, gathering power, preparing for some act.

Alexina was not sure at what point she noticed a change. It was not the Guardians who had changed, though they stood like statues, nor the power, for she could still feel it. Puzzled, she watched the little group. The air around them no longer shimmered; rather, it held a strange translucent immobility, as if it were an encasement of clear crystal.

A dreadful suspicion began to grow, taking shape even as the Guardians moved aside, their steps heavy, like automatons. Alexina saw Bron now, still sitting in his chair, exactly as he had been before. But this was no longer a defeated man. His eyes were open; the weariness had left him as if it had been wiped away, and all his power had returned. She could see it in his white face, shining against the darkness of its background. He looked as he had the first time she had seen him, in the link-dream: calm, brilliant, powerful. He was gazing directly at Alexina, and in his eyes she seemed to read triumph.

Alexina's bruised mind could not make sense of it. Where was the beaten exhaustion she had just seen? What had he done to the Guardians? Heads bent, faces shadowed, they looked like obedient mannequins—even Marhalt. Taryn, on the couch, was still unconscious. Bron rose from his chair and began to move toward her. Caught in the path of those black eyes, she was unable to stir.

Reaching her, he knelt by her side. His face wore an expression of concern.

"Are you all right, Alexina? You shouldn't be awake yet, you know."

She looked at him, unable to speak.

"It was very foolish of you to do that, but of course you don't understand the Stone. You're lucky you were freed in time, before your mind was destroyed. Only the nature of your power allowed you to survive as long as you did."

"Why should you care?" she whispered, her tongue rasping against the roof of her mouth. "You were going to kill me."

He actually looked surprised. For a moment he did not speak. Then he shook his head. "I was trying to rescue you when they stopped me. I care about your life, about your power, Alexina. Why should I have broken my concentration and risked capture if I didn't? I could have simply let it destroy you. The Guardians would still be outside if I had."

"You didn't know," she whispered. "When you looked at me, you couldn't move."

A shadow passed across his face, briefly. "Yes. I've never seen it before, another human being in link with the Stone. Those who link wear cloak and hood. It's an ancient tradition, but I see the reason for it now."

Alexina looked beyond him at the Guardians. She saw that their eyes were open and alive. She looked at Bron again, and as she did so her gaze swept across the couch where Taryn had lain. It was empty. She struggled to control a sudden surge of hope. She must play for time. If she could make him angry, unwary . . .

"I beat you," she whispered. "You and your secrets. I found the Stone. I woke it up."

Bron shook his head, unperturbed. "I admit I didn't expect you to break through to your power so soon, for after last night I was sure you weren't ready yet. But I'm not angry with you—I respect you for it. I have always respected your courage. As for finding the Stone—well, once you found your power, you could not help but sense the Stone. And I would have woken it myself, once the Guardians were taken care of. We're a bit ahead of schedule, that's all."

"What have you done to them?"

"I've put them in stasis."

"Will you . . . will you kill them?"

"No. There's no point to such violence. In any case, they can be useful. I'll plant a compulsion in them. They won't realize it until they've already passed through the Gate. They know about me now, about my power and my plans. They will return to their fellows and tell them. It will prepare my way."

"You're playing with them," Alexina whispered. "You have been all along."

"Yes," he said simply.

"But they'll come back."

"Yes. It may be necessary in time to move on to another place."

"They'll defeat you. They *will.*"

"No. That they can never do." Bron shook his head gently. "Alexina, you are still tied to them. It is understandable, for with them you found the first traces of your power. But they have deceived you. They lied to you about the link, about the nature of your power. They used you. They do not want you to have what is rightfully yours, just as they would not have allowed me to have it had they known. In time you will understand." He got to his feet and held out his hand. "Come now. Let me take you up to your room where you can rest comfortably. You need sleep to heal your mind."

She shrank away, pressing herself down into the velvet of the couch. "No. I don't want to come with you."

He sighed. "You might as well come willingly. You're in no condition to resist."

"No!" She squeezed her eyes shut. "Please let me go. Let me be free."

There was silence for a moment, and then she felt the air move as he knelt beside her again. "I see you have reached your power but not your will. You're still afraid; you don't yet know what you want. You must trust me in this, Alexina. I know you better than you know yourself. I know what you desire, and I can give it to you, your power and all the uses of it."

"You just want to use me. It's my power. I have the right to use it for myself! I'd rather not have it at all!"

"But you cannot use it yourself. You don't know

how. You will never be able to develop it as it should be developed. That would be a terrible thing, a terrible waste."

"I'll take that chance."

"Alexina," he said. His voice was gentle. "You don't know it yet, but you aren't part of your world. You're not like your people, any more than you're like the Guardians. What would you do with your power, alone in a place where every element of common sense tells your people nothing like it can exist? Your world is still as ignorant as the Guardians think it is. Can you imagine the burden of struggling against all that ignorance? Believe me, you're better off here, no matter what you think of me. When you have fully reached your power, then you can make the choice."

"I can't ever make a choice and you know it. Because of the link."

"Agree to stay here, swear on your power, and I will break the link at once and let you go forever."

"I don't believe you. You're lying."

"I have not lied to you, Alexina. I have told you the truth in everything."

But she could feel the link. He was using it even as he offered to break it, even as he protested that he had not lied. She could feel that coldness at the center of her mind, the strain of the pull that worked against all the resistance of her conscious will. Despair overwhelmed her, and she felt her bones turn to water. He was too powerful. She could not break away. It had been too long to hope for Taryn now. Gathering her last shreds of defiance, she met his dark eyes.

"No matter what happens, you'll never use me. I'll never help you with your plans, whatever they are. I won't make it easy for you in anything."

Still he was not angry. "In time," he said, "you will change your mind." Again he got to his feet. "No more talk now," he said firmly. "You need rest. Can you walk, or shall I carry you?"

Alexina shuddered. She would walk if it killed her. Brushing past the hand he held out to help her, she raised herself painfully to a sitting position, and swung her legs to the floor.

There was a sound from the direction of the hall. Bron whirled, catlike. Taryn stood in the doorway, pale, unsteady on his feet. In his hands he held the gun.

"Stop," he said. His voice was strained, almost unrecognizable. "Don't touch her."

There was a silence. Slowly Bron relaxed his tense stance and smoothed the momentary expression of surprise from his face.

"Well, well," he said. "You are very clever, Taryn. I didn't sense you at all."

"We know about barriers, don't we," said Taryn, his hoarse voice tense with hatred. "You're not as smart as you think you are. Now move away from her."

There was a pause and then, slowly, Bron stepped some distance away from Alexina, closer to Taryn. He stopped. Alexina sensed something, a building tension.

"Now release the Guardians," said Taryn, gesturing with the gun. "Go on, do it."

Bron was stepping toward Taryn again, very slowly. Alexina realized what she was sensing: He was gathering his power, concentrating his force. He was going to put Taryn in stasis too. She struggled to find her voice, to get to her feet, to warn him.

"You're being very foolish, Taryn," Bron was saying. His voice was calm, hypnotic. "Put the gun down before you hurt yourself. You don't know how to use it."

Taryn was backing away from him, his eyes fixed and wide. "Stay away," he tried to say, but it came out as a rasping whisper. "Stand still. I'm warning you."

Alexina sagged where she sat. It was over; Taryn would not shoot. Bron had won and he knew it. She could see it in the set of his body, hear it in the triumphant calm of his voice. He was even enjoying himself.

"Come now, Taryn. Put the gun down. You can stay with us, you know. I will train Alexina to her power, and I will train you to this world. There is so much to know, so many wonders to discover. Think about it. Think about the questions you've asked, Taryn, about having them answered. I know you better than you know yourself, because we are the same, you and I. You too were meant to come to me—"

Several things happened at once then. Thinking about it later, Alexina could not separate them, or remember the order in which they had occurred. She saw Bron advancing on Taryn, Taryn backing away, his eyes dilated and blank. She heard Bron's voice, quiet, cadenced, dropping almost to a whisper on his last words. As he spoke them he let loose a bolt of immobilizing power. But at the same moment a wild awareness returned to Taryn's face. Exactly then, almost as if in reflex, he fired the gun, even as the power knocked him to the floor. Bron cried out and crumpled, clutching his knee. Simultaneously, Alexina felt a tremendous impact in her own knee. It was her turn to cry out, instinctively grabbing at her leg. She looked at it, thinking that somehow the bullet had hit her too, expecting to see blood and shattered tissue—but the fabric of her jeans was unmarked and beneath her fingers her knee was whole. Still that unbelievable pain gripped her leg, spreading downward to wrap her calf in agony.

As Bron fell, something in the room snapped. Enclosed in pain, Alexina was aware of voices, motion. Hands gripped her shoulders, and through her tears, she looked up to see Marhalt. Behind him were the other Guardians, now free.

"What is it? What do you feel?" he was saying. Alexina could only gasp and clutch her knee. Marhalt pried her hands away and examined it. He turned and spoke over his shoulder. "The link," he said. "It must be broken, at once."

Hands lifted Alexina from the couch and carried her over to where Bron lay on the polished oak floorboards, his blood a spreading pool beneath him. Briefly, Alexina saw Taryn, sitting shakily in the doorway; Fico, his mouth open in a soundless cry, struggled in the grip of Loran. Alexina was lowered to the floor beside Bron. Squinting through her pain, she saw his face twisted in agony, a gray film overlaying its pallor. He was breathing in shallow gasps.

"Alexina." It was Marhalt. Alexina tried to listen to him. "It's the link that's making you feel this. You aren't hurt, but because of the link you're feeling his pain. Do you understand me?" Struggling for comprehension, Alexina nodded. "Now, in order to be free of the pain, you must break the link. If you don't you'll go on feeling it—and if he dies, you may die too. Do you understand? Do you?" Alexina nodded again. "We'll help you. We'll lend you our power. But to break the link, both people must be willing. You must wear down his will, make him *want* to let you go. Then, only then, can you be free. We'll try to lessen your pain so you can concentrate. Look into his eyes now. The link will tell you where to go."

Marhalt stooped and put his hands on either side of Bron's face, turning it so his eyes were toward Alexina. She did not think to be afraid of the link. She wished only to be rid of the agony in her leg. She sensed the rhythms of power in the air around her, aware that her pain was less, at least enough to make it possible to concentrate on something besides the hurt. As she looked into Bron's eyes, letting the cold of the link take her, she became aware of the pain as a separate thing, as Bron's pain rather than her own. She could feel the blood ebbing from his shattered knee. She could feel the rage of his helplessness. And she knew that he did not wish to let her go. He was fighting her; more than that, he was entangling her in the link, despite the pain that impaired his power. Too late, she realized what was happening. Panicked, she tried to pull away—but she was held fast, encased in the growing cold. His eyes pulled her in, told her to let go, to surrender her will to his. *You want to,* his eyes told her. *I know your true wish.* She felt herself weakening; the link pulled her inexorably forward.

There was a commotion, a struggle. From nowhere Taryn threw himself on Bron, grasping the dark robe in both hands, lifting him off the floor. Taryn's face was white, his eyes almost as black as Bron's.

"Let her go!" he half-cried, half-whispered, his voice completely strange. "Let her go, you pig! Let her go!"

Only seconds behind, Gwynys pounced on Taryn, breaking his grip, heaving him to his feet and holding his arms behind his back. She dragged Taryn away. There were a few scuffling sounds, and silence.

But the balance had shifted. Taryn's outburst had shaken free Alexina's will to resist, and the violent motion created a shattering surge of agony that engulfed Bron's senses like a tidal wave. Suddenly Alexina was able to stand firm, to pull back in equal measure to the forward impetus of the link. Deadlocked, an endless moment passed. Alexina could feel Bron struggling against his pain, striving for the concentration that would allow him again to beguile her; she feared her advantage would not last long. Desperately she gathered together everything she felt for him—her revulsion for the link, her hatred of his attempt to use her, her disgust for his motives and plans, her fear of his person. She concentrated it within herself and sent it out against him like a thrown fist. It hit him like the pain from his knee, and she saw the expression in his eyes alter—not to anger, not to surprise, but to something very much like . . . loss.

Time seemed to stop. And then, at last, Alexina felt something new. Bron's grip was easing. The cold was decreasing. He was letting go! She could still feel that he was stronger than she, yet he no longer tried to hold her. Did he understand? Had he allowed her to make a choice at last?

There was no answer. But as he receded, for a revealing instant she saw fully inside his mind. She saw his desire for the redress of centuries of wrong, his passion for change, his determination to smash the stratifying rock of tradition. She saw his belief in what he had taken it upon himself to do. She felt his rage at the destruction of careful plans, his despair at the dissolution of a great hope and the foundering of a structure upon the smallest of oversights. She felt the pain of failure, greater than all the physical pain in the world. And finally, she saw her own power through the medium of his mind: a beacon among candles, the possibility of partnership, the basis of devisings such as no one had ever dreamed. Stricken before the force of his emotions, Alexina could not pull away. They washed through her, shaking her to the core. It was as if he were giving her this glimpse on purpose, to show her what she was throwing away.

The pain was overwhelming his senses. He could no longer fight unconsciousness. He wanted it to be over, he wanted the pain to end. Abruptly it was all gone, and Alexina felt only the receding chill of the link. It was going now, dwindling, a pinpoint, but before it winked out of existence entirely, for an instant the dark eyes flashed faintly with their old light. It was just the barest breath, the tiniest spark. Alexina told herself later she must have imagined it.

It was gone now, all of it. Even the pain. Alexina moved slightly, experimentally. She was free.

She felt nothing now but exhaustion. She sagged as Marhalt drew her to her feet. Her legs would not support her. He gestured to Loran, who came and lifted her in his arms. She rested her head on his shoulder and closed her eyes.

Distantly she heard Marhalt speak. "There's nothing left to do now. She has breached his barriers. We can go."

With effort Alexina raised her head. "You can't just leave him like that," she said. "He's bleeding. . . . He needs a doctor—"

Marhalt looked at her. There was something in his eyes she had never seen before, and it told her to be silent. Loran began to carry her from the room. Over his shoulder, she saw Marhalt stoop to lift a large round object wrapped in a leather pouch. He gestured to Gwynys, who took Taryn's arm and guided him forward. Taryn's face was white as paper, his eyes vacant; he walked shamblingly along, unresisting.

Beyond them, Bron's crumpled figure lay twisted on its side, head thrown back, eyes closed. Fico was kneeling beside him, ministering to his knee. Alexina felt tears gathering in her eyes and rolling down her cheeks. She was not sure why she cried, nor of the source of the dreadful sadness she felt.

17

On the border between sleep and waking, Alexina dreamed. She saw a room without doors that was a shrine and a prison, a room filled to the ceiling with all the sadness of the world. The dream dispersed, but it left behind a feeling of distant pain. She started awake, sitting up and looking around her as if the stone walls might still be there. Instead she saw trees and grass, flooding sunlight, and the Guardians.

It all came rushing back: Bron, the locked room, the realization of her power, the Stone, Taryn with the gun. And with an incredible feeling of release, she realized that it was really over this time. Bron was truly vanquished. The Stone was rescued. And the link was broken.

Around her stretched the familiar shimmer of the barrier. Beyond it lay an open field golden with early afternoon sun; above it arched a blue sky heaped with clouds. A breeze whispered outside and the drone of a distant airplane was faintly audible. Around the fire, the Guardians sat immobile in meditation, surrounded by their camping gear. A pot was bubbling softly. Taryn lay wrapped in his blankets a short distance away.

Alexina breathed deeply, drinking in the peaceful familiarity. The nightmare of the past few days might never have occurred. It was as if something tightly knotted within her had been released, and it took her a moment to recognize this not as a feeling, but as the absence of one—the absence of fear. No longer did she need to ward off the link, the bewitchments of Bron. The woods beyond the camp were not pines, and the air was warm and filled with pleasant sounds. She was free.

Gwynys opened her eyes. She rose from her crosslegged position, filled a bowl from the steaming pot, and brought it over.

"Eat this," she said. "You must regain your strength."

Alexina took the bowl eagerly; she was ravenous. "How long have I been asleep?" she asked.

"Two days."

"Two *days?*"

"Your mind was badly taxed by the things that happened to you."

She turned abruptly and went back to the fire. Alexina watched her for a moment, puzzled. Gwynys had never been overly friendly, but her manner today was positively cold.

The other Guardians were stirring now, and Alexina watched as Marhalt and Loran got to their feet. Taryn too was extricating himself from his blankets. They put on their boots, and Marhalt picked up the leather pouch with its burden. Then the three passed in single file through the barrier, disappearing into the stand of trees that rose beyond the camp. They had not even glanced toward Alexina. Gwynys remained behind. She was staring into the fire, not meditating, but quite unapproachable even so.

It was curious. But Alexina felt too good to worry about anything. She ate slowly, savoring the warmth of the sun, the freshness of the air, the soft noises of the world outside the barrier. Gwynys appeared to be completely abstracted, but as soon as Alexina placed her empty bowl on the ground she was on her feet.

"Are you fit enough to walk now?" she asked.

Alexina got up, a little unsteadily at first, but the dizziness passed quickly. She nodded.

"Follow me, then."

They moved through the barrier into the woods. The sun was left behind.

"Where are we going?"

"You'll see when we get there."

"Nothing's wrong, is it? Is the Stone all right?"

"The Stone is safe."

"So . . . everything's okay?"

Gwynys nodded. She was walking faster now, and something in her bearing communicated the fact that she did not wish to talk. It was curious, but again Alexina let it go. She was content with what her senses brought her as they walked: the thud of their steps, the clean and slightly damp smell of leaves and vegetation, the single shafts of sun piercing the canopy of branches at intervals and stippling the ground underfoot.

They came at last to a little clearing. Alexina saw Loran and Marhalt sitting side by side on the ground. Taryn stood before them, his back turned. His head was bowed and his hands hung empty at his sides. Well ahead by now, Gwynys had already reached the other Guardians. She seated herself next to Loran.

It was Taryn's stance which first caught Alexina's attention and alerted her to something wrong. She came to a halt beside him, glancing at him sidelong. His face was pale and still, and he did not acknowledge her presence. She felt her skin prickle. There was a heaviness in the air, as if a storm were about to break.

"We have been waiting for you, Alexina. There is something you must witness."

Alexina's breath caught in her throat. Marhalt's words fell like hard, separate stones into the silence and his voice, very quiet, seemed to carry everywhere. His face was smooth and expressionless, yet somehow its very immobility was more intimidating than any emotion. His topaz eyes were like gems, brilliant and refractive. Before him lay the leather pouch. Alexina knew it contained the Stone, though she could no longer sense it.

Marhalt transferred his gaze to Taryn. "Come forward," he said.

Taryn obeyed, his steps jerky and mechanical.

"Take off your medallions."

Taryn's hands went to the chains around his neck and drew them over his head. He held out his arm and dropped the medallions on the ground between himself and Marhalt.

Marhalt spoke a few words to the others in their own language. They turned their eyes in unison upon the fallen medallions. There was a pause, and then, suddenly, the medallions burst into blue flame. It lasted only a second or two. When the flames winked out, the medallions were a twisted lump of metal, streaked with charring and smoking slightly from the great heat that had destroyed them.

"Take them up now, Taryn."

Again Taryn obeyed, stooping to the metal, picking it up without any sign of pain, slipping it into the pouch at his belt.

"You will carry this metal with you for the prescribed time, a symbol of our shame. When the day comes, you will bury it outside the Fortress, deep within the defiled ground. You may step back now."

Taryn did so. Alexina turned her head to look at his face. It was mottled red and pale. His eyes met hers, just for an instant. In them she saw blank despair and terrible humiliation, and very far behind it all, the dull glow of a banked and smouldering rage. Shocked, she looked at Marhalt.

"Do you understand what has happened here, Alexina?"

She shook her head.

"The medallions were the badges of Taryn's rank—as an apprentice to the Brotherhood of Guardians, and as an apprentice to the Suborder of Journeyers. We have destroyed them. Even the metal is tainted. It will be buried deep and never reclaimed. Taryn will never wear the silver again."

"You . . . you mean he can't be a Guardian anymore?"

"Yes."

"But . . . but why? Why now?"

"The medallions cannot be worn after they are forfeit. We waited only for you to wake, for you have a part in this."

"But what has Taryn done?"

Marhalt watched her, his face as still as granite. Beside him, Loran's and Gwynys's features mirrored his own.

"He touched and used a forbidden instrument. There in that house."

"You mean the *gun?*" A pause; no answer. "But he didn't even know what it was! And it was my fault, you shouldn't blame him—"

"We could not expect you to know better." Marhalt's voice was implacably calm. "But Taryn is—was—a Guardian. He knows the tenets of our Brotherhood. He performed a forbidden act in full knowledge that it was forbidden. There can be no forgiveness for his behavior."

Alexina shook her head, not believing what she was hearing. "But he saved my life! All our lives. If he hadn't used the gun we would still be Bron's prisoners, and he would still have the Stone!"

"Taryn performed a forbidden act. There were other options open to him. He chose not to use them. If it were an isolated action, rehabilitation might be possible, but as the culmination of a history of difficulties, that cannot be considered. In that house Taryn chose handpower over the power that is his heritage and his sacred trust."

"But he couldn't just stand by and do nothing!"

Marhalt simply looked at her, and at last the look dried the words of protest in her mouth. Could it really matter more that Taryn had used the gun than that he had saved them all, and risked his life to do so? Surely Marhalt could not be so unjust, so unkind—surely the Marhalt who had helped her through the journey and taken her hands from the Stone could not be so uncompassionate.

It was very quiet under the trees. The still faintly audible drone of the airplane touched the silence like a dream. The leaves moved on their branches, casting an ever-shifting pattern of shadow across the faces of the three Guardians. Alexina could feel the myriad patterns of significance that drifted around their little group, meanings beyond her grasp. And she felt a breath of real fear, like a cold hand laid along her cheek. Reality seemed to be shifting with the patterns of the leaves, and suddenly she did not know where she was. The man who sat before her was not Marhalt at all, but a stranger who wore his face.

"We come now to your transgression."

Alexina swallowed against the dryness of her throat. "Mine?"

"Yours. I tell you this only because I feel you should know what you cast aside through your disobedience. Punishment is not for you, for you are not one of us, and in a sense you are not responsible for your actions. But you must know what you have done."

His voice beat against her ears, and she had to strain to follow what he said.

"In all the time of this journey I gave you one order, one only. Yet you could not obey it. Why?"

Alexina struggled to control the tremor in her voice. "He . . . he hypnotized me. Through the link. He made me forget. I . . . I didn't know what I was doing. When I realized, it was too late—I was already inside . . ." Her words trailed off. The excuses sounded miserable even to herself, for she knew very well she had failed to be sufficiently on guard. Marhalt's unshifting eyes made her feel small and worthless.

"That is not why, Alexina. My order came to you through the power. Your power understood and remembered, even if your conscious mind did not. It was impossible for you to forget the order; you could only disobey it. Perhaps you really were not conscious of your motives. But your power acted for you, whether you knew it or not. Like called to like. The link could never have compelled you had you truly desired it not to."

"No," said Alexina, her voice weak. "No, it's not true."

"I gave you that order for a reason. In you there seemed to be power. Power like ours, I thought at first, despite the paradox of your background, power that could be nurtured and even freed from the corruption this world had wrought in you. You passed certain tests; you were brave and obedient along the journey. It all seemed to indicate good things. I allowed you to grow accustomed to the idea of power and to the variety of its uses. And then I imposed a real test. If your power had been like ours, if it had been true, my order would have been obeyed." He seemed to hesitate for a moment. When he spoke again his voice was softer. "I cannot say that I did not wish it to be so, Alexina. Perhaps for that reason I gave an order that should have been easy to follow. I gave you every chance of success."

Suddenly she could see again the Marhalt she knew, present behind the still face of the stranger. Desperately she reached out, calling to the man who had answered her questions, who had revealed to her the secrets of his world, who had comforted her through her fear of the link.

"Why didn't you tell me, Marhalt? Why didn't you let me know?"

He shook his head slowly. "Then the test would not have been a test. It was necessary that you obey or disobey *of your own nature,* not because you knew what was at stake. I could not have done it any other way." His face was closing again, anything familiar disappearing, leaving behind the rigid shell that locked away emotion. "And of your own nature, you disobeyed me. Because of that, you have forfeited all that might have come to you. And I know now that I was wrong. Your power is not like ours. It is not true. It is corrupt, a twisted reflection of real power, a horrible manifestation of your world and the forces in it. It was what was corrupt in you that *he* could reach, and through it, bring you to him. Your corruption has tainted everything you have touched. Taryn's difficulties were always known to me, yet I never despaired that he could overcome them. Without your influence he might never have acted as he did. Worst of all, however, is what you have done to the Stone. By your touch you have defiled it."

His words fell into the silence, soft and brutal, as stunning as blows. He could not really be saying these terrible things, comparing her with Bron . . . Could it be true? Was she corrupt? Could it be that by trying to rescue the Stone she had harmed it? Yet how could anything in her have touched or stained a power as great as the Stone's? And her own power . . . She could remember the clear exhilaration of it, the great flood of it through all the empty places in her soul. How could a feeling like that be corrupt? Defiance rose in her, and words sprang to her lips before she knew what she was saying.

"I gave the Stone back to you. I broke Bron's concentration so you could get through the hedge. I used my power to help you. If it hadn't been for me and Taryn, Bron could have held you off forever and the Stone would never have rested in your hands again! Doesn't that matter?"

But her words struck Marhalt's impenetrable regard and bounced back, like pebbles thrown at a wall. "It is one more sign of your corruption that he could deceive you so about his power. And about your own."

Alexina no longer knew what was true. She was dreaming, spinning down into a vortex of madness. The world had turned inside out: black was white and white was black and everything that was said meant exactly the opposite. She had not really woken up this morning, she told herself; she was still in the nightmare. But she knew it was not so. This was really happening.

Marhalt spoke again. "It is over now. You have failed the test. You have witnessed Taryn's divestiture. It remains only to return you to your people and leave this world forever."

"What . . . what will happen to Taryn now?"

"It does not concern you, Alexina."

Beside her, Taryn stirred. He lifted his head and looked directly at Marhalt.

"No," he said. His tone was harsh and strange. "No, it's not fair."

"Taryn," said Marhalt. He did not raise his voice, but the word carried the force of a blow. Taryn stiffened himself against it, his head still up, defiant.

"She is not responsible for what I did," he said. "She is not corrupt. What I did was out of my own will."

"It is enough, Taryn."

"No, it's not enough. I don't care what happens to me any more. I have nothing left to lose, you've made sure of that. You thought you'd beaten me, broken my will. But you haven't. I've been thinking while I've been standing here—things I never thought before. Things I should have thought long ago. I've been confused for a long time, but not any more. I have you to thank for that."

The color had returned to his face. He was standing very straight, his fists clenched by his sides, leaning slightly forward as if bracing himself against Marhalt's gaze. His words tumbled over each other, breaking free of their own weight, the long-delayed explosion of pressures grown beyond the capacity of what had always held them in.

"I'm not sorry for what I did. It wasn't bad, no matter what you say. I—we—saved you. You could never have beaten him. Without us you would still be outside the hedge, or on your way through the Gate driven by *his* power, *his* compulsion. I won't have Alexina blamed for anything that happened. We acted together, and we acted rightly."

The faces of the Guardians were fixed, without emotion. When Marhalt spoke, his voice was very soft. It carried a warning that was as palpable as an icy current in the air. "Taryn. You will go too far."

Amazingly, Taryn laughed. There was a sound of triumph in it. "No. No, I've never gone far enough! I wasn't able to before." He turned suddenly to Alexina and took both her hands. His touch was like fire. "They've lied to you, Alexina, they've lied all along. But I'm going to tell you everything that has been kept from you. I'm sorry I never told you before, when you could save yourself. I can't tell you how sorry I am for that, for lying to you too. You see, it was the link. They needed it. They couldn't sense him or the Stone in this world at all. So they restored your memory and brought you to the camp, and Marhalt put a compulsion on you. He fixed it in your mind, a compulsion to follow, a drive that would bring you after us without questioning, as if it were your own will. Without you, they could never have found him. And now—now they're going to take it all away. They'll take away the memory of all that has happened—and not just that. They'll take your power too, for they can't leave that behind. You'll be left with nothing, Alexina. Nothing! Do you understand what I'm telling you?"

Bewildered, she stared into his face, shrinking from the intensity of his eyes. "I . . . I don't know. . . ."

"*You* tell her then!" He dropped her hands and turned back to Marhalt. "Let her hear it from your own lips. Oh, Bron was so right about you! You're all the things he said you were. Whatever you do to me will just go to prove it. You're not punishing me because I did wrong. You're doing it because you want to get rid of me. I see it in your face every time you look at me. You want me gone because you're afraid, afraid of people like me, of people like Bron, people who ask questions and think the thoughts you won't let anyone think—"

"Taryn. That—is—enough."

Marhalt's voice was soft, but it was terrible. Behind it lay the crushing thunder of an avalanche, the burning cold of a polar winter. Taryn stopped speaking as if a hand had grabbed his throat. Slowly, the color ebbed from his face as the adrenaline from his outburst drained away. He stood spent and still, his head down and his hands limp, as he had been when Alexina first came into the clearing. Silence fell. Alexina could hear the sound of her own breath. The force that had stopped Taryn seemed to grip her too, like the first signal of a terrible pain. She met Marhalt's eyes.

"Is it true?" Her voice was a whisper. "A . . . a compulsion? You did something to make me follow you?"

His face showed her nothing. "Yes."

"How? How did you do it?"

"Through the language transfer."

"The *language* transfer?"

"We could not enter your mind without permission. You gave it to us then."

"But not for that! I didn't give you permission for that!"

He simply looked at her. The slight shock as he touched her forehead that first night, she thought, all the touches since then which had unaccountably raised her spirits and banished doubts—it must have been the compulsion all along, planted in her mind like a second, secret link. And Marhalt had put it there. Marhalt, whom she had trusted with everything that was hers. Marhalt, who she had believed cared about her. She had not thought anything could be worse than being called corrupt. The pain was growing, a terrible pressure along her nerves.

"You . . . you tricked me." Her voice shook. "You lied to me. You used me. And you'd never have told me, would you, not if Taryn hadn't said what he did."

"Alexina." Strangely, Marhalt's voice was gentle now. "Alexina, it was necessary. We had a mission to complete, a Quest more important than any of the small human lives sent out to accomplish it, yours *or* mine. Nothing could stand in the way of that purpose. Nothing could be left to chance. There were certain things you could not be told, certain things that had to be kept from you. Things you could not have understood."

"Couldn't you have *tried* to make me understand? At least try, instead of using a . . . a cheap trick!"

"It is not as simple as that. Do you think we could simply have laid it all out for you and asked you to give us the link of your own will? Asked you to allow us to test your power? You were too afraid, too handpower-bound. We and our Quest were far outside the range of your experience or comprehension. How could you have understood what we sought or its true importance or the sanctity of power? We could not trust your free will in this matter, for you did not understand enough to exercise it."

"But you never *let* me understand!" It came out as a half-sob. "You never helped me at all! You just assumed that because I was handpower-born I couldn't understand anything. You never even gave me a chance to make a choice. I *would* have understood. I would have followed you, I would have given you the link willingly even if I were afraid! Why didn't you just try asking me? All my life I waited for something like this, for people like you. All my life I dreamed about power. I didn't need any compulsion! You saw inside my mind. You saw everything I was or thought. Didn't you see that too?"

Her voice broke. Still Marhalt's face held no remorse, only pity, the pity a man might feel for a caged animal.

"I saw everything inside your mind, Alexina. I saw that you had power, that you dreamed as you said. It was what allowed the compulsion to work at all. But I also saw your world, your world with its ignorance and fear and corruption. You are of your world, you cannot escape it. Because of that you could not have understood, no matter what we told you. You could not have followed, no matter how much you wished to. Your world would not have allowed it. The compulsion was necessary, as was the way in which we placed it."

"You're wrong. You're wrong."

"I am not wrong. But in the end it does not matter. Only the Quest matters. And power."

Alexina could just make out his face through the blur of tears. The pity was gone now, and only the inhuman stillness, the iron implacability, remained. Understanding was a bleak and terrible wind sweeping through her soul, stripping away illusion. She knew now that Marhalt had never really looked at her. When his topaz eyes rested on her, they had seen not a human being, but the stigma of the handpower-born. She knew now that he had given her a test she could only fail. She had never been anything but a tool for him, for all of them—a tool like the ones they scorned so, a divining rod to be used and then discarded when its use was done. And in her innocence she had thought herself one of them. The tears spilled down her cheeks. Alien, expressionless, the three Guardians faced her, and she knew that she had never seen them either. Yes, Marhalt had shown her compassion, kindness, patience, warmth—but that had been the mask, that had been the stranger. This was the real Marhalt. The world had been reversed all the time, and she had not known it.

Marhalt was unfolding himself now, getting to his feet, coming toward her.

"Please believe that I am sorry for what I must do now, Alexina. I had hoped to wait. But Taryn has forced my hand."

His arm was outstretched. His shadow moved before him over the leaf-strewn ground, reaching out for her, holding her helpless. The air seemed to shake slightly. She felt his power. He would touch her now, as he had touched her before, the touch that soothed fear and brought oblivion. His topaz eyes were locked to hers, and in them she saw nothing she recognized as human. Her future flashed before her—a life without power, without memory of the most important thing she had ever experienced, an eternity spent in a small antechamber without access to the great vistas that made up her true self.

No, she thought, I can't let it happen. She tried to raise her barriers, to close the doors that guarded her mind. But she was weak, depleted by the experiences of the past days and by betrayal. She could not find her power. His fingers approached, closing in on her forehead, outstretched to drain her of so much that mattered.

And then, in the instant before his finger touched, she felt something from outside. A great gathering of power, a joining of an enormous and all-encompassing awareness to hers. Marhalt's power reached out for her mind. Her barriers slammed shut. She felt a tremendous shock, a blow that resounded through her entire being, and then nothing at all.

18

Alexina was in a round room at the center of a maze of passages. The room was hung with costly tapestries and the floor was deep with rich rugs. In the middle, a pillar rose from the floor. She was sitting on this pillar, her legs drawn up to her chin and her arms around her knees. The room had no door and no window; those who entered must pass through the very stone of the walls. It was home and prison at the same time. She had lived there a very long time. She had been gone, and now she had returned, and she would never leave again. Sadness filled her, not for herself but for the others, for the world, for existence itself, for the great emptiness that cried out for balance. The sadness seemed to spread outside her and fill the entire world. In turn the world turned back and filled her. It poured in and poured out again, a constant elemental flow, a great river of being—not blocked, as it had been before, yet still not free, for it was only a part of what it could have been.

The dream had the power of a call, and it began to bring Alexina up toward consciousness. Just before she woke completely she was aware, briefly, of a prickling sensation in the air around her. When she sat up and looked around, it was already gone. She put her hand to her head. What had happened?

Groggily she got to her feet. She had a sense of déjà vu as she did so, as if she had been in this place many times before. But it was not déjà vu. She was standing, she realized, in the pine wood adjacent to the Krantzes' farm. She could just see the meadow through the trees, and, farther on, the farm itself.

Stupefied, she stared around her. How had she gotten here? Where were the Guardians? But even as she thought it, she knew. That strange sensation as she woke—it must have been the Gate, or rather, its closing.

Alexina's legs were weak, and she sat down. It seemed that only a moment ago she had stood in a different wood, watching Marhalt approach, his hand outstretched to take her memory and her power. The last thing she could remember was the shock of impact as she flung up her barriers to protect herself. Now, all at once, she was here, and they were gone. She remembered none of the trip back. Could it be that she had been unconscious for a week, maybe two—the whole of the journey back?

Alexina put her hand to her face, feeling an unfamiliar sharpness to her cheekbones, tangles in her hair. She clenched her fists. They had left her here to wake alone, dropping her on the ground like a lump of dirty linen. It was the final cruelty, the final manipulation in the series of callous actions that had brought her on the journey. She had an image of them, very clear, climbing up the cliff to the cave, opening the Gate, leaving her world forever with, they thought, no trace to mark their passage through it. Yet, Alexina thought, with a bitter combination of triumph and anger, there *was* a trace. Herself. Somehow, miraculously, her barriers had protected her and her memory was intact.

Now what? The farm? Disbelief swept over her.

How could she go back? How would it be possible to live there again after all she had experienced? Yet she had nowhere else to go. She was more practical than to think she could run away. After a while, her feet dragging, she walked through the trees to the edge of the meadow. The farm lay inside its ring of mountains, a peaceful jumble of buildings. She could see the long field where vegetables grew. It seemed so normal and familiar. She might never have gone away at all; she might just be returning from an afternoon trip to the cave.

Yet something was different. It took a few moments to realize what it was, or rather that what she was seeing as difference was actually something missing. Somehow, during her absence, the farm had lost its ugliness. The meagerness, the dilapidated and sagging wornness of it that had always assaulted her gaze, no longer seemed to matter. Instead, gilded with the afternoon sun, the air all around it quivering faintly as heat rose from the grasses, it looked almost beautiful, and completely, invitingly serene.

A dream-feeling took her, or rather a waking-from-a-dream feeling. She felt like a traveler in an enchanted land, regaining consciousness to find that not one night but a hundred years have passed. She was aware of a chill in the breeze, of touches of red and gold at the edges of the leaves. How long had she been gone? Several weeks at least. It had been late July when she left, but she had lost track on the journey and even now she could not isolate days and nights into an orderly stream of time. Julia and Charles must be terribly worried. They might think she was kidnapped, even murdered.

Alexina could feel the world of the farm reaching out for her, feel the multitude of its mundane obligations. The other, timeless world in which she had lived for a little while was beginning to slip away. She looked at the boundary between meadow and wood and thought: That line is a Gate. If I go through, it will close up behind me forever and I will never get back again.

She stood, still hesitating over the first step. But within her something moved toward acceptance. The journey was over. The enchantment was gone. Her own world had reclaimed her, and it was time to return. Fighting it would do no good.

Resolutely, Alexina straightened her shoulders and stepped out at last into the sunlight.

* * * *

She was not sure what she had expected on her return—anger, perhaps hysterics—certainly not the shocked silence the sight of her produced. She walked through the meadow, through the gate and the backyard, into the kitchen by the back door, just as she had done a hundred times before. Julia and Charles were sitting at the kitchen table having lunch. Charles's face went very still and he froze, fork halfway to his mouth. The color drained from Julia's cheeks. She dropped her cutlery and clasped her hands to her heart.

"A-Alexina!" Julia gasped, stammering a little. "Is it really you?"

"Are you hurt?" It was Charles. He was on his feet. "Are you all right?"

"Yes." Alexina cleared her throat. "Perfectly all right."

"But you look . . . you look . . ." Julia's voice trailed off, and she stared at Alexina's face, her tangled hair, her dirty clothing.

"Where have you been all this time, young lady?"

demanded Charles, regaining some of his normal composure.

"I'm sorry. I can't tell you."

"What do you mean, you can't tell me?"

"I just can't."

"That's all you have to say for yourself?"

Alexina looked down. "I'm sorry," she said again.

There was a pause. Then, "Go to your room, Alexina," Charles said quietly.

Alexina obeyed. She still felt as if she were dreaming. Like everything else, her room was familiar yet alien. The coverlet and rug were still faded and worn, but the abundant sunlight lit them to a richness they had never possessed before. Alexina sat down on the edge of the bed, and waited numbly for the inevitable confrontation.

The sun had moved quite a way across the floor before she heard footsteps in the hall. Julia entered the room. She stopped, just inside the door.

"You've lost a lot of weight," she said at last.

Alexina nodded.

"Are you sure you're . . . all right?"

Alexina heard the delicate significance in Julia's voice. "I'm fine," she said. "Really."

There was another pause, and then Julia came to sit beside Alexina on the bed. Alexina stared at the bars of sun on the floor.

"We thought you might be hurt, even dead. No note, no letter or word in all this time. The police are looking for you."

Alexina looked at her miserably. "I'm sorry."

Julia shook her head. She sounded as if she were struggling for words. "Can you *imagine* the worry you caused us? How could you do such an inconsiderate thing? How could you be so irresponsible? And now you walk in here as if you'd just been away for an afternoon, and you won't even say where you've been!"

"I know I've been awful," said Alexina dully. "I know you were worried about me. I know there's no excuse. I know I can't even ask you to forgive me."

"I don't know what to say to you, Alexina." Julia seemed at a loss. "You've apologized, but it's just not enough. It's not as if you stayed out too late or skipped school."

"I know. I do know, Julia. There's just . . . nothing to say."

There was a pause, and then Julia sighed. "You're a hard one to know, do you realize that? I tried to show you I was there for you, but you didn't seem to want to see it."

Alexina did not answer.

"But you're not as good at hiding things as you think, Alexina. I could see it all in your face. You were unhappy here. You never quite managed to fit in. Maybe you didn't try hard enough, or maybe I didn't help you enough—I don't know. It doesn't matter now." She reached out and put her hand under Alexina's chin, turning her face so that she had to look into Julia's compassionate brown eyes. "I want you to know that I know why you ran away. I don't want to speak badly of my own sister, but she laid the groundwork for it. She could have done so much more for you—left you alone less, maybe. And I imagine you needed a lot more comforting in the beginning than you ever got." She shook her head. "I saw how sad you were in the days before you left here. There's no excuse for what you did. But sometimes I think . . . if I'd talked to you directly, if I hadn't been waiting for you to come to me . . . all this might never have happened."

Alexina looked at Julia. They thought she had run

away! She felt a mad impulse to burst out laughing. But tears took over instead. The bars of sun ran together on the floor, and she began to sob rackingly. She was conscious that Julia reached out and drew her into an embrace, holding her gently as she cried for everything that had been lost. Julia's arms were comforting, yet the things for which she offered comfort were not the things for which Alexina wept.

After a while Julia straightened up and held Alexina away from her, wiping her wet cheeks with the corner of an apron.

"Can you tell me where you've been now?"

Alexina swallowed. She had to lie. There was no avoiding it. "I . . . I went cross-country. I was in Chicago for a while . . . then Michigan. For a while I was in an abandoned house in the woods." It was not quite a lie, even if it left out everything essential. She would play along with what they thought. It was the easiest way. What had really happened must be her secret, always. At the loneliness of that, fresh tears rose to her eyes and trickled down her cheeks.

"Oh, Alexina," said Julia. "I can't find it in my heart to scold you any more. You're back, that's the important thing. You did a terrible thing, but you've been through a terrible time—I can see it in your face. You look . . ." her voice faded, as if she could not put it into words. She sighed. "Perhaps that's punishment enough."

Alexina stared at her knees. There was a pause. Then Julia spoke resolutely.

"We won't talk about it any more now. I hope one day you'll be able to tell me everything, but I won't force you. Some things . . . some things are very hard to talk about at first."

Julia's understanding only made Alexina feel miserably guilty. "Thank you," she said huskily.

Julia got to her feet, smoothing her apron. "You look at least ten pounds thinner. Clean yourself up a bit and then come down to the kitchen and I'll fix you the best meal you've had in weeks."

After Julia had gone, Alexina got up and went to look in the mirror. She stood for some time, staring at herself, appalled. Her fingers, meeting unfamiliar contours as she woke, had not lied. She was thin and haggard, her hair tangled and lank with dirt, her clothes grimy and stiff. Her eyes seemed to have receded into her head, set deep in dark-ringed sockets. It hardly seemed to be her face at all. It reminded her of photographs of farmers during the Oklahoma dust bowl. Slowly she put her hands to her cheeks. She felt strange, disembodied. This was not the self she remembered, the self she had last seen in the candlelit glass of Bron's mansion. This person was a stranger. It was more than weariness or lack of food. She felt she had somehow fundamentally changed. She must have, to wear this face.

She took a shower, scrubbing at the dirt and tangles, wishing it was as easy to remove other traces of the journey. She dressed in clothes she had left behind, dismayed at the looseness with which they hung on her body. She did not want to go downstairs. All she wanted now was to sleep, even if she had been sleeping for two weeks. But she must eat, to please Julia. Slowly she started down the hall. The door to Toby's room stood open slightly. Curious, she pushed it open and peered inside. It looked as it always had, except that his books and personal things were gone. Had he managed to leave, then, as he had planned?

Julia set before her a large bowl of soup, biscuits and preserves, slices of ham, and a wedge of custard pie. Alexina worked her way through it without much enthusiasm. Julia went about her kitchen chores, maintaining a sympathetic silence that was somehow almost as painful as the conversation they had just completed. At last Alexina pushed her plate away. Julia looked around.

"Good," she said. "you've eaten it all. Can I get you anything else?"

Alexina shook her head. "Julia, is Toby . . . I mean, did Toby go away?"

Julia's eyes were keen. "So you knew about that."

"Well, it was a sort of accident. I found out by chance."

"Yes, he did go. Only two weeks ago, in fact. I've just had a letter from him. Would you like to see it?"

Alexina nodded. Julia went upstairs, and in a few minutes came down again with an envelope. She handed it to Alexina.

The letter was not long. It described Toby's classes, his living arrangements, and the people he had met. It gave a telephone number. There was no reference to her own absence, or to the fact that he had left without permission himself. Alexina put the letter down.

"Is Charles very angry?"

Julia was back at the counter, chopping something. She nodded. "He'll get over it. I had a feeling that Toby was going, you know. I wasn't surprised when he did. Though it was a bit much losing both of you within a month."

The guilt flooded back. Alexina got up from the table. "I'm feeling a bit tired now. I think I'll sleep for a while."

"All right. Sleep as long as you like."

Her slumber was immediate and dreamless, and she slept the clock around, from early afternoon until late the next morning. She woke confused, not knowing where she was. Where was the canopy of trees or sky, where was the hardness of the ground, why was the light so strange? But at once recognition returned, and with it despair, a hollowness right at the center of her being. She clasped her arms around her knees and put her forehead against them, willing away tears. For a long moment it was utterly impossible, completely wrong, that she be here. Bleakly she raised her head. Through the windows she could see the familiar slice of meadow and mountain and sky, splashed with bright color here and there from the changing leaves. The sun reached through the window and rested on the faded rug by the bed, a bar of deep crimson. Alexina thought of the last time she had sat in this bed, of the ugliness she had seen all around her. Today, as bad as she felt, she simply could not see it any more. Was she too unhappy even for that?

She got up, dressed, and went downstairs. Julia fixed her an enormous breakfast, and she spent the morning helping with light tasks. In the afternoon, Julia took her to the police station so that a report could be made out. She was asked a lot of questions, but at last, pronouncing himself satisfied, the detective allowed them to go. They returned to the farm, and Julia cooked dinner with Alexina's help. At ten o'clock they all went to bed. It had been a short day—yet Alexina could not remember when the hours had seemed so long.

* * * *

So, gradually, Alexina slipped back into the routine of life at the farm, with scarcely a ripple to mark her return. Her chores were just as they had been, and her schedule, once school resumed, was also the same. Except for the hollow place inside her, and the replacement of Toby by a live-in hired man, she could sometimes almost imagine she had never been away at all. But she *had* been away. A great deal had happened and she had no choice but to try to come to terms with it.

She thought often of Bron. Was he still alive, or had he bled to death on the floor of his mansion? Somehow, she thought not. And she was quite sure that, as he had said, the forces of her world would not rob him of his power. Sometimes she wondered why he had let her go. Even weakened by his pain he could have held her. She shuddered slightly when she thought of this, as if the cold of the link were passing over her again. She knew the link was broken. Yet occasionally she could almost feel it, as if something rooted in the deepest parts of her unknown self still drew her to where he was, far away, in his silent house that now had no center. She was profoundly grateful it was only a memory.

For so long she had feared and hated Bron. It was not easy to stop. But she was aware that her hatred had been carefully fostered, her fear made into one more tool for the Quest. He had shown her much in that one glimpse inside his mind; slowly, it was changing her view of him forever. She knew now how much of what he told her had been true.

Marhalt had lied; Bron had told the truth. Yet did it really make a difference? Perhaps Bron really had wished for partnership, but in the end, he too had wanted to use her, to make her a part of his mysterious and still-unknown plans. Of all of them, Taryn had been the only one who had not wanted to use her. Only he had seen her as she really was.

Alexina felt like weeping when she thought of Taryn. What would they do to him, back in his world? Any lingering hope must have been killed by his final outburst. He had said, once, that he had done nothing for her. But it was not true. He had brought her her first taste of power. He had followed her into the woods to protect her, despite his fear. He had saved her—and the Guardians—from Bron. For it all he had been cast out of the Brotherhood, his badges reduced to scrap. And what had she ever done for him, apart from leading him deeper into the morass? If only she could take back some of her actions. If only she had not let him accompany her to Bron's house, if only she had taken the gun away from him. Perhaps it really would have been better for both of them if the Guardians had never regained the Stone, even if it meant that she and Taryn were still with Bron. Poor Taryn had never been at home in his world anyway. Better in this one, where the powers that fascinated him so could be used without punishment, where he need never keep part of himself a secret.

The images crowded around her. Often they were powerful, so that she felt she might almost turn and see them. Yet sometimes they were oddly indefinite. There was so much she still did not understand, questions which would remain questions forever. More and more it was as if she had read it all in a book: something that had really happened, but in another time, another place—and to another person.

Where was the girl who had embarked on the journey—the eager, bold, resourceful girl who had realized her power in the heart of an enchanted mansion, who had found and become one with the Stone? Alexina remembered this girl as if she were not herself. She could seldom find any sign of her in the drab, dull, hollow person she had become. Had her perception before the mirror been a true one, had she somehow changed beyond recognition in the time she had been away? The same mirror told her that she was gaining back the lost weight, that her eyes were no longer dark-rimmed, that her hair was as lustrous as it had always been. Yet the foreignness behind the image persisted. It was akin to the estrangement of before, yet not the same.

She began to fear it was because her power had left her. She could remember her power—finding it, using it, understanding it—but of its actual presence she had felt no trace since awakening on the hillside above the farm. The passing days brought no change. Even the *waiting* which had marked the incipience of power over so many years was gone. There was just . . . nothing, empty spaces, the vague memory of enormous possibilities that had been hers for a small time. Had Marhalt, failing to remove her memory, still managed to take her power? She knew she must reach within herself to find out for sure. But she was afraid to try, afraid to face the certainty of final proof.

The dream returned now and then, the dream of the small prison-shrine and the terrible sadness that filled it. Alexina understood that she was dreaming of the Stone. The original dream had been more than vivid: It was as if the Stone had cried out as it passed from her world, and only she had heard. Each time it returned it was a little less clear. It was fading, dropping away into the well of memory. When it ceased, the Stone would be just one more distant image. Alexina fought against this, willing herself to dream the dream, calling back the link experience in all its magnitude, complexity, and terror. But the images continued to lose their definition. Time smoothed them out, like sandpaper.

Still, with all that was being lost, something was also gained. The images of the Stone's awakening—flooding indiscriminately into Alexina's consciousness, floating there confused and jumbled in the days after her awakening—gradually ordered themselves into a pattern of new understanding. It was not an easy pattern, and for a time Alexina doubted her own insights. Her world had no access to the Stone, and ignorance was not surprising in her people. But Marhalt—how could it be that he, too, was blind? She remembered his Tale, his words about handpower and the split and her world: false visions. Or, rather, half visions: half the truth, as his world was only half the world. The Stone had shown her, beyond doubt, that the Guardians' world with its brutal Limits was no more possessed of balance than her own, where anything beyond scientific proof was dismissed. Handpower without mindpower was only part of what could be, but mindpower without handpower was just as poor a version of reality. How could Marhalt, how could the Guardians, linking with the Stone through the centuries, fail to see this? How could they dismiss the desolation of the Stone's loss, the thinness of their own reality? Surely, in all the long years, she could not be the only one who had understood.

Bron had understood. He had understood even before he took the Stone. But he too had chosen to use its power wrongly. He had tried to trap it, to enslave it to his machines. Alexina was certain it could not have worked. Surely only the merest fraction of all that power and knowledge could be caught on disks, on tapes, in crystal. Surely the sheer volume of that torrent would have shattered the machines as it had almost shattered her.

It did not matter. None of it mattered any longer. Back in their world, the Guardians were embarking again on their work of denying wholeness to their people. Her own people continued their pursuit of the myth of progress. Each world traveled the path it had chosen, turning away from that portion of reality deemed nonexistent or corrupt. One day the Gates would close forever, and the worlds would be completely separate. Not because of any inevitable process of corruption or progress, Alexina knew now, but because of *choice*, because of man's unceasing effort to make things as he thought they ought to be.

Choice had split the worlds. And perhaps that one choice, between two kinds of powers, had not been the only one. Perhaps beyond this world lay dozens, even hundreds of others, peeled off in succession through choice after choice, parallel but separate like the layers of an onion or an infinite set of nesting boxes. And perhaps which world you lived in depended on what you excluded, what you did not see—so that it was all just a matter of *looking* one way rather than another. Could reality really be so tenuous? Or could it even be that, beneath successive levels of illusion stacked one upon another like sheets of soft tissue paper, there lay one original earth? And all men walked upon it, no matter what they saw, passing through each other like ghosts or breaths of wind. Perhaps there were many Gates, hundreds or even thousands, Gates that were not physical but openings on a new perception. Perhaps every mind was a Gate, and all of life was a process of passing through. . . .

Alexina could not sustain such thoughts for long. They made her giddy, as if the earth were ready to slip away beneath her feet. Reaching out for balance, it would all disappear: Confronted with the solid and unassailable realness of the farm and its people and its neverending tasks, the images would slip still further away. If the Stone had been there, she could have asked it. Or if she had had her power, she could have reached with it toward those possible other worlds.

But her power was gone, and so was the Stone. The days passed and the routine endured. She was alone, as so often before in her life, with no outlet for her thoughts. She missed Taryn more than she would have thought possible. Even Toby would have been comforting. She tried to lose herself in work—schoolwork, farm work. But she was always aware of the days stretching ahead of her, a long, gray, featureless plateau. She had climbed the highest mountain she would ever climb. From its vantage point, the whole world looked flat.

19

Jessica wrote twice after Alexina's return. The first letter expressed relief, and gave vent to some perfunctory scolding. Alexina could detect little real emotion in the dry phrases. Julia told her that Jessica had been "frantic," but the letter sounded the very opposite, and Jessica had certainly not paused in her work for Alexina's sake, nor rushed back from abroad to see if she could help. The letter stipulated that Alexina must see a psychiatrist. Alexina could almost hear the thought processes behind that: all those weird books, Jessica was thinking, all that time alone in her room—escapism. The infection must now be excised. Accordingly, an appointment was made with a doctor in Bradenton. Alexina was not pleased, but there was no way to escape it.

The second letter, arriving a few weeks later, was a surprise. Jessica wrote that she had obtained permission for Alexina to join her. An English tutor would be arranged, and a larger apartment had been promised. Alexina read the letter over and over. Jessica must have gone to a lot of trouble, she thought. More surprising than the letter, however, was her own ambivalence about the move. Before, she knew she would have jumped at the chance. Now, however, when she really thought about it, she was not sure. Did she not want to go abroad? Did she not want to be with Jessica? Or could it be that she did not want to leave the farm?

No, that couldn't be. The farm was a constriction and a prison. Yet, looking at it in the glory of the late September sun, surrounded by blazing autumn foliage, she could almost begin to feel otherwise. Without knowing why, she viewed everything through changed eyes. The ugliness that had been so oppressive before had never returned. She had begun to think it part of the change that included herself, an odd external counterpart to the dullness within. Now, the letter before her, she examined her mixed emotions. She hated it here—didn't she? If she didn't, what did she feel? She did not know. She put the letter in the bottom of her bureau drawer. A week later she was no closer to a decision.

In mid-October Toby returned home for four days. Clearly he wished to make peace with his father, and hoped that Charles had at last accepted the situation. But Charles had not. While there were no confrontations, the tension between Toby and his father was obvious. They hardly spoke, except to exchange mundane remarks about the farm. For the first time Alexina saw Toby uncertain, not in control. His attempts to bring up his college life were met with impenetrable silence from Charles and worried looks from Julia.

Alexina was surprised by how glad she was to see Toby, and to her further astonishment they got on very well, though they were cautious, recalling the old days. Toby told her a good deal about his studies and his new friends. She sensed that he found in her a relief from the tension of the house, for she was the only person who could listen to what he had to say without discomfort.

It was not until the last day of his visit that the more dangerous subjects were broached. Alexina had been sorting apples into bags for the produce stand,

and Toby had volunteered to help. They worked in companionable silence, surrounded by the perfume of the apples, and Alexina found herself thinking that she would miss him when he left the next day. It was suddenly very easy to fall into self-pity, to make a pattern out of the departures and abandonments in her life.

Toby sighed suddenly. "This hasn't been an easy visit," he said slowly.

"I've noticed."

He had stopped sorting. He was holding a pink-blushed Golden Delicious apple in his hands, turning it around and around. "I just don't know what to do," he said. "I've tried to talk to him about it, but I can feel the wall go up when I do. It's like he's closed himself up to me. I feel like a stranger."

"He'll come around," said Alexina unconvincingly. "He has to care that you're happy."

"I *am* happy. For the first time in my life, actually—because I'm doing what *I* want. I just wish he could accept me for what I am. If only we could have a decent quarrel, get it all out in the open. Anything would be better than this . . ." He gestured wordlessly. "I can't expect anything from my mother, either. She's caught in the middle."

"But she understands," said Alexina. "Maybe she'll be able to change his mind in the end. Anyway, it's a fact now. There's nothing to do *but* accept it."

"You don't know my father," said Toby. His expression was inward and there was a grimness to the set of his mouth. Suddenly, painfully, Alexina was reminded of Taryn, speaking of Marhalt and his obediences. But Toby moved and the moment was gone. He stopped turning the apple in his hands and began to eat it.

"Maybe you're right," he said, munching. "About

my mother, I mean. Maybe she *can* bring him around. My mother's an incredible woman."

"Yes," said Alexina. Toby looked at her speculatively.

"You know, I keep thinking of that night you came to tell me you were leaving. You seemed to know exactly what you were doing. It was like you'd worked it all out in advance. I don't mean to pry, Alexina, but I'm curious as anything. What was it all about?"

"I can't tell you. I'm sorry."

"That's what you said that night." He chewed his apple, his gray eyes narrow. "It's what Ma said you told her at first when you came back."

"You talked about it with her?"

"Sure. She wondered if I might know something. I didn't tell her about that night, Alexina. It was something you said in confidence. You kept *my* secret."

"Thanks."

"She thinks you ran away. You didn't, did you?"

"No. There was something I had to do. Like I told you that night."

"Was it anything to do with all that sneaking around before you left?" Alexina felt herself reddening; she could not help it. Toby pounced. "Aha! You're protecting someone!"

"I am not! You don't know what you're talking about, so kindly keep your conclusions to yourself!" Some of the old sharpness had been in his voice, and her words shot out before she could stop them. With an effort she closed her mouth. It was so easy to fall back into the old patterns. "Please don't ask me to talk about it, Toby. I just can't. I did know what I was doing, and I didn't run away. And that's all I can tell you."

There was a pause. Toby finished the apple and

flung the core away. He watched it arc toward the woods, falling somewhere in the meadow. "It's just that it's all so mysterious! You're acting like the heroine of some romantic novel. You know, the secret mission, the mysterious motive. And I still have that weird feeling I ought to know what it was all about—or I would if I thought hard enough."

Alexina looked at him. He did not have the memory, but he was still aware that something ought to be there. She found herself wishing he did remember. It would have been good to tell someone. Would it be possible to use telepathy to unlock the images of Marhalt, Taryn, the globe of light? But then she thought, My power is gone. The hollow feeling, obscured somewhat today and over the other days of Toby's visit by his company, was there again. The bright afternoon seemed to darken a little and, without meaning to, she sighed.

"Did something happen to you out there?" said Toby. His voice was gentle. "Something bad, like my mother thinks?"

"She thinks that?" Alexina looked up at him and then shook her head. "No. Not like she thinks."

"Something did happen, though. I can see it in your face." He was studying her. "You look . . . I don't know. Older, maybe. Though that's not it either."

Alexina felt a sudden overwhelming urge to tears. She struggled against the lump in her throat, turning back to the apples. He seemed to sense her feelings and did not press the matter. They finished their task in silence, each absorbed in thought. Toby's mind too seemed to have returned to his troubles, for his face was preoccupied. Once more, fleetingly, Alexina was reminded of Taryn.

Toby left the next morning. Charles did not come

out to say good-bye. Alexina saw Toby's face in the pickup window as Julia drove him to town, scanning the house to see if by some chance his father had relented and come to watch him go.

* * * *

It was Sunday, and as the day dragged on the Sunday dullness seemed particularly oppressive. Alexina did her chores and wandered restlessly around the empty house for a while. She sat down to try to read, but she could not concentrate. The memories were crowding around her with especial closeness today: The images came thickly, with the vividness they rarely possessed any more. It was as if Toby had been a trigger, bringing Taryn back to her almost in the flesh, and with him the others. She gave up on her book and sat remembering, and the room around her disappeared. Still she felt that sense of unresolved restlessness. Impulsively, she decided it was time she paid a visit to the cave.

She had not returned to it since she found herself at the farm. She had not been able to face the thought of all the memories it would bring. But today, perhaps because Taryn and the others were so very close in her mind, she felt the moment was right at last.

She walked through the meadow, as she had so often, avoiding automatically the places where she knew there were brambles or rabbit holes. She reached the cliff she had climbed so many times; her fingers instinctively found the familiar holds. At the top of the cliff she turned and looked outward, as she had always done. There was the farm in its meadow, the rows of dark mountains marching off toward the horizon, the faraway glimmer of the lake where Marhalt had told his Tale. It was overcast today and clouds lay heavily on the peaks, drifting down into the hollows between the hills. She had forgotten how high it was, how to stand there felt almost like flying. A chill wind was blowing.

She turned and began to walk slowly along the ledge, shivering a little. Here was the spot where she had felt the opening of the Gate for the first time. Here was the place where she had bolted up the cliff to escape Bron and Fico. Here was the curve of rock, beyond which lay the cave.

Alexina's pace slowed as she approached the outcrop, and for a moment she stopped altogether. She felt an odd reluctance to take the last step. Don't be a fool, she told herself. What are you afraid of? She took a deep breath, and resolutely rounded the corner.

It was just as she remembered: the grassy patch before the opening, the sifting of pine needles around the entrance, the little pools of wax where her candles had burned, the bare stone of the floor. The back extended into mysterious depths, in which, somewhere, lay the Gate. Here she had first seen Taryn, had unpacked food for him and dressed his wounds. Here she had experienced telepathy for the first time. Every inch of the cave was charged with memories. But though she could remember where power had been, no breath of power, no trace of it, could be felt. There was nothing to say that here had stood a Gate between two worlds, that here an incredible journey had begun.

Alexina knew now what she had been afraid of—exactly this. The cave was just another empty place, another dimming memory. All it told her was that this was truly the end, that nothing had been left behind. There were no Guardians, there was no Gate, and she had no power. There were only the crowded fading images, and the void where power had been.

Alexina stood for a while longer, caught in a kind of apathy. The sun came out from behind the clouds and shone full into the cave, a long bar of tawny light that stretched all the way to the curve of the back wall.

It was time to go. She started to turn away—but as she moved she caught a flash out of the corner of her eye. She turned back. There it was again: She thought she could see something glinting on the floor toward the rear. For an instant time telescoped. Her heart was pounding, and her breath came short. She did not dare to hope. It was probably just the tab from a soft drink can. But she moved slowly forward for a better look. And when she saw what was on the stone floor, she fell to her knees and sat motionless, barely breathing.

A formless mass of metal, streaked heavily with charring so that its color barely showed, lay in a hollow of the stone. The remains of Taryn's silver medallions, the wreckage of his hopes. Why was it here? Had the Guardians dropped it as a final sign of contempt before they left her world, giving Taryn's silver to the powers they believed he had chosen? But no, for Marhalt had said the metal must be buried in his own world. They would never have willingly left this behind. It must be . . . it must be that somehow Taryn had contrived to place it here. He had left it behind for her to find.

Slowly Alexina reached out and picked up the lump of silver, rubbing at the black stains. They did not change. The silver rested heavily in her hand, a little warm with the sun. It was a message to her, she was sure. A message of survival perhaps, a sign to her that he had not given up his brave words. Perhaps he had even escaped the Guardians. Perhaps he was safe, somewhere in his world where they could not reach him. Yes, that must be it. The Guardians did not know the silver was here—they would never allow it to remain if they did. And that must mean they did not know where Taryn was either.

Alexina felt as if a great weight had been lifted from her, for she knew now that Taryn's spirit had not been broken, that he would hold to his new vision and, in his own way, work to achieve it. She hoped he would find what he needed, what he desired. She could almost feel him beside her now. Some of his soul must still be there in the lump of metal they had tried to destroy. She could almost hear his voice, as if through the silver he were trying to tell her something else, something besides the fact that he was safe, something important.

Almost unconsciously, Alexina lifted the heavy metal in her hands and rested it against her throat, as if closer contact would make it possible to understand. It struck briefly cold against her skin, warming quickly with her body heat. She was gazing directly into the sun now, irradiated in the flood of golden light that filled the cave. It seemed that the light was not just light, but a force, a force that poured into her and spilled out around her, as if she herself were the point on which it focused. Her eyes, dazzled, seemed to see not just light but dimension, many dimensions sheaving away in infinite progression, a multiplicity of images that, through the act of simply looking, became one. For just the barest instant she felt the full force of power, spreading out around her like the sun. If she could keep her eyes open just this way, she would always see and feel just this; if she could go on looking forever, the great harmony would always be hers.

Alexina blinked, and the instant was gone. She was kneeling on the hard stone floor of the cave, enclosed in warmth and light, her hand clasped against her throat. The silver she held was warm beneath her fingers, warmer than her body, as if it had absorbed some of the heat of the sun. She lowered her hands and looked at it. It gleamed, clean and uncharred. The marks of the fire were gone.

Alexina felt a little weak. She was not quite sure what she had experienced. It had been too brief, too intense, gone as quickly as a breath. But at the heart of it had been power. *Her* power. For that moment it had returned, flooding through her as it had in Bron's house. She could no longer sense it. It had withdrawn almost as soon as she touched it, as the setting sun was withdrawing from the cave. But it *had* been there, beyond doubt. And if that was so it could be there again; she could reach for it in longer and longer instants, until it filled her whole being once more. It was still hers. Marhalt had not taken it after all.

Alexina closed her eyes for a moment. She felt something that was wider and more peaceful than joy, something that was rooted in the very core of her being. Her power had never left her at all—it was just that it could not be reached by the ordinary, easy roads, the roads she was used to traveling. Like the Quest itself, it must be a search, an adventure. Taryn knew, she thought. That's why he left his silver—so I could know it too. The lump of metal was cooler now, and she felt its heaviness as a seal upon her, a sign that all things could be achieved.

The sun had nearly set behind the mountains. The cave was dark again and the chill had returned. Alexina got to her feet, a little stiffly. Once more, she thought, Taryn had given her a thing beyond gratitude, and she had given him nothing in return. She wished there had been a time along the journey when she could have done something for him, just once. She wished there were something she could leave for him now that would tell him she was safe too. She looked down at the silver in her hand, and her eyes fell on her watch. She remembered his awe as she told him how common watches were in her world. Impulsively, she unclasped it from her wrist and laid it gently on the stone, still warm with the last traces of the sun. The watch might lie there forever, Taryn might never again come through the Gate, but it pleased her to think it was there for him if he ever did. In a way, it did not matter. Through what he had left for her she would always feel him, somewhere in his world that lay above, beneath, interwound with hers. Maybe someday she would see him again, if she learned to look the proper way. And maybe one day the Gate would not be necessary.

Alexina walked along the ledge and climbed down the cliff, passing the spot where she had woken from her long sleep, crossing the borderline between trees and meadow. Before her lay the farm, darkening as the darkness of the mountains came down with the evening. There was a light in the kitchen window and through it she could see Julia, preparing dinner. The light reached out to her with welcome and a promise of warmth as she hurried toward it.

epilogue

Bron walked the corridors of his candlelit house. In that way, not much had changed. Still clad in one of his dark robes, his black hair falling about his face, he paced slowly through the rooms and halls of his empty domain. He limped now. The knee had healed, but the return of his power had been too late to completely restore the shattered bone.

His power was intact, and his strength was slowly returning. Soon all would be as it had been.

He had not realized this at first. While he was lying delirious with infection, the knowledge of failure tormented him more than his physical pain. Faces crowded about him, crying out, reproaching him, lamenting his defeat. He saw the faces of his family—his mother and sister, dead in an epidemic of the plague; his father, crippled with the mining trade. He saw the faces he had grown up with, or had met in growing up, the desperate hungry faces of the people of his world. And sometimes, he saw still other faces—not of his world at all, but of other places unknown, yet still crying out for wholeness. For a week he was only half-sane, and only the devoted ministrations of Fico kept him alive.

But he survived. The knee healed, the madness receded. One day, he braved a visit to the basement.

He gazed around the white-tiled room, at the silent machines, at the violated adaptor gaping among the memory banks. And suddenly he realized. The machines—they had been running! When she touched the Stone it had still been inside the adaptor, and the machines had come to life as it awoke. In the horror of the moment, in the empty immensity he had seen in her eyes, he had forgotten.

It came to him then, like a reprieve, that he might not have failed after all. It would be infinitely more difficult, of course. He had needed the great power of the Stone. But part of the Stone was still here, in this world, caught in the memory banks of the computer complex. Through the machines, it might be possible to regenerate some of that power, some of that knowledge. What he had here might still help him unlock the secrets of the worlds.

He left the basement, feeling reborn. The work could be begun. It would have to wait until he was completely healed, but that would not be long. He would leave the adaptor as it was, a reminder of the perils of overconfidence. He would never allow himself to fall into that trap again.

Often he thought of Alexina. He regretted terribly what had happened, the waste and the loss of a great hope—not simply for himself, but for her. He knew as surely as if he had seen it happen what the Guardians had done to her, unable to accept either her true nature or her knowledge of them. The likelihood was that she would never again find her way to her power, living out the rest of her life with most of her being in darkness, like a clay vessel that holds a secret wealth of gold. If only he had had more time. If only he had been able to work on her barriers, on the lies she had been told. Now and then he toyed with the idea of searching her out and bringing her back to herself. After all, the link was still there. . . . Sometimes he could almost feel it, as if she were calling to him. Maybe . . . one day.

And so Bron paced his empty house, waiting for the time to be right to begin his great work of joining. He readied his mind, opening it to vision; he sensed the worlds all around him now, close together, intertwined. Sometimes he paced luxurious candlelit rooms; sometimes he walked across long-abandoned stone floors; sometimes he found himself in still other rooms even less familiar. He knew that for a long time yet the barriers would stand, and the people would suffer. But he was close to the secret, very close. For he had learned the proper way of looking—and that, after all, was the first step.

About the Author

VICTORIA STRAUSS was born in Exeter, New Hampshire. She has also lived in Alabama, New York, Indiana, New Jersey, Ireland, England, and Germany. At seventeen, before entering Vassar College, she took a year off to write her first book, *The Lady of Rhuddesmere,* which has been nominated for the Dorothy Canfield Fisher Award.

Ms. Strauss now lives in Poughkeepsie, New York, with her husband and two cats.